A TEXT BOOK OF

MOBILE APPLICATIONS

(ELECTIVE - IV)

For

SEMESTER – II

FINAL YEAR (B.E.) DEGREE COURSE IN COMPUTER ENGINEERING

As Per the New Revised Syllabus of Savitribai Phule Pune University, Pune.

(2012 Pattern)

SANDEEP U. KADAM
M. E.. (Computer Engg.)
Assistant Professor & HOD,
Computer Engineering Dept.,
D. Y. Patil College of Engineering,
Ambi, Talegoan Dabhade, Pune.

DEEPA J. PANDYA
M. Tech. (IT),
Assistant Professor,
Computer Engineering Dept.,
D. Y. Patil College of Engineering,
Ambi, Talegoan Dabhade, Pune.

N3746

MOBILE APPLICATIONS (BE COMP. SEM. II) **ISBN 978-93-5164-885-7**

Second Edition : January 2017

Published By :

NIRALI PRAKASHAN

Abhyudaya Pragati, 1312, Shivaji Nagar,
Off J.M. Road, PUNE – 411005
Tel - (020) 25512336/37/39, Fax - (020) 25511379
Email : niralipune@pragationline.com

DISTRIBUTION BRANCHES

PUNE

Nirali Prakashan : 119, Budhwar Peth, Jogeshwari Mandir Lane, Pune 411002, Maharashtra
Tel : (020) 2445 2044, 66022708, Fax : (020) 2445 1538
Email : bookorder@pragationline.com, niralilocal@pragationline.com

Nirali Prakashan : S. No. 28/27, Dhyari, Near Pari Company, Pune 411041
Tel : (020) 24690204 Fax : (020) 24690316
Email : dhyari@pragationline.com, bookorder@pragationline.com

MUMBAI

Nirali Prakashan : 385, S.V.P. Road, Rasdhara Co-op. Hsg. Society Ltd.,
Girgaum, Mumbai 400004, Maharashtra
Tel : (022) 2385 6339 / 2386 9976, Fax : (022) 2386 9976
Email : niralimumbai@pragationline.com

DISTRIBUTION BRANCHES

JALGAON

Nirali Prakashan : 34, V. V. Golani Market, Navi Peth, Jalgaon 425001,
Maharashtra, Tel : (0257) 222 0395, Mob : 94234 91860

KOLHAPUR

Nirali Prakashan : New Mahadvar Road, Kedar Plaza, 1st Floor Opp. IDBI Bank
Kolhapur 416 012, Maharashtra. Mob : 9850046155

NAGPUR

Pratibha Book Distributors : Above Maratha Mandir, Shop No. 3, First Floor,
Rani Jhanshi Square, Sitabuldi, Nagpur 440012, Maharashtra
Tel : (0712) 254 7129

DELHI

Nirali Prakashan : 4593/21, Basement, Aggarwal Lane 15, Ansari Road, Daryaganj
Near Times of India Building, New Delhi 110002
Mob : 08505972553

BENGALURU

Pragati Book House : House No. 1, Sanjeevappa Lane, Avenue Road Cross,
Opp. Rice Church, Bengaluru – 560002.
Tel : (080) 64513344, 64513355,Mob : 9880582331, 9845021552
Email:bharatsavla@yahoo.com

CHENNAI

Pragati Books : 9/1, Montieth Road, Behind Taas Mahal, Egmore,
Chennai 600008 Tamil Nadu, Tel : (044) 6518 3535,
Mob : 94440 01782 / 98450 21552 / 98805 82331,
Email : bharatsavla@yahoo.com

niralipune@pragationline.com | www.pragationline.com

Also find us on www.facebook.com/niralibooks

Dedicated to…

Our Students...

… Authors

PREFACE TO THE SECOND EDITION

We are glad and excited to announce that the First Edition of this book received an overwhelming response from the engineering student community, compelling us to release its **Second Edition** within a very short period of time.

This thoroughly revised **Second Edition** has been **updated** with **additional matter**, many solved problems, including **all University Examination Papers** and Numerous Exercises for practice.

Special care has been taken to maintain high degree of accuracy in the theory and numericals throughout the book.

We take this opportunity to express our sincere thanks to Dineshbhai Furia of Nirali Prakashan, a reputed pioneer in the publication field. Our special thanks to Jignesh Furia for their effective cooperation and great care in bringing out this revised edition. We also appreciate the efforts of M. P. Munde and the entire staff of Engineering Books Deptt. of Nirali Prakashan namely Mrs. Deepali Lachake (Co-ordinator) and Mrs. Shilpa Kale for bringing this book to the students in a timely manner.

We sincerely hope that this "**Second Edition**" will also be warmly received by all concerned as in the past.

Valuable suggestions from our esteemed readers to improve the book are most welcome and highly appreciated.

Pune **–Authors**

PREFACE TO THE FIRST EDITION

It gives us great pleasure to bring out the book on **"Mobile Applications"**. This book is strictly written as per the New Revised Syllabus of Savitribai Phule Pune University, Pune (2012 Pattern) for the Students of Final Year Degree Course in Computer Engineering.

The book is as per New Revised Examination Scheme which has been implemented from this academic year. According to this, In-Semester Examination carries 30 Marks over first three units and End-Semester Examination carries 70 Marks over entire syllabus of which the first three units will carry 20 Marks and units 4, 5 and 6 will carry 50 Marks.

We have given **Sample Question Papers of In-Semester University Examination (30 Marks) and End-Semester University Examination (70 Marks) in this book for practice.**

The subject matter is presented in simple form so as to enable the students to understand the subject easily. Sufficient care is taken to present the subject matter in the point wise form in most of the Units. The book consists of six units, which cover the entire syllabus.

This book has been written to satisfy the needs of undergraduate syllabus of the Computer Engineering Course in most of the Universities. We are quite sure that this book will serve its purpose very well for Computer and IT Engineering Students.

We are grateful to Principal **Dr. S. D. Shirbahadurkar** for his continuous motivation while writing this book. Also, it is important to mention invaluable moral support of our beloved family members, who consistently encouraged us for better work.

We are also thankful to **Mr. Ashok Bodke** and **Mr. Nilesh Deshmukh** Marketing Executives, Nirali Prakashan for providing us good support and valuable guidance to write this book.

We gratefully acknowledge co-operation from **Shri. Dineshbhai Furia, Shri. Jignesh Furia, Mrs. Nirali Verma**, **Shri. M.P. Munde** and **Mrs. Deepali Lachake** (Co-ordinator) of **Nirali Prakashan.**

Despite the best efforts taken by authors, it is possible that some unintentional errors might have taken place. Authors would gratefully acknowledge if any of these is pointed out.

15 February 2016

Pune **Authors**

SYLLABUS

Unit I: Introduction **6 Hrs**

Mobile Development Importance, Survey of mobile based application development, Mobile myths, Third party frameworks, Mobile Web Presence and Applications, Creating consumable web services for mobile, JSON, Debugging Web Services, Mobile Web Sites, Starting with Android mobile Applications.

Unit II: Mobile Web **6 Hrs**

Introduction, WAP1, WAP2, Fragmentation Display, Input Methods, Browsers and Web Platforms, Tools for Mobile Web Development.

Unit III: Application Architectures and Designs **8 Hrs**

Mobile Strategy, Navigation, Design and User Experience, WML, XHTML Mobile Profile and Basics, Mobile HTML5, CSS for Mobile, WCSS extensions, CSS3, CSS for mobile browsers, HTML5 Compatibility levels, Basics of Mobile HTML5: Document Head, Document Body, HTML5 Mobile Boilerplate, the Content, HTML5 Forms: Design, Elements, Attributes, Validation.

Unit IV: Devices, Images, Multi-Media **6 Hrs**

Device Detection, Client-side Detection, Server-side Detection, Device Interaction, Images, Video, Audio, Debugging and Performance, Content Delivery, Native and Installed Web Apps.

Unit V: Advanced Tools, Techniques **8 Hrs**

J2ME programming basics, HTML5 Script Extensions, Code Execution, Cloud based browsers, JS Debugging and profiling, Background Execution, Supported Technologies and API, Standard JavaScript Behavior, Java Libraries, Mobile Libraries, UI Frameworks: Sencha Touch, JQueryMobile, Enyo, Montage, iUI, jQTouch, JavaScript Mobile UI Patterns.

Unit VI: Advanced Applications **6 Hrs**

Geolocation and Maps app, Offline Apps, Storage, and Networks, Distribution and Social Web 2.0

CONTENTS

✠ ✠ ✠

Unit I

INTRODUCTION OF MOBILE DEVELOPMENT

1.1 MOBILE DEVELOPMENT IMPORTANCE

Core development of software for smart phones and gadgets is nothing but Mobile app development. It is a technique of software development of mobile and the main fundamental concept is derived from it. The main thing is that developing of different mobile applications that will run on mobile platform is primarily called mobile apps development.

Right now, most popular and well-known mobile operating systems are iOS android, windows and blackberry. Each operating system follows own rules and development procedures when to develop a particular application on different platform. For example, we an android application cannot run in windows or iOS platform.

Languages Used

The development is entirely depends upon the language of the mobile OS like, Apple iOS is based on C language and Android uses Java to develop their OS. So, "C" is the preferred language for the application development that will be used in apple iOS. Same thing is said on android.

Wide Area

There are unlimited mobile applications are spread out worldwide and at present, chatting, cooking, matrimony, shopping, money making, share market news, banking , etc are all at our hold. For many reasons there is increasing demand of up-graded version of mobile apps. New versions create interests among users; they experiment with it and express their reviews through internet. Hence it covers a very wide area of requirements and development of software.

Useful for Business

Mobile web is very useful for the business and many other areas. The customers in today's world are on the move and they're using mobile application platforms to get there. Mobile apps allow customers to have all information at their fingertips. Also, it is important that app works on multiple mobile application platforms. We all know that the first place customers go to search for a product or service is online. If business is available online and plus users have an app that they can download to their devices, business will make really good impression. At a glance they will be able to see and open business app and purchase from it.

Benefits of Mobile Apps for Businesses:

- Build loyalty
- Reinforce organizational brand
- Increase business visibility

- Increase business accessibility
- Increase sell-through
- Increase exposure across mobile devices
- Connect organization with on-the-go consumers

Not only will that business have benefits, but customers as well.

Benefits of Mobile Apps for Customers:

- Easy access to business inventory
- Get notifications of special events, launches, etc.
- Have one-touch access to organizational contact information
- Get directions to business location from wherever they are.
- Make fast, seamless appointment scheduling

Until now, it should be really clear - the future of business depends on ability to get business implanted on the smart phones of customers all over the world.

1.2 SURVEY OF MOBILE BASED APPLICATION DEVELOPMENT

Mobile app development survey has been, conducted by ComboApp (U.S.) in 2011. This survey covers multiple mobile app platform's development aspects. The major idea behind this extensive questionnaire was to make sure it presents all major mobile app platform developer's concerns, highlights their biggest challenges and provides a picture of what the mobile app development consists of nowadays. With such a large and ever-changing market environment, direct information is essential for new and revolutionary business practices. Total number of app developers took part in this survey are 3070.

1. Which Markets does Company/Organization Operate in?

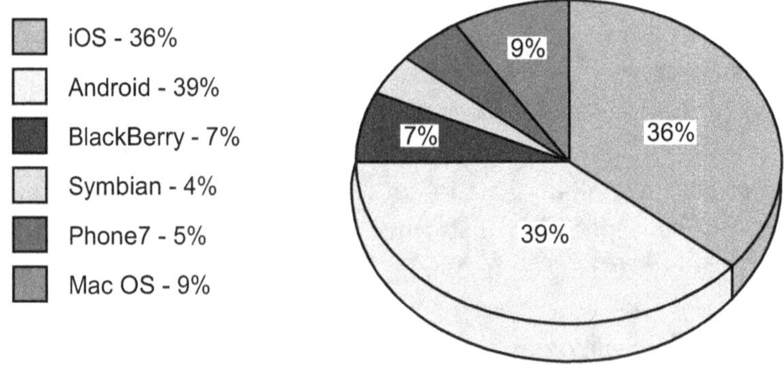

Fig. 1.1

The percentage of participants operating in specific platform's markets is presented in Fig. 1.1. A large majority of today's app developer's operations center on the iOS and Android platforms.

2. What is Primary Motivation for App Development?

Among polled responses profit is clearly the central factor motivating app developers. One of the most important implications of this is that business motivators such as point brand recognition and company portfolio extension are all significantly less pronounced among individuals or organizations who seek to develop mobile apps.

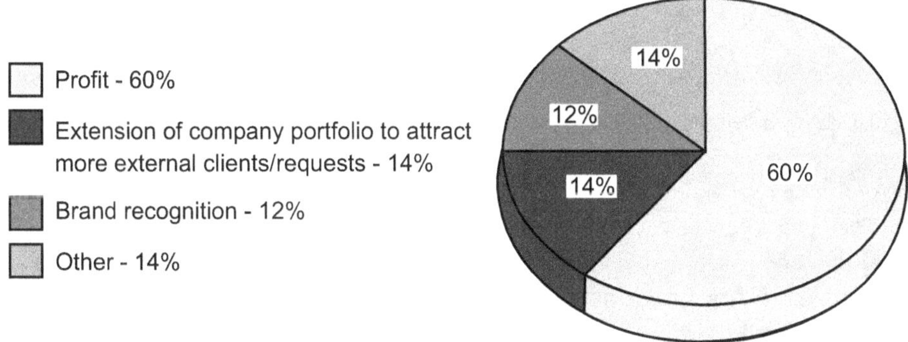

Fig. 1.2

3. Are Currently or in the Near Future, Adopting HTML-5 as a Platform for Building Cross-Platform Applications?

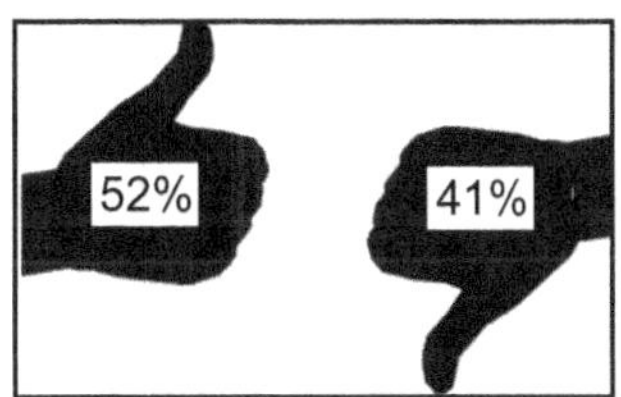

It seems like the app development community is divided almost equally between a faction of people who believe in developing native apps for different platforms and others who consider investing resources in cross-platform apps the better approach.

Both points of view have their respective pros and cons individual developer's choice can be dictated by their experience with HTML-5 development as well as either a strong belief or skepticism regarding the maximum advantages of the native app development approach.

4. Which of the Following Promotional Methods Found to be most Effective in Publicizing Products or Applications?

According to developer feedback, two leading promotional methods for mobile apps have emerged - banner ads inside existing apps / games and promotion via Social Networking channels. Collected data proves that banner ad cross promotion is an effective and affordable tool for marketing a majority of apps and games. Likewise, Social Media channels such as Facebook, Twitter and YouTube also represent highly effective marketing tools. Furthermore, these channels allow developers to reach abroad audience without employing a big budget.

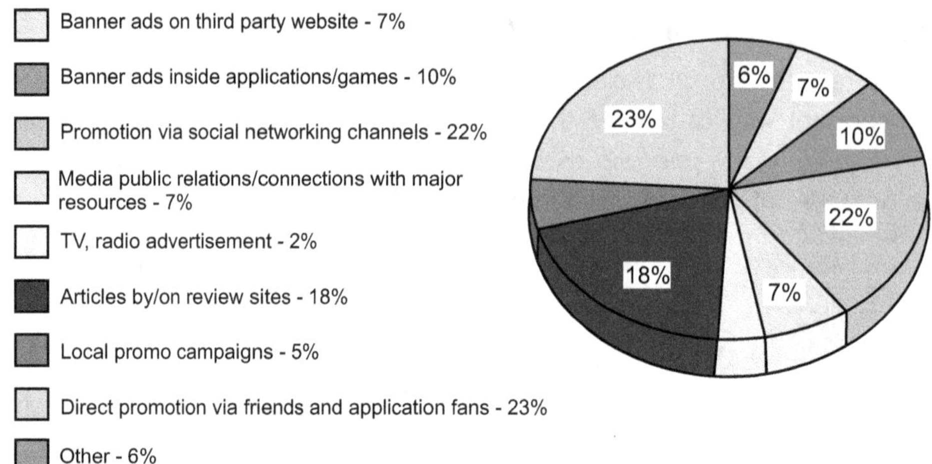

Fig. 1.3

5. In the Future, if Applications/Games Become or Continue to be Successful, they will:

54% of developers do not consider the popularity of given apps and mobile games currently or in the near future as important influences for instating price increases. Given this information there are not many reasons to believe that app users will be willing to spend more when shopping throughout the mobile marketplace currently or in the near future.

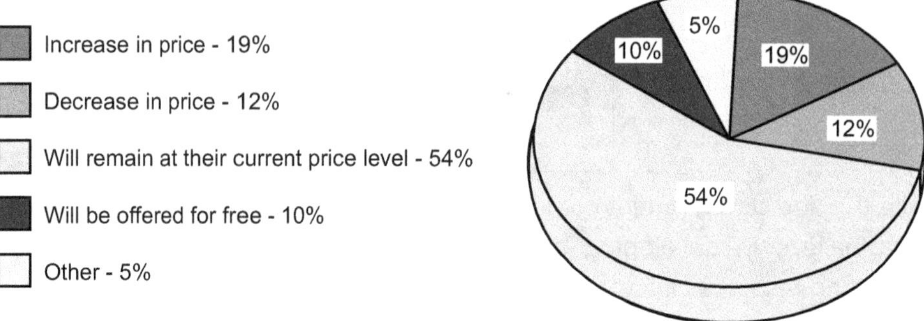

Fig. 1.4

6. What is most challenging in the Mobile Application process?

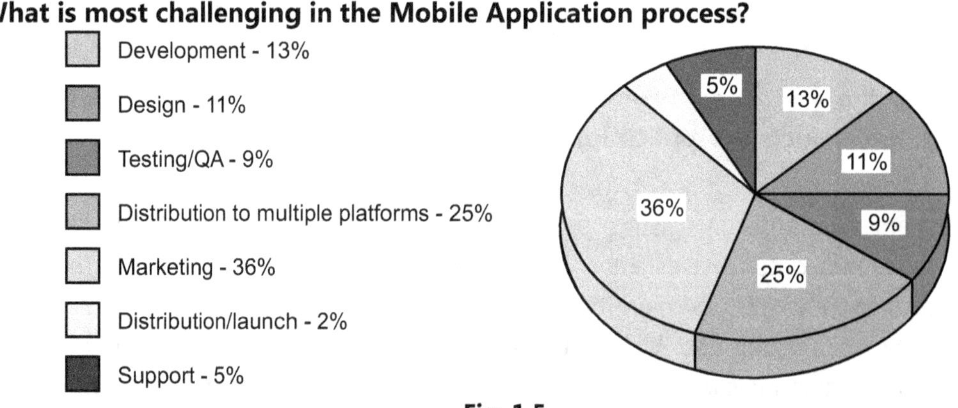

Fig. 1.5

The challenges associated with effective app marketing and distribution across multiple platforms has emerged as a primary obstacle facing app developers today. It is clear that at this point app developers are equipped with professional SDK tools and as a whole the app development process itself does not present a significant challenge.

On the other hand app marketing is consistently a source of serious concern. A further implication of this reality is that it marks a great opportunity for app marketing agencies to offer developers feasible and easily implemented solutions to these problems.

1.3 MOBILE MYTHS

There are many myths associated with mobile application. It's cheap, it's easy, it's unnecessary, you can not do it without large team, you should not pay for it, etc.

Myth 1: It is Inexpensive to Develop a Mobile Solution

Mobile development is not cheap. Iterative design and development can be expensive. Major cost needs to be sustained to employ the expertise of mobile application agency and get software development. Cost for planning, design, features, app administration, testing, deployment, infrastructure is required. Infrastructure includes basic controls, data storage, third party integration, access to enterprise data and data encryption.

Myth 2: It's Easy to Develop a Mobile Solution

Many people make a mistake of equating physical size to development speed and cost. Because a mobile app is so small, it must be easy to create than traditional development. That's not true. Creating a mobile app is often more complex than traditional development

Myth 3: We do Not Need a Mobile Presence

In most cases you need both, native apps and mobile websites. A native app is designed to accomplish particular tasks effectively. Native apps are great for interacting with existing customers and allowing them to access business in a way that is comfortable to them. On the other hand, mobile websites are going to allow you to perform better in search ranking which will help customers find you in a mobile-friendly way on search engines

Myth 4: Great Features = Successful Apps

Contrary to the opinion of some bunch of great features do not make an app great. With new apps and great features coming out everyday, it can be easy to get wrapped into feature types. It is important to differentiate between a feature and a benefit. No matter how cool some app features are, a mobile app is purpose driven. If it does not offer the user a smoother and better experience, it will not be used.

Myth 5: Once the Mobile Application Development is Completed, Job is All Done

It's not enough to develop an app only. Invest an effort, time and resources on marketing and promoting app. There are thousands of apps on the app store which are quite similar. Online marketing is necessary to sell the apps.

Myth 6: Building for One Platform is Enough

There is no single platform that can fulfill all development needs. The main determining factor when it comes to selecting mobile platform is target audience. If want app to target the mass market, want to build for both Android and iOS. Android and iOS have the largest user base compare to windows and Blackberry.

1.4 THIRD PARTY FRAMEWORKS

There are number of third-party frameworks for mobile development. The idea of the "write once and deploy to many languages" is the key force driving this frameworks. There are few different types:

- Translated Framework
- Web Framework
- Interpreted Framework

Translated frameworks take a single language and use a one-for-one replacement to develop a binary in the native language. Web frameworks use the native language's control for displaying web content and stick developer-generated HTML web applications in it. Interpreted framework use rewrite of the .NET framework to interpret the code in a native application. Right now the Mono products are the only ones that fall into this category.

Titanium Mobile Framework

The framework is an open source mobile application framework that provides an environment to create native apps for several mobile platforms. It utilizes Javascript API and the build process creates source code in the languages build to. Titanium effectively translates its specific JavaScript objects into native objects.

JavaScript calls to Titanium API are mapped to native code in the Titanium framework and generate native components. Events on those components are sent back to the code in JavaScript where we can handle them.

PhoneGap

PhoneGap is open source set of tools created by Nitobi Solutions that enables to create mobile app for multiple devices by utilizing the same code. PhoneGap is hybrid mobile applications framework that allows the use of HTML, CSS and JavaScript to write applications that are based on the open standards of the web. The final application is wrapped within a platform native 'web view' browser object and becomes a stand alone web application with the ability to access some device specific features.

MonoDroid and MonoTouch

The Mono project itself is an open source implementation of the .NET framework so that C# based .NET applications can be developed on systems other than windows.

MonoTouch: MonoTouch initially developed by the Mono team. It was their way of developing iOS apps using .NET and specially the Mono framework.

MonoDroid: It enables users to develop and distribute android application using windows and visual studio environment.

JQuery

It is robust and touch optimized framework built with HTML5 to create cross-platform mobile apps. It uses HTML5, CSS3 and JavaScript to accomplish its work for laying out pages with minimum scripting. JQuery Mobile supports a wide range of different platforms, from a regular desktop, smart phone, tablet or an e-reader device.

IONIC

It is one of the most promising HTML5 mobile application frameworks. It provides many UI components to develop rich and interactive apps. It is having highly mobile optimized library of CSS, HTML and JS components. If concerned with app performance, Ionic is the right framework.

1.5 MOBILE WEB PRESENCE AND APPLICATIONS

Mobile website is similar to any other website in that it consists of browser-based HTML pages that are linked together and accessed over the Internet (for mobile typically WiFi or 3G or 4G networks). The obvious characteristic that distinguishes a mobile website from a standard website is the fact that it is designed for the smaller handheld display and touch-screen interface.

Mobile Apps are actual applications that are downloaded and installed on mobile device, rather than being rendered within a browser. Users visit device-specific portals such as Apple's App Store, Android Market or Blackberry App World in order to find and download apps for a given operating system. The app may pull content and data from the Internet, in similar fashion to a website or it may download the content so that it can be accessed without an Internet connection.

Which is Better – an App or a Mobile Website?

When it comes to deciding whether to build a native app or a mobile website, the most appropriate choice really depends on end goals. If developing an interactive game an app is probably going to be best option. But if goal is to offer mobile-friendly content to the widest possible users then a mobile website is probably the way to go.

In some cases may decide need both a mobile website and a mobile app, but it's pretty safe to say that it rarely makes sense to build an app without already having a mobile website in place.

In general, a mobile website should be considered first step in developing a mobile web presence, whereas an app is useful for developing an application for a very specific purpose that cannot be effectively accomplished via a web browser.

1.5.1 Mobile Web Presence

Mobile web is extremely versatile and accomplishes what it sets out to do, which is to make websites scale and translate well to a mobile device in the hands of as many users as possible. Easily searched and found by search engines and web browsers, mobile optimized websites are inexpensive to create and should be considered part of the website development process. A website that is not optimized for mobile access will likely see traffic fall, as mobile is now a major driver in web traffic growth.

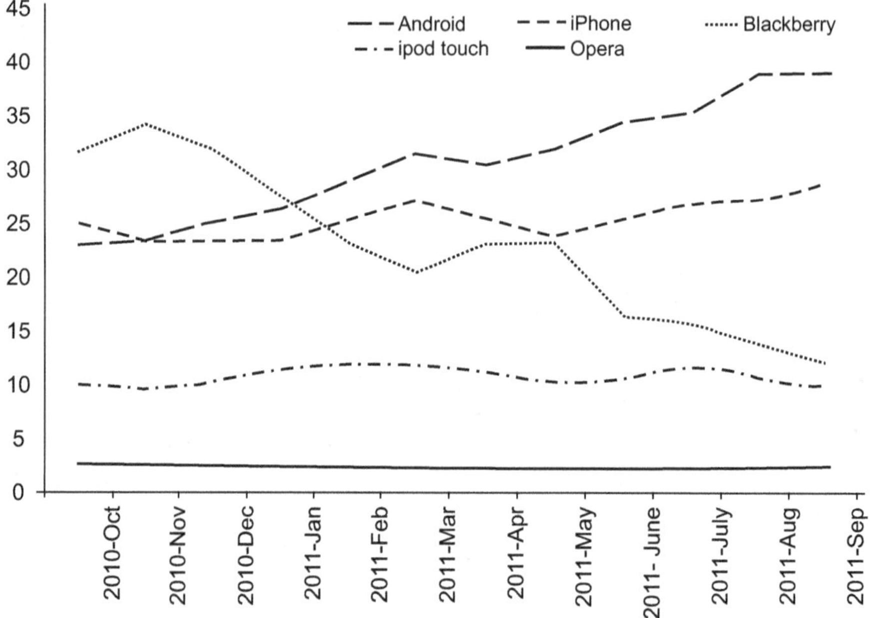

Fig. 1.6: Top five mobile browsers

Mobile browsers have been built to render websites not intended to be displayed on small devices; tools to zoom, pan, scroll and highlight links help make browsing normal websites more tolerable. Fig. 1.6 shows the top five mobile browsers. In 2011 notice the increase of usage from the Android browser and the decrease of usage from the BlackBerry browser, which coincides with the Android bumping BlackBerry off the top spot for market share for mobile devices in 2011.

Advantages

- **Development:** Mobile sites share a common publication format, resulting in all mobile devices generally reading them the same way. Simply put, can reach more devices with a single development effort. Also, mobile web development allows for freedom to innovate and refine without requiring the approval that apps require.
- **Discoverability:** Mobile sites are accessible on any device with a mobile browser, so they do not rely on users to find and download them, thus having a significant advantage when it comes to being found in major search engines like Google and Yahoo. Mobile web also makes it easy to share a site or product via social media like Twitter and Facebook.
- **Cost:** Mobile sites cost less to develop, deploy, manage and maintain than mobile apps. They are faster to implement because they build off of existing website. The common use of HTML and CSS means that development only needs to happen once to be available on all mobile devices.

- **Performance/Supportability:** Mobile sites are cross platform compatible, allowing for easy, real-time updates and immediate deployment to the public.

Disadvantages

- **User Experience:** HTML coding and limited control of the phone's interface can restrict presentation capabilities, as well as the inability to support Flash and JavaScript. These factors can adversely affect ease of use and personalization compared to customized apps.

1.5.2 Mobile Applications

A mobile application can be an opportunity to improve interaction with customers, create brand awareness and even create additional revenue. The following scenarios tell where a native app would be the best solution:

- Require graphics and processing power
- Require the use of the device's camera or microphone
- Require access to the device's address book or media library
- Require use of push notifications
- Need to run as a background service
- Want to design a game

It is predicted that mCommerce will surpass eCommerce in the near future. Apps or "native apps," can be a powerful tool, especially for retailers. But before creating an app, need to know target audiences; they are the driving force behind the decision to create an app. Mobile apps can offer a way for customers to connect with a brand, if done correctly. Just because you develop an app does not mean it will be successful: it must provide value.

In a June 2011 study, mobile analytics company Flurry found that time spent using mobile applications surpassed time spent using the mobile browser only in the United States; other countries have not become as "app crazed" as the United States. Fig. 1.7 shows these figures. With users spending this much time in mobile applications, it's worthwhile looking into creating a mobile app if business domain has a good fit.

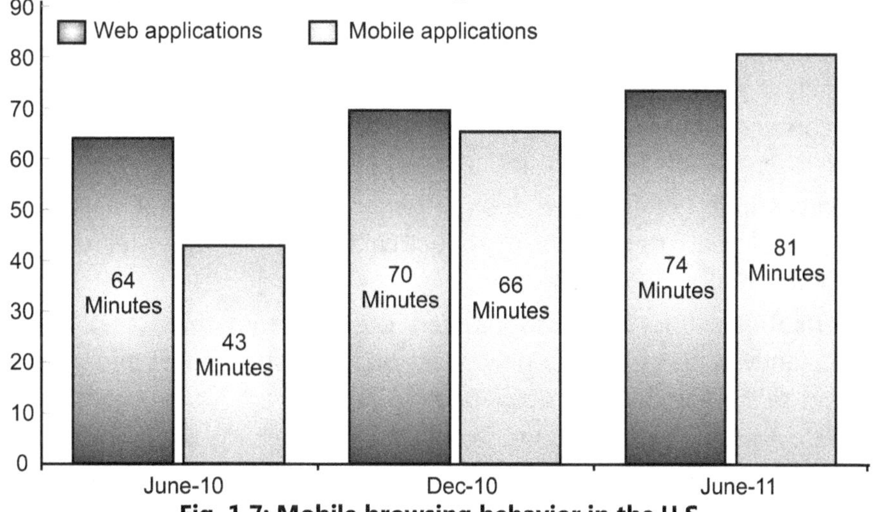

Fig. 1.7: Mobile browsing behavior in the U.S.

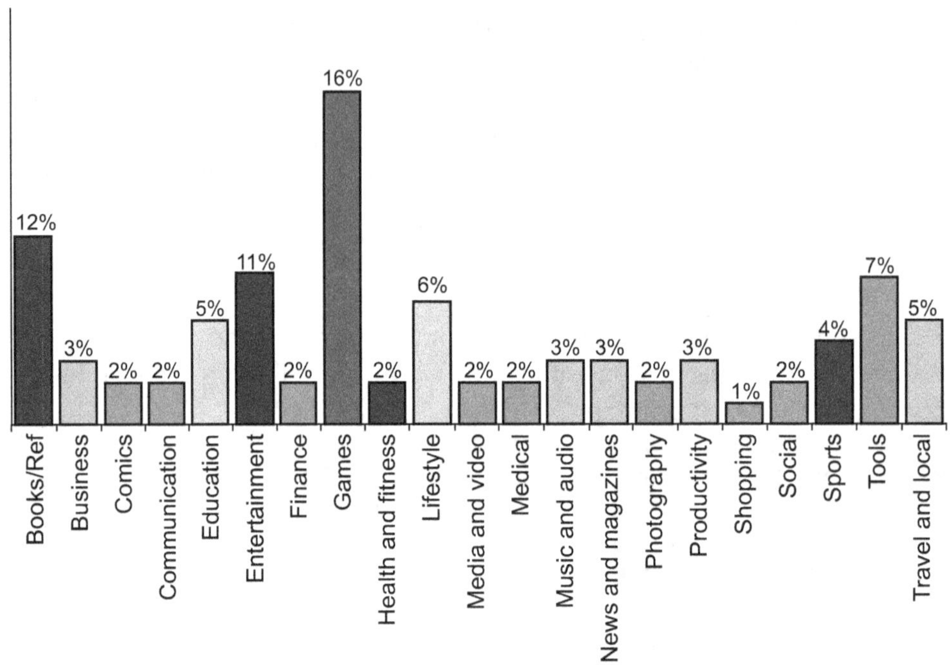

Fig. 1.8: Types of apps in the markets

When development of mobile app is finished and the app is being deployed to the market, required to put it into a category within the market to allow users to discover app more easily. Within all markets, apps are divided into categories and some categories are more popular than others.

It's common across all of the markets to see games being a large percentage of the types of apps available for the platform. Fig. 1.8 shows a distribution of apps among the Android Market provided by Android Zoom.

Advantages

- **User Experience:** Mobile apps are developed to enhance a users' experience to lead to an end result, especially for retail sites. Apps give the developers more control over the display of content – images, text, as well as audio and video. Apps are easy to download and provide user-friendly functionality.
- **Offline Processing:** With mobile apps, internet access does not always have to be available for customers to view their product catalog or use other features that will still provide a good shopping experience.
- **Push Notifications:** Push notifications alert users of something that they should be aware of instantly: a new e-mail, a new tweet or some other bit of information that may be important to the app that was downloaded.
- **Increased Customer Feedback:** Businesses often hope to build brand loyalty through apps. When loyalty has been achieved, can capitalize on this loyalty within the app, asking for feedback about company.

Disadvantages

- **Development:** Mobile apps take more resources to develop because of their customization and the various devices they need to be developed for. They must also meet requirements and be submitted and accepted by a rigorous approval system and there is the chance that an app could be dismissed / declined.
- **Discoverability:** Assuming app makes it through a stringent approval process, how will customers know about it? Marketing app is necessary in getting people to discover it and download it and need to invest in this. It can include links from website, advertising, viral campaigns and word of mouth.
- **Cost:** Apps are typically built for multiple mobile device platforms and are custom developed per a specific client and a specific goal i.e. more conversions, more subscriptions, more in-store visits, etc., therefore taking more time and costing more money.

1.6 CREATING WEB SERVICES FOR MOBILE

Many of today's mobile applications are personalized and are not useful if they can only access the data on the phone. For a user to get, for example, sports scores, retrieve stock quotes or perform accounting work; the mobile device needs to communicate with one or more servers. The best way to achieve this communication is through web services.

1.6.1 What is a Web Service?

A web service enables two electronic devices to communicate over the Internet. The World Wide Web Consortium (W3C) defines web service as "a software system designed to support interoperable machine-to-machine interaction over a network." In practice this means a server communicating over port 80 or port 443 in plain text to the client.

Other methods of communication are Remote Procedure Calls (RPC), the Distributed Component Object Model (DCOM) and the Common Object Request Broker Architecture (CORBA). These methods of communication do not work well through the Internet due to firewalls and the data formats they use. Typically their data formats are specific to whatever tool created the service and it becomes a significant challenge to have a Java application read data from a .NET or C++ application. Finally those technologies do not work well through the Internet because they are not designed to work with the Hypertext Transfer Protocol.

1.6.2 Web Service Languages (Formats)

One of the reasons web services have been so successful is because of their self-describing nature.

For example, Instead of giving a number like 5 and hoping the user of the web service knows that 5 is a weight, an age or dollars, the 5 is described in a service like this:

```
<length measurement="inches">5</length>
```

This states clearly the measurement is for length and is 5 inches. The two self-describing formats that have taken off for web services are XML and JSON.

eXtensible Markup Language (XML)

XML was designed as a way to describe documents, but it took off as a data interchange format after it was introduced. XML was envisioned to be a simple human-readable language; for example, a person object can be represented like this in XML:

```
<person>
<firstname>David</firstname>
<lastname>Smith</lastname>
</person>
```

And the same person can also be represented like this:

```
<person firstname="David"lastname="Smith" />
```

XML enables to define the language systems used to communicate by creating an XML Schema Document (XSD). This enables software to verify an XML document conforms to a predefined contract. For example, the XSD can specify that the cost of a movie must be a number. XSD also provides the benefit of enabling tools to generate code based on the XSD. Programmers can increase productivity by feeding their programming tool an XSD file and getting back code they can immediately use to interact with the data. Without the XSD file programmers have to write code to understand the XML.

It has many tools around it XPath, XQuery, XSLT and XSD. Since it is a mature language, many systems work well with XML. These advantages make XML a good choice for data interchange and it may even be required for some projects to work with existing systems.

eXtensible Stylesheet Language Transformations (XSLT)

XSLT is used to transform a document into another representation. Initially it was proposed as primarily changing XML data documents into representations for human consumption, such as XHTML. Another common use is applying an XSLT transformation to one application's XML output to be used by another application that does not understand the original representation.

The following example shows how XSLT can transform an XML data fragment for display on a web page.

This fragment: <person><age>30</age></person>would better be displayed on a web page like this:<span>Age:30</span>

The following XSLT will loop through each element in the XML with the name of person. Within each person node, the XSLT will then output the span tag with the value of the age element included within the span tag.

```
<xsl:template match="/">
<xsl:for-each select="person">
<span>Age:<xsl:value-of select="age"/></span>
```

```
</xsl:for-each>
</xsl:template>
```

XQuery

XQuery is used to retrieve a subset of data from a full XML document, like a SQL query is used to retrieve a subset of data from a database.

This example shows how to get the total amount paid for this sample order:

```
<order>
<item price="50" currency="USD" name="metal gear" />
<item price="25" currency="USD" name="plastic gear" />
</order>
```

The following XQuery returns the sum:

```
Sum(doc('orders.xml')/order/item/@price)
```

JavaScript Object Notation (JSON)

JSON was created in 2001 and came into use by Yahoo in 2005. JSON has few rules, few base types and is human readable. JSON schema enables document validation, but this is rarely used. JSON is a great format for transmitting data between systems because it is simple, text based and self-describing.

A person can be represented in JSON like this:

```
{
firstName :"David",
lastName :"Smith"
}
```

1.6.3 Creating an Example Web Service

To understand the concept let us create a web service to provide stock price information. The clients can query about the name and price of a stock based on the stock symbol. To keep this example simple, the values are hard coded in a two-dimensional array. This web service has three methods:

- A default HelloWorld method
- A GetName method
- A GetPrice method

Take the following steps to create the web service:

Step 1: Select File -> New -> Web Site in Visual Studio and then select ASP.NET Web Service.

Step 2: A web service file called Service.asmx and its code behind file, Service.cs is created in the App_Code directory of the project.

Step 3: Change the names of the files to StockService.asmx and StockService.cs

Step 4: The .asmx file has simply a WebService directive on it:

```
<%@ WebService Language="C#" CodeBehind="~/App_Code/StockService.cs"
Class="StockService" %>
```

Step 5: Open the StockService.cs file, the code generated in it is the basic Hello World service. The default web service code behind file looks like the following:

```
using System;
usingSystem.Collections;
usingSystem.ComponentModel;
usingSystem.Data;
usingSystem.Linq;

usingSystem.Web;
usingSystem.Web.Services;
usingSystem.Web.Services.Protocols;

usingSystem.Xml.Linq;

namespaceStockService
{
  // <summary>
  // Summary description for Service1
  // <summary>

  [WebService(Namespace = "http://tempuri.org/")]
  [WebServiceBinding(ConformsTo = WsiProfiles.BasicProfile1_1)]
  [ToolboxItem(false)]
  // To allow this Web Service to be called from script,
  // using ASP.NET AJAX, uncomment the following line.
  // [System.Web.Script.Services.ScriptService]

public class Service1 : System.Web.Services.WebService
  {
    [WebMethod]

public string HelloWorld()
    {
return "Hello World";
    }
  }
}
```

Step 6: Change the code behind file to add the two dimensional array of strings for stock symbol, name and price and two web methods for getting the stock information.

```
using System;
usingSystem.Linq;

usingSystem.Web;
usingSystem.Web.Services;
usingSystem.Web.Services.Protocols;

usingSystem.Xml.Linq;

[WebService(Namespace = "http://tempuri.org/")]
[WebServiceBinding(ConformsTo = WsiProfiles.BasicProfile1_1)]

// To allow this Web Service to be called from script,
// using ASP.NET AJAX, uncomment the following line.
// [System.Web.Script.Services.ScriptService]

public class StockService : System.Web.Services.WebService
{
publicStockService () {
    //Uncomment the following if using designed components
    //InitializeComponent();
  }

string[,] stocks =
  {
    {"RELINCE", "Reliance Industries", "1060.15"},
    {"ICICI", "ICICI Bank", "911.55"},
    {"JSW", "JSW Steel", "1201.25"},
    {"WIPRO", "Wipro Limited", "1194.65"},
    {"SATYAM", "Satyam Computers", "91.10"}
  };

  [WebMethod]
```

```
public string HelloWorld() {
return "Hello World";
  }

  [WebMethod]
public double GetPrice(string symbol)
  {
    //it takes the symbol as parameter and returns price
for (inti = 0; i<stocks.GetLength(0); i++)
    {
if (String.Compare(symbol, stocks[i, 0], true) == 0)
returnConvert.ToDouble(stocks[i, 2]);
    }

return 0;
  }

  [WebMethod]
public string GetName(string symbol)
  {
    // It takes the symbol as parameter and
    // returns name of the stock
for (inti = 0; i<stocks.GetLength(0); i++)
    {
if (String.Compare(symbol, stocks[i, 0], true) == 0)
return stocks[i, 1];
    }

return "Stock Not Found";
  }
}
```

Step 7: Running the web service application gives a web service test page, which allows testing the service methods.

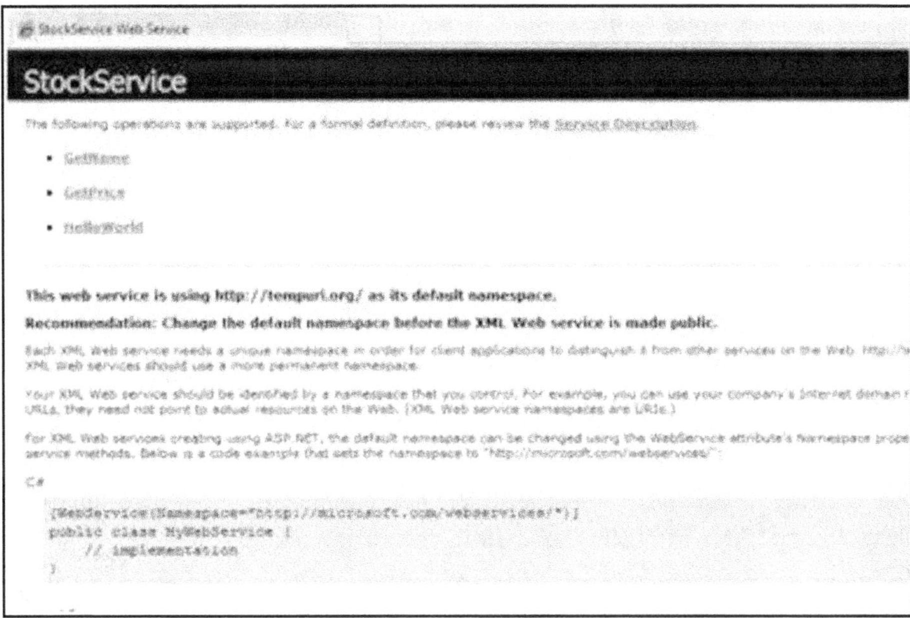

Step 8: Click on a method name and check whether it runs properly.

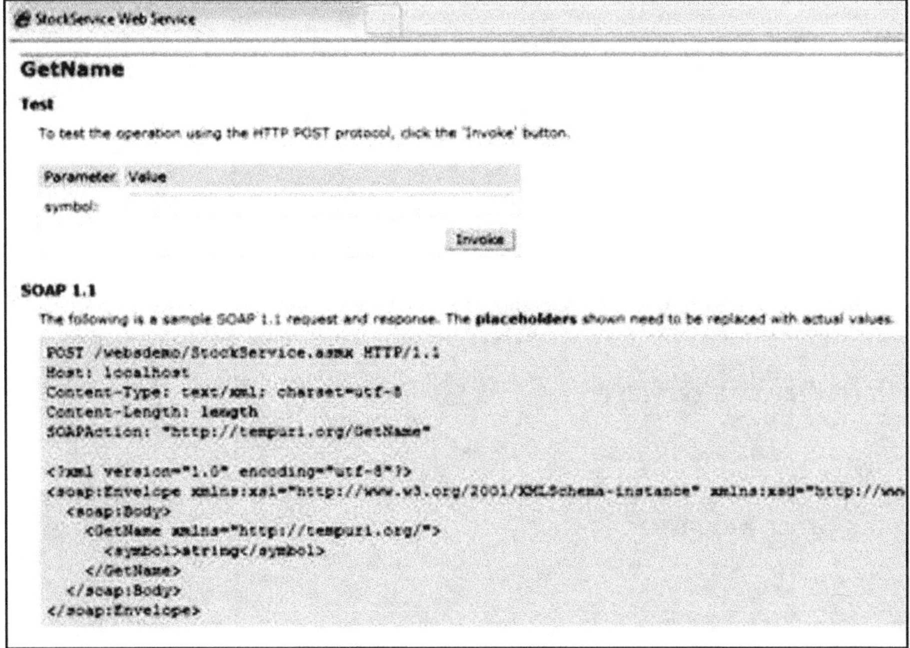

Step 9: For testing the GetName method, provide one of the stock symbols, which are hard coded, it returns the name of the stock.

http://localhost:1081/websdemo/StockService.as...

```
<?xml version="1.0" encoding="utf-8" ?>
<string xmlns="http://tempuri.org/">Satyam Computers</string>
```

Consuming the Web Service

For using the web service, create a web site under the same solution. This could be done by right clicking on the Solution name in the Solution Explorer. The web page calling the web service should have a label control to display the returned results and two button controls one for post back and another for calling the service.

The content file for the web application is as follows:

```
<%@ Page Language="C#" AutoEventWireup="true" CodeBehind="Default.aspx.cs"
Inherits="wsclient._Default" %>

<!DOCTYPE html PUBLIC "-//W3C//DTD XHTML 1.0 Transitional//EN"
"http://www.w3.org/TR/xhtml1/DTD/xhtml1-transitional.dtd">

<html xmlns="http://www.w3.org/1999/xhtml" >

<head runat="server">
<title>
    Untitled Page
</title>
</head>

<body>

<form id="form1" runat="server">
<div>

<h3>Using the Stock Service</h3>

<br /><br />

<asp:Label ID="lblmessage" runat="server"></asp:Label>
```

```
<br /><br />

<asp:Button ID="btnpostback" runat="server" onclick="Button1_Click" Text="Post Back"
style="width:132px" />

<asp:Button ID="btnservice" runat="server" onclick="btnservice_Click" Text="Get
Stock" style="width:99px" />

</div>
</form>

</body>
</html>
```

The code behind file for the web application is as follows:

```
using System;
usingSystem.Collections;
usingSystem.Configuration;
usingSystem.Data;
usingSystem.Linq;

usingSystem.Web;
usingSystem.Web.Security;
usingSystem.Web.UI;
usingSystem.Web.UI.HtmlControls;
usingSystem.Web.UI.WebControls;
usingSystem.Web.UI.WebControls.WebParts;

usingSystem.Xml.Linq;

//this is the proxy
using localhost;
namespacewsclient
{
public partial class _Default : System.Web.UI.Page
  {
```

```
protected void Page_Load(object sender, EventArgs e)
    {
if (!IsPostBack)
      {
lblmessage.Text = "First Loading Time: " +  DateTime.Now.ToLongTimeString
      }
else
      {
lblmessage.Text = "PostBack at: " + DateTime.Now.ToLongTimeString();
      }
    }
protected void btnservice_Click(object sender, EventArgs e)
    {
StockService proxy = new StockService();
lblmessage.Text = String.Format("Current SATYAM Price:{0}",
proxy.GetPrice("SATYAM").ToString());
    }
  }
}
```

Creating the Proxy

A proxy is a stand-in for the web service codes. Before using the web service, a proxy must be created. The proxy is registered with the client application. Then the client application makes the calls to the web service as it were using a local method.

The proxy takes the calls, wraps it in proper format and sends it as a SOAP request to the server. SOAP stands for Simple Object Access Protocol. This protocol is used for exchanging web service data. When the server returns the SOAP package to the client, the proxy decodes everything and presents it to the client application.

Before calling the web service using the btnservice_Click, a web reference should be added to the application. This creates a proxy class transparently, which is used by the btnservice_Click event.

```
protected void btnservice_Click(object sender, EventArgs e)
{
StockService proxy = new StockService();
lblmessage.Text = String.Format("Current SATYAM Price: {0}",
proxy.GetPrice("SATYAM").ToString());
}
```

Take the following steps for creating the proxy:

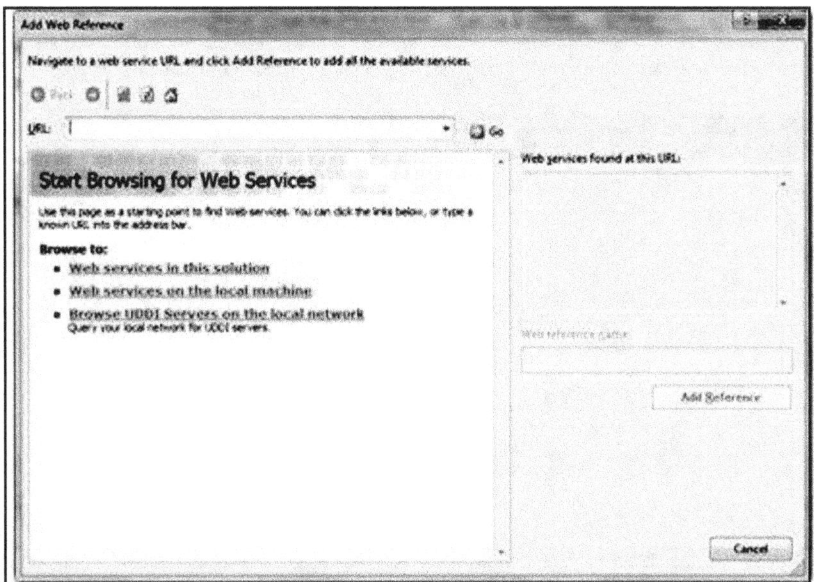

Step 1: Right click on the web application entry in the Solution Explorer and click on 'Add Web Reference'.

Step 2: Select 'Web Services in this solution'. It returns the StockService reference.

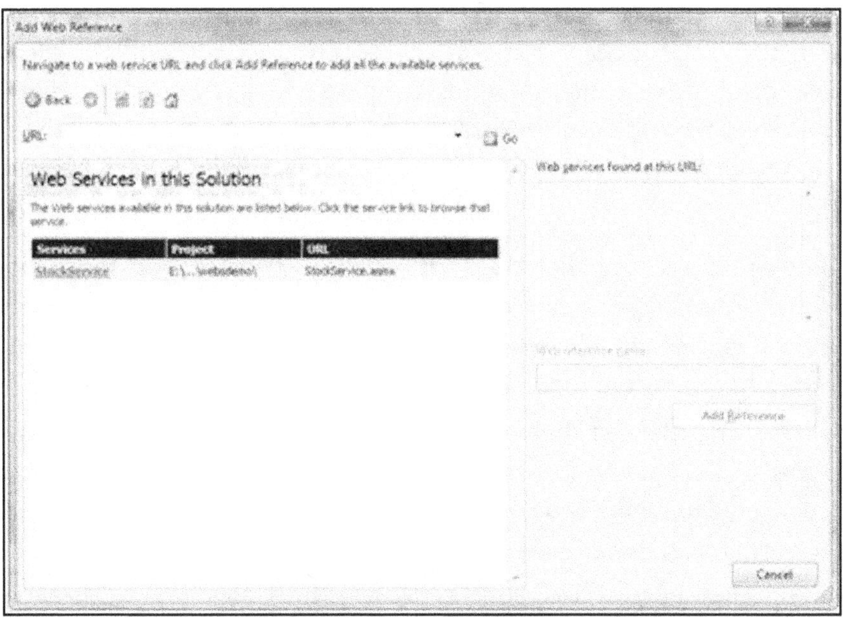

Step 3: Clicking on the service opens the test web page. By default the proxy created is called 'localhost', you can rename it. Click on 'Add Reference' to add the proxy to the client application.

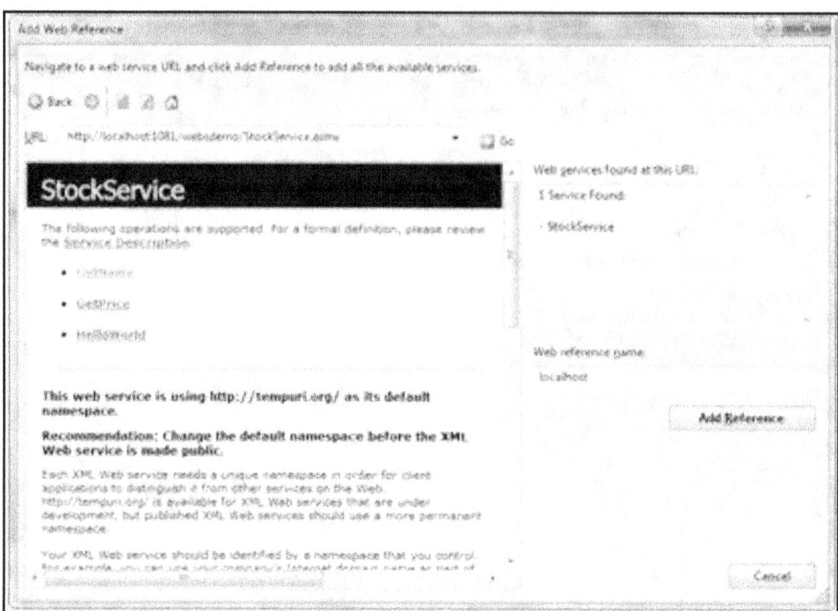

Include the proxy in the code behind file by adding:

```
using localhost;
```

1.7 DEBUGGING WEB SERVICE

All developers are not perfect and the web service create will not work exactly correct the first time try to test it. Understanding why a web service is not working correctly can be difficult because most of the code running is standard software and not code written. Most of the code delivering web services consists of the libraries being leveraged; the platform the code is running on, the webserver code running and the operating system code.

1.7.1 Fiddler

Fiddler is a free Windows tool that does just that. Find installation instructions and the download at http://www.fiddler2.com. Fiddler shows the raw HTTP traffic for the Windows system on which it is running. This means the tool will show the raw HTTP service request and HTTP response if the system running Fiddler is the one making the request.

Unfortunately, when developing mobile applications, Fiddler will not be able to show the HTTP traffic because it is coming from an external device. Fiddler has another feature called Composer that allows the creation and execution of a raw HTTP request. The Composer feature enables testing and debugging of services.

The two most important features of using Fiddler to debug web services successfully are the filters and Composer. When Fiddler is running it captures all the HTTP traffic on the machine on which it is running. This is typically too much data, which obscures the web calls that are important. Fiddler has the concept of filters, which enable a user to hide HTTP traffic that is not of interest.

The other feature is Composer. Composer enables putting together the exact HTTP request to have executed. This is useful for understanding why a web service call is not working; especially requests that use HTTP accept headers, because those requests cannot be executed by a default web browser. Fiddler is a must-have tool for debugging on the Windows platform.

1.8 JSON (JAVASCRIPT OBJECT NOTATION)

JavaScript Object Notation (best known as JSON) is a lightweight data interchange format known to be compatible with almost every language in common use. It is sometimes used in JavaScript as a replacement for other transport formats, like XML.

JSON is syntax for storing and exchanging data, it is an easier-to-use alternative to XML. The JSON format is syntactically identical to the code for creating JavaScript objects. Because of this similarity, instead of using a parser like XML does, a JavaScript program can use standard JavaScript functions to convert JSON data into native JavaScript objects. It has been extended from the JavaScript scripting language. The filename extension is **.json**.

It is used while writing JavaScript based applications that include browser extensions and websites. It is primarily used to transmit data between a server and web applications. Web services and APIs use JSON format to provide public data.

The following example shows how to use JSON to store information related to books based on their topic and edition.

```
{
  "book": [
    {
      "id":"01",
      "language": "C++",
      "edition": "third",
      "author": "Herbert Schildt"
    },
    {
      "id":"07",
      "language": "C",
      "edition": "first",
      "author": "E.Balagurusamy"
    }
  ]
}
```

JSON is like XML because,

- Both JSON and XML is "self describing" i.e. human readable
- Both JSON and XML is hierarchical i.e. values within values
- Both JSON and XML can be parsed and used by lots of programming languages
- Both JSON and XML can be fetched with an XMLHttpRequest

It is differ from XML because,

- JSON does not use end tag
- JSON is shorter
- JSON is quicker to read and write
- JSON can use arrays

The biggest difference is: XML has to be parsed with an XML parser, JSON can be parsed by a standard JavaScript function.

Why JSON?

For AJAX applications, JSON is faster and easier than XML:

Using XML we can fetch an XML document, use the XML DOM to loop through the document and extract values and store in variables. Using JSON we can fetch a JSON string, parse the JSON string.

JSON Syntax

The JSON syntax is a subset of the JavaScript syntax. JSON syntax is derived from JavaScript object notation syntax:

- Data is in name/value pairs
- Data is separated by commas
- Curly braces hold objects
- Square brackets hold arrays

JSON data is written as name/value pairs. A name/value pair consists of a field name (in double quotes), followed by a colon and followed by a value:

```
"firstName":"John"
```

JSON names require double quotes. JavaScript names do not.

JSON values can be:

- A number (integer or floating point)
- A string (in double quotes)
- A Boolean (true or false)
- An array (in square brackets)
- An object (in curly braces)
- null

JSON objects are written inside curly braces. Just like JavaScript, JSON objects can contain multiple name/values pairs:

```
{"{firstName":"John","lastName":"Smith"}
```

JSON arrays are written inside square brackets. Just like JavaScript, a JSON array can contain multiple objects:

```
"employees":[
    {"firstName":"John", "lastName":"Smith"},
    {"firstName":"Michael", "lastName":"Richard"},
    {"firstName":"Peter","lastName":"Jackson"}
]
```

In the example above, the object "employees" is an array containing three objects. Each object is a record of a person (with a first name and a last name).

JSON Uses JavaScript Syntax, so, very little extra software is needed to work with JSON within JavaScript. With JavaScript you can create an array of objects and assign data to it, like this:

```
var employees = [
  {"firstName":"John", "lastName":"Smith"},
   {"firstName":"Michael", "lastName":"Richard"},
   {"firstName":"Peter","lastName":"Jackson"}
];
```

The first entry in the JavaScript object array can be accessed like this:

// returns John Smith

employees[0].firstName + " " + employees[0].lastName;

It can also be accessed like this:

// returns John Smith

```
employees[0]["firstName"] + " " + employees[0]["lastName"];
```

Data can be modified like this:

```
employees[0].firstName = "Gilbert";
```

It can also be modified like this:

```
employees[0]["firstName"] = "Gilbert";
```

A common use of JSON is to read data from a web server and display the data in a web page. For simplicity, this can be demonstrated by using a string as input (instead of a file).

JSON Example - Object from String

Create a JavaScript string containing JSON syntax:

```
var text = '{ "employees" : [' +
'{ "firstName":"John" , "lastName":" Smith " },' +
'{ "firstName":"Michael" , "lastName":"Richards" },' +
'{ "firstName":"Peter" , "lastName":"Jackson" } ]}';
```

The JavaScript function JSON.parse(*text*) can be used to convert a JSON text into a JavaScript object:

```
var obj = JSON.parse(text);
```

Use the new JavaScript object in your page:

```
<p id="demo"></p>
<script>
document.getElementById("demo").innerHTML =
obj.employees[1].firstName + " " + obj.employees[1].lastName;
</script>
```

1.9 MOBILE WEB SITES

With the rise of mobile browsers, people need to be able to access website and, at a minimum, be able to browse it smoothly to find the information they need. Taking it a step further and providing an optimal mobile user interface or specialized mobile content, can provide a great experience and enhance the reputation of organization.

Creating a mobile website depends on the functionality of current website, the platform and development standards with which it was created and the purpose that users have for visiting the website.

Choosing a Mobile Web Option

If organization is itching to be mobile, but does not have a focused purpose or resources to develop a mobile app, a mobile website can be a great place to start.

Adaptive mobile websites automatically adjust current website when viewed on mobile screen sizes, modifying the layout, sizing and spacing to make it more mobile-friendly.

Dedicated mobile websites require a completely separate mobile website and mobile web apps employ HTML5 functionality and specific UI elements to create an app-like experience on the web.

The following table lists the pros and cons of the various mobile web development options.

	Adaptive Mobile Website	**Dedicated Mobile Website**	**Mobile Web Application**
Pros	• Maintain only one website • Quick and least expensive to implement	• Good website performance • More perfected mobile UI • Fairly inexpensive to implement	• A website that can behave like an app • Less development cost than native app • Works across platforms
Cons	• No use of native device functionality • Not optimal performance • Some layout restrictions	• No use of native device functionality • Maintain two websites	• Not in app stores • Can not use all mobile features

1.9.1 Adaptive Mobile Websites

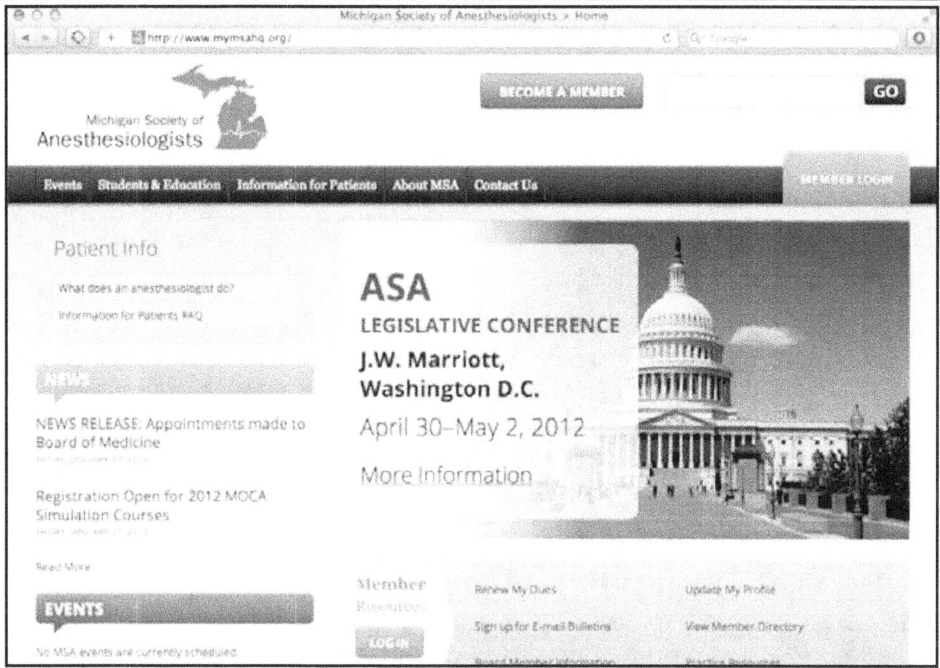

Fig. 1.9: Adaptive website example, viewed in a full-sized desktop browser

An adaptive mobile website is a great first project for mobile and it allows steps to be taken incrementally toward an optimal mobile UI. Adaptive mobile websites use CSS media queries to serve different style sheets based on the size or type of browser or device detected viewing the site (see Fig. 1.9 and 1.10).

With CSS, content and presentation layers are kept separate; media queries change website layout and appearance without content modification. No browser detection or site redirection is needed; the optimal website layout appears automatically when media query parameters are met.

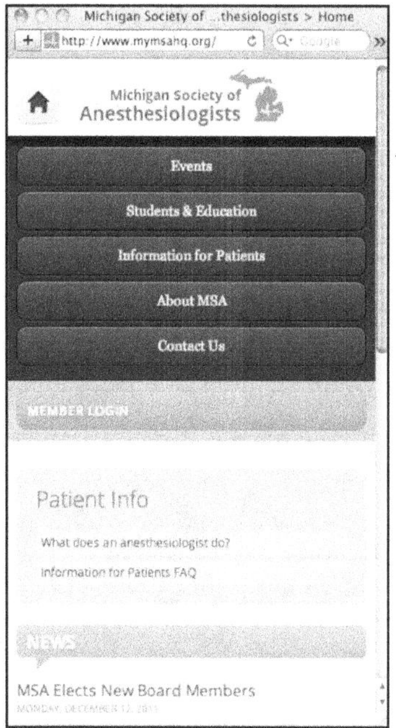

Fig. 1.10: Adaptive website example, viewed in a mobile-sized browser

1.9.2 Dedicated Mobile Websites

Need to decide how want to change, rearrange or remove content from your website for the mobile version. The difference is that building the dedicated mobile website from the ground up, so very few restrictions and it is easier to pay attention to the details that create the optimal mobile browsing experience. This is also a good opportunity to undertake a fully responsive site design, to cover the range of phone and tablet device differences.

When planning a brand new mobile website, designing ahead is a must. A designer does not need to think about restrictions like the flow of columns: there is much more freedom to design a mobile site as perfectly as possible. Choose only a small number of key pages on the mobile site. This might allow the menu to fit horizontally across the mobile site, when the desktop version may have too many links.

Because a dedicated website will not mirror desktop content, it is also a good idea to provide site content to mobile users. Rewrite mobile content to be shorter and appeal to any mobile-specific user needs.

1.9.3 Mobile Web Apps with HTML5

Mobile web apps can provide useful alternatives to native mobile apps. With a excess of new tools attaching the HTML5 and JavaScript capabilities of modern mobile browsers, dynamic web applications can stand up to any native app. It can take much less time for an experienced web developer to create a mobile web app that works across platforms than to develop the same app natively for the same variety of device platforms.

What Exactly Is a Mobile Web App?

Whereas a mobile website exists to improve the mobile functionality of an existing website, a mobile web app exists to perform a specific mobile function. A mobile web app should be more comparable to a native app than to a website. A web app cannot handle some functions or might not have the capability to access the device to perform them.

Use many of the already-discussed techniques like adaptive images and media queries. Like a dedicated mobile website, a mobile web app will most likely be designed only for mobile phones and possibly tablets. Creating all of HTML pages and use media queries to target different orientations and screen sizes. Then, using HTML5 and JavaScript, add advanced functionality that more closely relates to a native app.

1.10 STARTING WITH ANDROID MOBILE APPLICATIONS

Among the many reasons to target the Android platform, first and foremost is cost. On average you can get an Android smartphone for a fraction of the cost of an iPhone. They may not have commensurate features, but thrift is a major component for new smartphone buyers.

Next is flexibility. More types of Android devices are available, so if application fits a specific role market, there is probably a device that support needs already in production.

HTC, LG, Motorola and Samsung are the major players in the Android smartphone market.

Archos, Dell, Samsung and Toshiba hold the largest pieces of the Android tablet market.

1.10.1 Getting Tools for Android

This section summarizes the installation instructions from the Android Developer section:

1. Downloading and Installing JDK

The first thing that do to develop Android applications is to visit http://www.oracle.com/technetwork/java/javase/downloads/index.html and ensure that the Java JDK installed. Because so many different acronyms and versions appear on the Java download website.

The JDK is the Java Development Kit. This package need to do any Java development on machine, Android or otherwise. Be sure to look for the Java Platform, Standard Edition JDK.

2. Downloading and Installing Eclipse

After successfully installed the JDK, need a development environment. The open source IDE Eclipse is recommended by Android directly in its documentation. Not limited only to Eclipse, but the tooling has been honed over time to be the easiest solution to get up and running. Fig. 1.11 shows the Eclipse download page (www.eclipse.org/downloads). Download the version of Eclipse Classic that is appropriate for operating system.

Fig. 1.11: Eclipse download site

3. Downloading and Installing the Android SDK

After installed the Eclipse IDE, need to install the Android Software Developer Kit (http://developer.android.com/sdk/index.html). This includes all the tools necessary to build Android apps, because the SDK is not built directly into Eclipse. Fig. 1.12 shows the Android SDK download page; make sure to get the right version for OS.

Download the Android SDK

Welcome Developers! If you are new to the Android SDK, please read the steps below, for an overview of how to set up the SDK.

If you're already using the Android SDK, you should update to the latest tools or platform using the *Android SDK and AVD Manager*, rather than downloading a new SDK starter package. See Adding SDK Components.

Platform	Package	Size	MD5 Checksum
Windows	android-sdk_r16-windows.zip	29562413 bytes	6b926d0c0a871f1a946e65259984701a
	installer_r16-windows.exe (Recommended)	29561554 bytes	3521dda4904886b05980590f83cf3469
Mac OS X (intel)	android-sdk_r16-macosx.zip	26158334 bytes	d1dc2b6f13eed5e3ce5cf26c4e4c47aa
Linux (i386)	android-sdk_r16-linux.tgz	22048174 bytes	3ba457f731d51da3741c29c8830a4583

Fig. 1.12: Android SDK download page

4. Downloading and Configuring the Eclipse ADT Plug-in

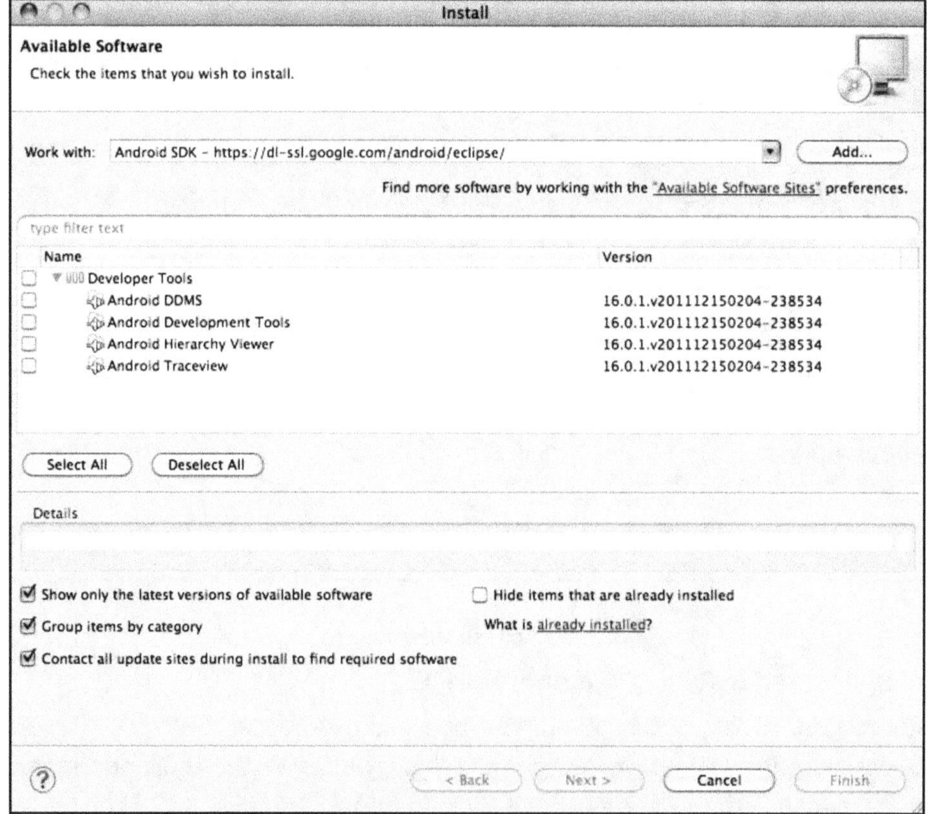

Fig. 1.13: Installing the ADT plug-in

After installed the Android SDK, need the ADT plug-in. What this does is add the features necessary to create Android Projects, because they are not bundled with the base Eclipse install. Additionally, the plug-in adds debugging tools to Eclipse to help during the Android development process. Fig. 1.13 shows the interface for installing the ADT plug-in. Also use this interface when upgrading ADT.

Use the Update Manager feature of Eclipse installation to install the latest revision of ADT on development computer. Follow these steps:

1. Start Eclipse and select Help ➪ Install New Software.
2. Click Add in the top-right corner.
3. In the Add Repository dialog box that appears, enter ADT plug-in for the name and the following URL for the location: https://dl-ssl.google.com/android/eclipse/
4. Click OK. If trouble acquiring the plug-in, try using "http" in the Location URL instead of "https" ("https" is preferred for security reasons).
5. In the Available Software dialog box, select the checkbox next to Developer Tools and click Next.
6. The next window shows a list of the tools to be downloaded. Click Next.
7. Read and accept the license agreements and then click Finish. If get a security warning saying that the authenticity or validity of the software can not be established, click OK.
8. When the installation completes, restart Eclipse.

Once downloaded the ADT plug-in, need to set it up to talk to the Android SDK that downloaded earlier. This allows Eclipse to build, run and debug Android applications without needing to open a terminal or command shell. Fig. 1.14 shows where you need to add the link to the Android SDK in the Eclipse preferences.

After successfully downloaded the ADT, the next step is to modify ADT preferences in Eclipse to point to the Android SDK directory (see Fig. 1.14):

1. Select Window ➪ Preferences to open the Preferences panel. In Mac OS X, click Eclipse ➪ Preferences.
2. Select Android from the left panel.
3. See a dialog box asking whether to send usage statistics to Google. If so, make choice and click Proceed. Cannot continue with this procedure until click Proceed.
4. For the SDK Location in the main panel, click Browse and locate downloaded SDK directory.
5. Click Apply and then click OK.

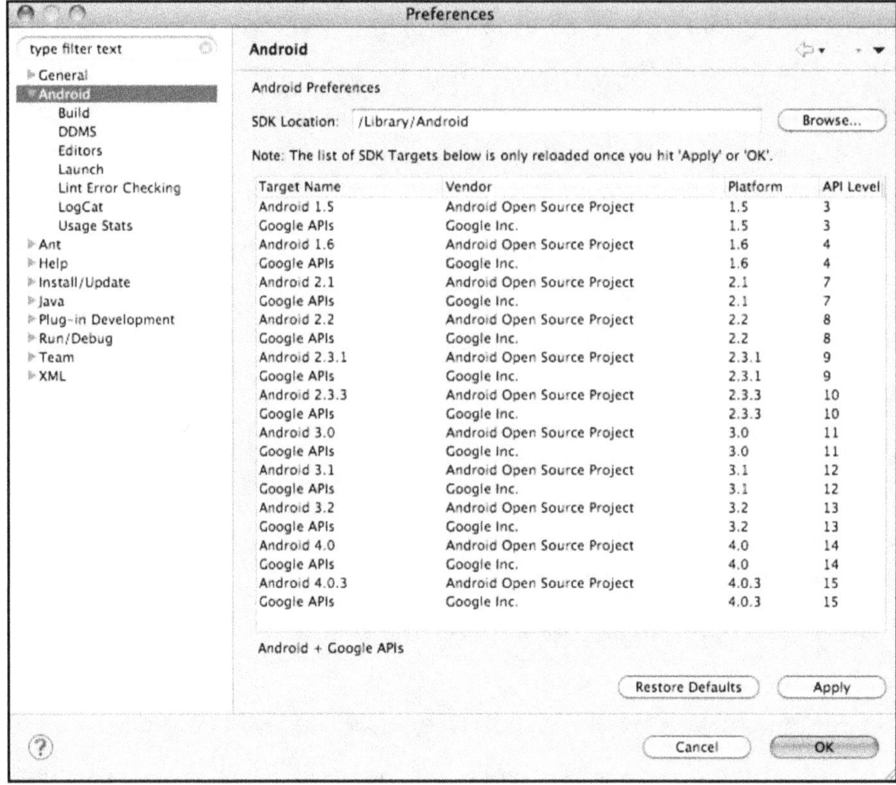

Fig. 1.14: ADT configuration screen

5. Installing Additional SDK Components

The last step in preparing development environment for Android is to download additional Android OS packages. This enables to build applications that target that OS and also gives the tools need to emulate a device running that OS on which to test all applications, whether or not they have been targeted to that OS version. Fig. 1.15 shows just how many options have when looking to target Android OS versions.

Correctly configuring and using this tool will ensure that all the latest SDKs and utilities afforded. Note that not necessarily need all of the versions of the SDKs listed in Fig. 1.15; this was merely to illustrate the full breadth of options.

Loading the Android SDK Manager in Eclipse takes only a few steps:

1. Open Eclipse.
2. Select Window ➪ Android SDK and AVD Manager.
3. Select Available Packages in the left panel. This reveals all of the components that are currently available for download from the SDK repository.
4. Select the components like to install and click Install Selected.
5. Verify and accept the components (ensure each one is selected with a green checkmark) and click Install. The components will now be installed into existing Android SDK directories.

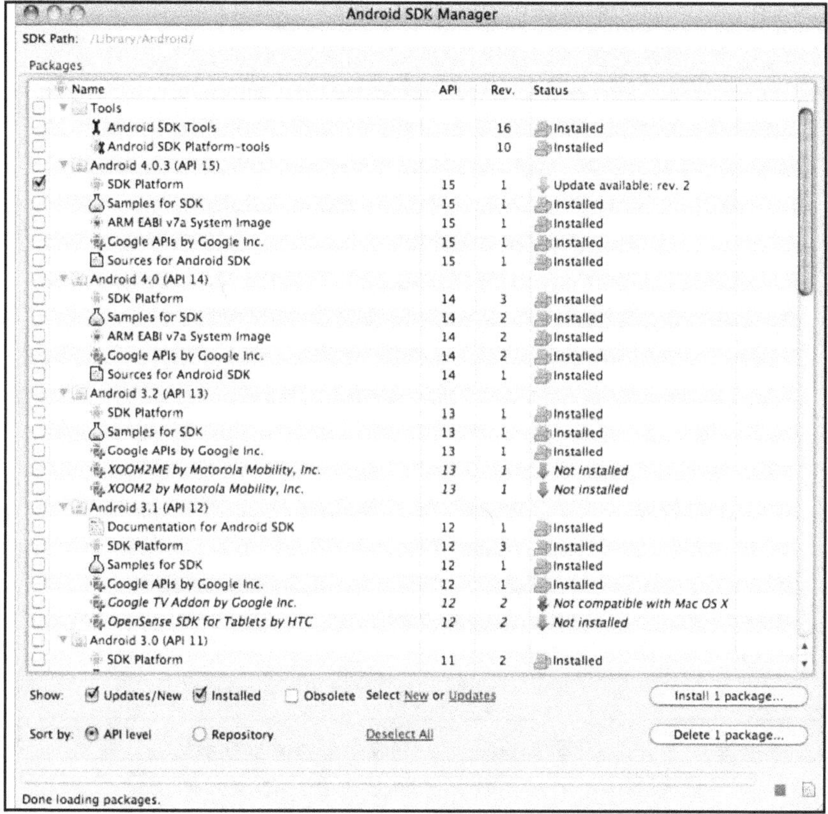

Fig. 1.15: Working with the SDK manager

1.10.2 Development

The following sections discuss the application layout and Android app development.

1. Creating a New Project

First things first- need to create a new Android project. The line highlighted in Fig. 1.16 is the type of project want.

First need to name application and add it to a workspace. Think of a workspace as the folder in which application resides.

After, named application need to give it a package name, set the minimum SDK required to run application and name the initial Activity that will run when application runs. If want to add a test project to workspace. Fig. 1.17 shows a completed Application Info step in the new project wizard.

An important note at this point: Make sure that package name is unique. The standard format for package names is com.company Name.application Name. This must be unique because that is how it is known on the Android device and in the Android Market. When make updates can make them only within package name. If change package name there will be no upgrade path between versions.

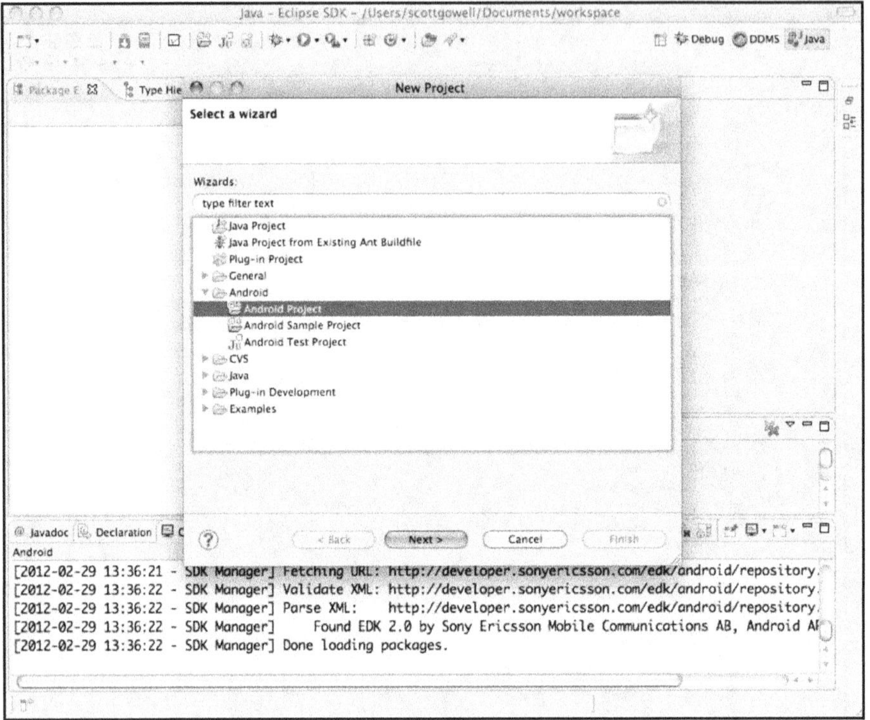

Fig. 1.16: Creating a new android project

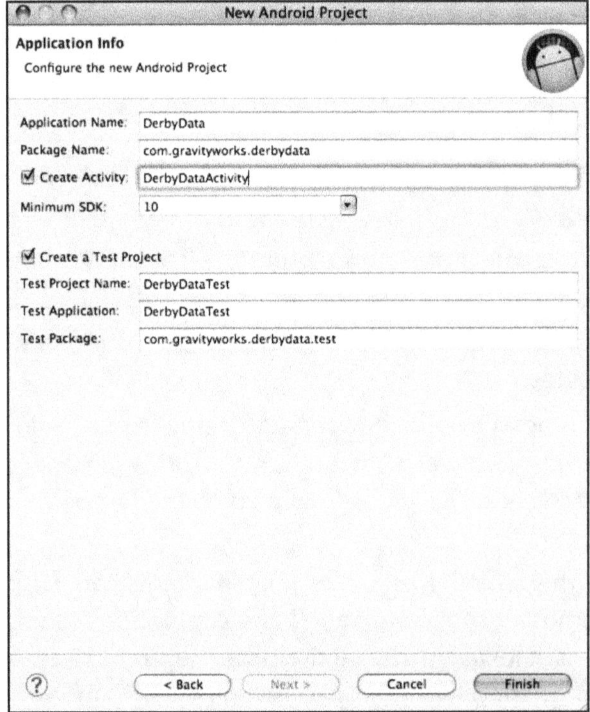

Fig. 1.17: Configuring application information

The screen show all of the SDKs that installed that you can target when creating application. This step is also very important when building application. The minimum SDK version set specifies the lowest possible version of the SDK in which application will run and it is the primary version in which application will run. Android 1.5 is the lowest version of the SDK still supported and Android 4.0.3 (at the time of this writing) is the highest.

2. Project Structure

The major sections to note in Fig. 1.18 are the src and res folders and the Android Manifest.xml file. It shows the project layout for the application that has been building in the previous steps.

All of the code lives within src folder, under Package Namespace. Folder holds layouts and resources for different hardware specs. HDPI, LDPI and MDPI are the resolutions for which can create images. The layout subfolder holds all of XML layouts. These are how application gets rendered. All of XML layouts are stored in the layout subfolder of res and code will be linked under the namespace in src folder of the project view.

The Android Manifest is the heart of application. It holds the entire configuration of app the permissions request, the application attributes and links to instrumentation to be attached to app. Edit this in Eclipse's Manifest Editor or in XML because that is how it is saved.

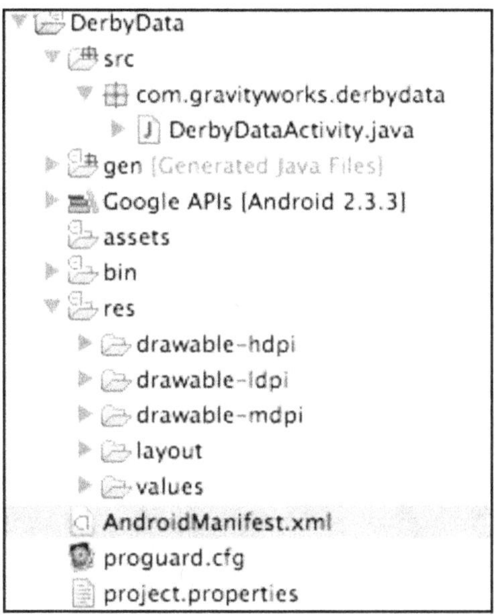

Fig. 1.18: Basic projectStructure

XML Editor is shown in Fig. 1.19. As make changes in the other tabs they are reflected here. If feel more comfortable editing the XML by hand can use this interface to add, update and remove properties as see fit.

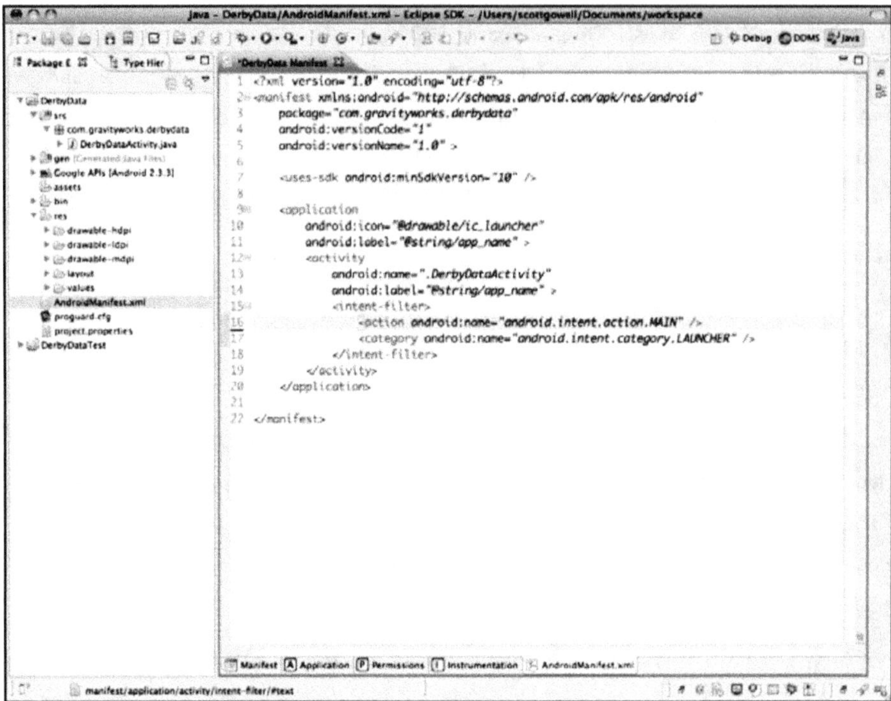

Fig. 1.19: Android manifest XML editor

3. Creating an Android Virtual Device

To create an Android Virtual Device (AVD) in order to debug application in the emulator, because this "device" is what the emulator runs. Creating an AVD is quite easy. Eclipse includes a tool called AVD Manager (click Window Manager ➪ AVD Manager). Need to name AVD instance, choose its OS version (Target), pick a skin (with which you can customize the look and feel of the emulator) and resolution and specify the hardware details for the device (amount of RAM, size of SD card and sensors like Accelerometer and GPS). Once configured it to specifications, click Create AVD and you are all set. Creating a new AVD with the appropriate specs and then selecting the skin gives, an emulator that looks just like the devices are testing for.

4. Debugging

Debugging in Eclipse is easy. Instead of running application, click Debug As and off and running. Set breakpoints in code by selecting them by the gutter next to the line numbers and as code progresses it will break at all steps.

In addition to breakpoint-based debugging, also have access to the Dalvik Debug Monitor Server (DDMS) perspective in Eclipse (see Fig. 1.20). Use DDMS to view the heap usage for a given process (running app or anything running inside the virtual machine), track memory allocation of objects inside an app, interact with the file system of the device running the app (emulator or actual), view running threads for an application, profile methods using tracing, read log messages using LogCat and emulate phone and sensor data (SMS, phone calls, location [GPS]).

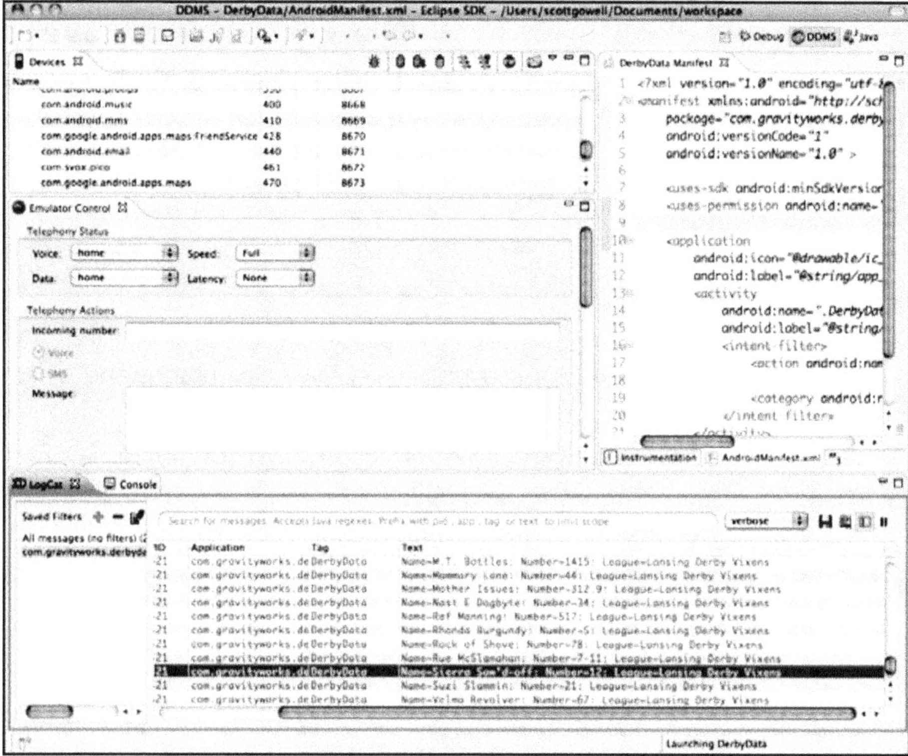

Fig. 1.20: DDMS perspective

1.10.3 Connecting to the Google Play

This section explains what is necessary to publish application to the Google Play. There is also the Amazon Android Marketplace, which has other requirements. Here, we will see the basic Google Play distribution process.

Getting an Android Developer Account

Signup is a snap for a dev account. Just make sure have a Google account either Gmail or Google Apps, one-time registration fee, head to https://play.google.com/apps/publish/signup and all are set.

Signing Application

Signing application with Eclipse is a relatively simple process:

1. Right-click on project in the Package Explorer and select File ⇨ Export.
2. Select Export Android Application.
3. Complete the steps of the wizard and have a keystore and a signed release build of app ready for the market.

When created keystore, make sure to guard it safely. It is the file that use to sign application every time update and if lose it cannot upgrade application in Google Play.

QUESTIONS

1. Give the importance of Mobile Development. How it is useful for the business world?
2. State the mobile myths associated with mobile application development with the reality.
3. Explain following types of frameworks for mobile development:
   (a) Translated Framework
   (b) Web Framework
   (c) Interpreted Framework
4. Differentiate Mobile Web and Mobile Application. Give advantages and disadvantages of both.
5. Explain Java Script Object Notation (JSON) with an example. Compare JSON with XML.
6. Explain Titanium, JQuery, PhoneGap, and Ionic frameworks.
7. Explain following with advantages and disadvantages:
   (a) Adaptive mobile website
   (b) Dedicated mobile website
   (c) Mobile web application

Unit II

MOBILE WEB

2.1 INTRODUCTION

The mobile web is one of those over-used terms that have lost all of its meaning, or worse yet, continues to confuse and spread the mobile myth. If you were to ask to define what the mobile web means, you would get as many different answers as people you asked.

The mobile web, from a user's perspective, is basically just web content accessed from a mobile device. From a developer's perspective, however, the mobile web definitely does exist, and it's a group of best practices, design patterns, and even new code that we need to learn.

2.1.1 Differences

An experienced web developer or web designer may feel confident about creating mobile web experiences. It seems like the same thing in a smaller package, right? Wrong. The mobile web is really different.

Some of the main differences from the desktop web include:

- Slower networks with higher latency.
- Slower hardware and less available memory.
- Different browsing experience.
- Different user contexts.
- Different browser behavior (for example, do you know that usually only the current tab on a mobile browser is active and running effectively?).
- Too many mobile web browsers, with different versions on the market at the same time.
- Some browsers are too limited, some browsers are too innovative.
- Several browsers without identity, documentation, or developer tools.
- Differences in testing and debugging.

2.2 WAP

This is recent history: the first mobile web platform was developed less than 15 years ago. Analyzing this history can help you to understand the technologies behind the mobile web, and compatibility issues.

2.2.1 What is WAP?

The Wireless Application Protocol is a standard for application-layer network communication in the mobile world. With the exception of i-mode protocol used in Japan and briefly in other countries, WAP is the primary protocol used by operators worldwide.

The WAP standard describes a protocol suite that allows the transportation of information between a device and the Internet via a WAP gateway, and a list of standard recommendations for the content to be transmitted. It was created by the WAP Forum.

For many years the term "WAP" was used incorrectly, to refer to a document type ("a WAP file") or a website as a whole. WAP has two main versions: 1.1, released in 1998, and 2.0, released in 2002 (this is the actual standard). Many users are not even aware of the existence of the newer version, and today it has been replaced by classic HTTP web browsing.

2.2.2 WAP1

- A wide range of operators started to offer mobile web browsing, with one or two devices with Wireless Application Protocol (WAP) browsers. At that time, mobile devices connected to the Internet using a voice call as a modem communication. So, every minute you were connected, was charged as a voice call minute. This early version of the mobile Internet was a failure. It was expensive and did not offer any useful services. The overall user experience was very poor.
- A few years later, 2.5G technologies such as the General Packet Radio Service (GPRS) appeared on the market. These technologies allowed us to browse the Internet (even WAP1 sites) and be charged according to the number of kilobytes transferred; no matter how many minutes we were connected to the Internet. This first mobile web was defined by the WAP1.0 standard which, in practice, never existed on the market, having quickly been replaced by WAP1.1.
- WAP1.x is not recommended today, as it has been replaced by new technologies. Some WAP1.x browsers were so simple that they didn't even have a "back" feature the developer was responsible for providing a link back to the previous page.
- Mobile browsers in this era were called "WAP browsers" and websites using this standard were called "WAP sites" "WAP" was used instead of "web". This created a perceived distinction between the two WAP appeared to be different from the Web. At this time, the de-facto standard for publishing WAP sites on the Internet was the use of the wap subdomain.
- Most low-end and mid-range devices on the market today still support WAP content, but the browsers on newer smartphones like the iPhone, and Android and Windows Phone devices don't support WML content anymore.

2.2.3 WAP2.0

WAP2.0 was released in 2002. The first WAP2.0 devices appeared in 2002, and almost every device on the market today is WAP2.0. This standard is nearer to the web standards than the previous version and allows HTTP communication between the device and the server. The WAP gateway acts only as a proxy in the operator network.

WAP2.0 deprecated WML and created XHTML MP (Mobile Profile), along with other companion standards. Surprisingly, after this new standard was released the word "WAP" dropped out of usage and "mobile web" started to be used. So, if we talk about a "WAP site" today, it will be understood that we are referring to a WAP1.1 website.

Many sites continued to use the wap subdomain for mobile websites, while others started using the other de-facto standard for publishing mobile websites, the m subdomain ("m" for mobile). For example, today we can access the Google Mobile website using http://m.google.com, or the popular Facebook social networking site using http://m.facebook.com

WAP Push

WAP push is a standard available since WAP1.2 that allows content to be pushed to a mobile device at any time. A WAP push is generally an SMS (Short Message Service) message to a special port with a URL to content or a website.

When a device receives a WAP push, it asks the user if he wants to go to that URL. Content portals use this method to push games, ringtones, and other premium content when you ask for that content using SMS. There are also some silent pushes from the operator that the user doesn't receive any feedback about.

WAP Link is a similar solution, but it sends an SMS to the user's inbox. The message contains a URL. Modern devices AutoDetect URLs inside the text messages and convert them into links that the user can click on. Modern smartphone platforms support push messages using an operating system layer that is out of the scope of carriers, working through TCP protocols.

2.3 FRAGMENTATION

Fragmentation in this context refers to how the market is "fragmented" in pieces supporting different interfaces, hardware, operating systems, and abilities offered to developers.

2.3.1 Display

A mobile device has a very small screen compared with a desktop. In desktop development 19-, 21-, and 25-inch screen sizes (diagonally) and in mobile development 1.5, 2.5, or 4 inches. It's really a big difference. Similarly, while in desktop development we refer 1024 × 768-pixel resolution, in mobile development about a quarter or half of that or in some cases, double that.

Resolution

Resolution is the primary concern in mobile design. How many pixels (width and height) are available on a given device? This was the only portability problem for many years in the area of mobile development.

There are no mobile device standards regarding screen resolution. One phone-sized device may have a resolution of 128 × 128 pixels, and another 720 × 1280. The third generation iPad has a 2048 × 1536 screen. But if we talk about devices sold from 2009, we can separate most of them into these groups:

- Feature phones: 128 × 160 or 128 × 128 pixels.
- Social phones (group #1, non-touch): 176 × 220, 176 × 208, 240 × 320 or 320 × 240 pixels.

- Social phones (group #2, touch): 240 × 320, 320 × 240 or 240 × 400 pixels.
- Touch-enabled smartphones (group #1, low resolution): 240 × 480, 320 × 480 or 360 × 480 pixels.
- Touch-enabled smartphones (group #2, higher resolution): 480 × 800, 480 × 854, 540 × 960, 640 × 960, 640 × 1136, 720 × 1280 or 768 × 1280 pixels.
- Tablets: 1024 × 768, 1024 × 600, 1280 × 800, 1920 × 1200 or 2048 × 1536 pixels.

Touch-only devices typically have a higher resolution than devices with a keyboard because no space needs to be reserved for the keypad. Most screen sizes have recognizable names that you will find in technical documentation and inside emulator settings. Table 2.1 shows the most important names you need to understand and their relation to DPI (dots per inch) for typical smartphones on the today.

Table 2.1: List of Screen Resolutions Available on the Market for Smartphones and Tablets, in Portrait Mode

Short Name	Name	Resolution	Aspect Ratio	Sample Devices	Average Screen Size	PPI
QQVGA	Quarter Quarter VGA	120 × 160, 128 × 160	4:3	Nokia C1-01, LG LX150	1.5″ – 1.8″	111 – 133
QVGA	Quarter VGA	240 × 320	4:3	Nokia Asha 300, Sony	2.4″	166
WQVGA	Wide Quarter VGA	240 × 400	5:3	Samsung Wave 2	3″	155
FWQVGA	Full Wide Quarter VGA	240 × 432	~16:9	Samsung F490	3.2″	155
LQVGA	Landscape Quarter VGA	320 × 240	4:3 land scape	BlackBerry 8320 (Curve), Sony Aspen	2.5″	160
HVGA	Half VGA	320 × 480	5:3	Apple iPhone 3GS, BlackBerry 9550 (Storm 2)	3.2″ – 3.5″	165-180
nHD	Ninth of High Definition	360 × 640	16:9	Nokia 808 PureView, Nokia N8	3.0″ – 3.5″	210-250

Short Name	Name	Resolution	Aspect Ratio	Sample Devices	Average Screen Size	PPI
WVGA	Wide VGA	480 × 800	5:3	Samsung Galaxy SII, Nokia Lumia 900	3.7″ – 4.3″	220-252
FWVGA	Full Wide VGA	480 × 854	16:9	Nokia N9, Motorola Droid X, Sony Xperia Play	3.9″ – 4.3″	228-251
VGA	Video Graphics Adapter	640 × 480	4:3 land scape	Nokia E6	2.5″	320
DVGA	Double Size VGA	640 × 960	3:2	Apple iPhone 4S	3.5″	330
WDVGA	Wide DVGA	640 × 1136	16:9	Apple iPhone 5	4″	330
QHD	Quarter High Definition	540 × 960	16:9	Motorola Droid RAZR, HTC Sensation	4.3″	256
WSVGA	Wide Super VGA	600 × 1024	~5:3	BlackBerry PlayBook, Samsung Galaxy Tab 7″	7″	170
HD	High Definition	720 × 1280	16:9	Galaxy Nexus, Sony Xperia S, Samsung Galaxy SIII	4.3″ – 4.8″	320 – 342
Sq.HD	Square HD	720 × 720	1:1	BlackBerry Q10	~3.5″	~300
XGA	Extended Graphic Adapter	768 × 1024	4:3	iPad 2, iPad mini, HP TouchPad	7.0″-9.7″	163-132
WXGA #1	Wide XGA	768 × 1280	15:9	Samsung Galaxy Tab 10.1, Motorola Xoom, Nexus 7, BlackBerry Z10	4.2″-10″	356-151

Short Name	Name	Resolution	Aspect Ratio	Sample Devices	Average Screen Size	PPI
WXGA #2	Wide XGA	768 × 1366	16:9	Microsoft Surface	10.6″	148
WXGA #3	Wide XGA	800 × 1280	16:10	Nexus 4	4.8″	320
Full HD	Full HD 1080p	1080 × 1920	16:9	Sony Xperia Z	5″	443
WUXGA	Widescreen Ultra XGA	1200 × 1920	16:10	Kindle Fire HD 8.9″	8.9″	254
QXGA	Quad XGA	1536 × 2048	4:3	iPad 3rd gen.	9.7″	256
WQXGA	Wide Quad XGA	1600 × 2560	16:10	Nexus 10	10″	300

Physical Dimensions

The resolution isn't the only thing we can talk about with regard to a mobile device's screen. One feature as important as the resolution is the physical dimensions of the screen in inches or centimeters, diagonally or measured as width × height, or the relation between this measure and the resolution, which is known as the PPI (pixels per inch) or DPI (dots per inch).

This is very important, because while our first thought may be that a screen with a resolution of 128 × 160 is "smaller" than a screen with are solution of 240 × 320 that may be a false conclusion. Consider the iPad2 and the third generation iPad: they have resolutions of 1024 × 768 and 2048 × 1536, respectively, in the same 9.7″ screen. Also, you can find on the market 10″ tablets with only as many pixels as a high-resolution 4.5″ smartphone.

We can categorize screen sizes as follows:

- Small phone screens: from 1.5″ to 3″
- Normal/medium phone screens: from 3″ to 4″
- Large phone screens: from 4″ to 5″
- Small tablet screens: from 5″ to 8″
- Large tablet screens: from 8″ to 11″

Every screen size type can have different density options:

- Low density: 100 to 130 PPI
- Medium density: 130 to 180 PPI
- High density: 180 to 270 PPI
- Ultra-high density: more than 270 PPI

That's why, on the market, we can find medium phone screens with medium density, high density, and ultra-high density with resolutions of 320 × 480, 480 × 854, and 640 × 960, all having the same physical screen size, meaning more or fewer pixels in the same area.

Pixel Density Ratio

To solve the problem of having different-resolution devices in the same device category, some mobile browsers support a feature called device pixel ratio. This is a multiplier that, when available, is automatically applied to our web content.

Be careful to not confuse device pixel ratio with pixel aspect ratio, which describes how the width of one pixel relates to its height.

When this feature is available inside a browser, instead of working with physical dimensions we are working with something known variously as device-independent pixels, density-independent pixels, CSS pixels, or virtual pixels. That means that if we define something to be 100 pixels wide and 20 pixels high, we are not talking about real device pixels. Instead, our measures will be multiplied by the current device pixel ratio, so it may be 150 × 30 pixels on a 1.5 pixel ratio device or 200 × 40 pixels on a 2 pixel ratio device.

Table 2.2 lists the device pixel ratio values that are most common on mobile devices currently on the market as of the beginning of 2013.

Table 2.2: Most Common Device Pixel Ratio Values and Sample Devices

Device Pixel Ratio Value	Resolution	Platform Using the Value	Sample Devices
0.75	Low	Android	Samsung Galaxy Mini, Motorola Charm, Sony Xperia Mini
1	Medium	iOS, Android, BlackBerry, Symbian	iPhones 3GS, iPad mini 1st gen., Nokia 500, LG Optimus One, HTC Explorer, BB torch 9810
1.3 to 1.4	Medium	Symbian, Android tablets	Nokia N8 (1.3), Nexus 7 (1.325...)
1.5	High	Android, symbian, MeeGo	Samsung Galaxy SII, LG Optimus, Nexus One, Sony Xperia Play, Nokia E6, Nokia N9
2	Ultra high	iOS, Android	iPhones 4S, iPhone 5, iPad 3rd and 4th gen., Galaxy Nexus, Galaxy SIII
2.1 to 2.5	Ultra high	Android, BlackBerry	Galaxy Nexus, Galaxy SIII, BlackBerry Z10
3	Ultra high	Android	Sony Xperia Z

Aspect Ratio

A device's aspect ratio is the ratio between its longer and shorter dimensions. There are vertical or portrait devices whose displays are taller than they are wide, there are horizontal or landscape devices whose displays are wider than they are tall, and there are also some square screens. To complicate our lives as designers even more, today there are also many devices with rotation capabilities. Such a device can be either 320 × 240 or 240 × 320, depending on the orientation. Our websites need to be aware of this and offer a good experience in both orientations.

The most recognizable aspect ratios are:

- Standard 4:3, used in classic TV and old CRT computer monitors
- Standard 3:2, used in classic 35 mm film
- Wide-screen 16:9, used in standard high-definition TV
- Wide-screen 15:9, used in LCD desktop computer monitors
- European wide-screen 5:3, used in Super 16 mm film

The other important part of aspect ratio in terms of mobile phones is the phone factor.

You will encounter all of the following:

- Phones and tablets with portrait (wider than high) and landscape (higher than wide) modes
- Phones with screens wider than they are high, such as most BlackBerry smartphones before BB10
- Phones with screens higher than they are wide with no rotation mechanism, such as most feature phones.

While your first thought may be that most mobile devices should be wide-screen because they are "modern," you should check that for example, every iPad on the market right now is using the standard 4:3 aspect ratio, and the iPhone 4S uses 3:2.

2.3.2 Input Methods

Today, there are many different input methods for mobile devices that change how a mobile web app should be developed. A given device may support only one input method, or many of them. Possibilities include:

- Numeric keypad
- Alphanumeric keypad (ABC or QWERTY)
- Virtual keypad on screen
- Touch
- Multi-touch
- External keypad (wireless or not)
- Handwriting recognition
- Voice recognition.

And of course any possible combination of these, like a touch device with an optional onscreen keyboard and also a full QWERTY physical keyboard (see Fig. 2.1).

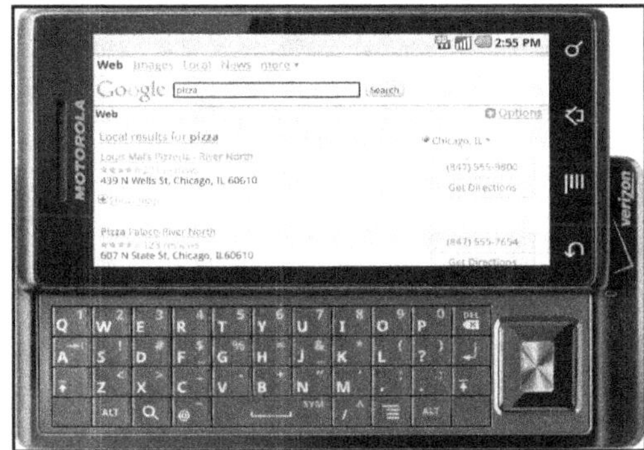

Fig. 2.1: The Motorola full slider QWERTY keyboard

Fig. 2.2: The iPhone and iPod touch virtual keyboard

If you are thinking that QWERTY sounds like a Star Trek Klingon's word, go now to your keyboard and look at the first line of letters below the numbers. That's the reason for the name; it's a keyboard layout organized for the smoothest typing in the English language, created in 1874. This layout is preserved in many onscreen keyboards (see Fig. 2.2).

2.4 BROWSERS AND WEB PLATFORMS

Understanding the big picture about platforms, operating systems, brands, and models is important for getting started in the mobile market, but the most important information for us will be which mobile browser or platform is used.

All mobile devices come with one preinstalled mobile browser, and very few of them can be upgraded or uninstalled. There are some exceptions: the browsers included with iOS, Windows Phone, Symbian, and Android (up to 4.0) are upgraded when you update the operating system firmware.

To complicate the situation, almost every device on the market allows users to add an alternative web browser, and some carriers, like Vodafone in Europe, include a copy of an alternative web browser customized for that operator, such as Opera Mini or Mobile, along with the factory-installed browser.

2.4.1 Web Platforms that are Not Browsers

You may be thinking that "Platforms that aren't browsers?" Well, that's true. That is, in some situations our content will be executed not in a browser, but inside some other native app or platform that can take web development to a different level.

While the market doesn't have concrete names for all of these things yet, we are going to talk about the following:

- Browser-based websites or web apps
- Web views
- e-books.
- HTML5 apps
- Native web apps

While browser-based websites or web apps is the easiest category to understand, with mobile web technologies including HTML5 we can deliver experiences that can get users out of the browser.

2.4.1.1 HTML5 Web Apps

Some platforms allow users to create application-like experiences by using the browser as the installation platform, and providing from then on a full-screen experience based on the browser. Usually this category involves installation through the browser itself or a store accessed via the browser. We don't need to compile or sign anything, and usually it involves away to define the package of files to use and the metadata.

There may be some confusion between these HTML5 web apps and hybrid or native apps. In the latter case we are creating HTML5 apps but wrapping them inside a native app, including compilation, signing, and native store distribution.

HTML5 web apps are hosted-based (must be hosted on a web server) and distributed through the browser, and there is no way to call native code outside of the HTML5 APIs available.

iOS Web Apps

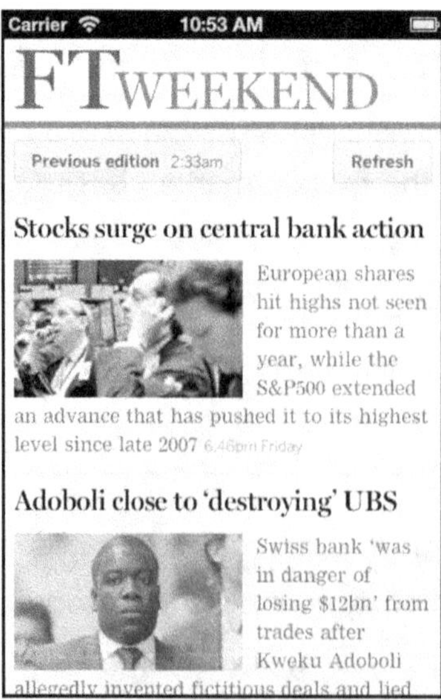

Fig. 2.3: iOS web app of financial times

On iOS devices we can upgrade a mobile website to a full-screen HTML5 app with a series of meta-tags and techniques. With this technique (Apple calls it a web app), the user can install an icon in the Home screen, sharing the space with the native apps.

Mixing this technique with HTML5 APIs, we can create an offline experience like that the user gets with any installed application. Fig. 2.3 shows an example of an iOS web app.

Chrome Apps

Google Chrome started with the idea of HTML5 apps on the desktop and notebook side, even delivering a store for app distribution, the Chrome Web Store. Today the Chrome app platform is available on Windows, Mac, Linux, and Chrome OS, and inmid-2012 Google announced that Android would be supported soon. Chrome apps are also known as packaged apps.

Once an app is installed in the system, it can be launched from Chrome or a system icon, and using HTML5 and Chrome APIs it can leverage a full-screen and offline experience.

Firefox Open Web Apps

Firefox supports on all of its platforms desktops, tablets, and smartphones the ability to create apps and distribute them through the Mozilla Marketplace. Every application is based on HTML5, with an app manifest defining all the information needed to install the application and run it out of the scope of the browser. We can expect these apps to work on Firefox OS, Firefox for Android, and desktop Firefox.

Samsung Web API

In early 2013 Samsung released an SDK to create web apps for smartphones and smart TVs using web technologies and a JavaScript API. It's compatible with devices such as the Galaxy SIII and Galaxy Note II, and it can also communicate with a Samsung smart TV. The platform supports mobile web apps, TV web apps, and convergence web apps, which inter work between a Samsung Smartphone and a TV.

2.4.1.2 Web Views

- A native application is compiled and signed using official SDKs and non-web programming languages, such as C, Objective-C, Java, or C#. Almost every native mobile platform includes a control or component that allows web content to be embedded inside a native application. This component is generically known as a web view.
- While sometimes the rendering engine in a web view is exactly the same as the one used in the browser, in some situations the behavior in terms of markup, APIs, and performance can be quite different.
- Even if you are not creating a native application with a web view inside, your website may be rendered in a web view: some social media related native apps for iOS, Android, and other mobile operating systems use this mechanism to show web content to users instead of opening the default web browser.

- Examples of web views in action include most social networking applications for smartphones and tablets. Usually there is a way to open the link in the web browser, but the default initial behavior is to open the URL inside a web view. In Fig. 2.4 we can see this in action in the Twitter application for iPod.

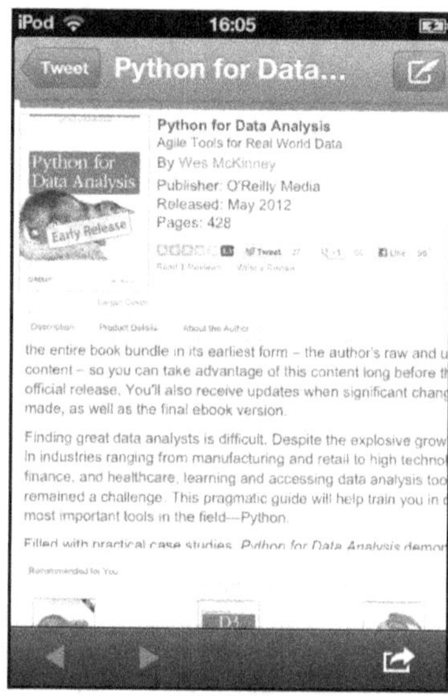

Fig. 2.4: Web page is loaded in a web view, not in the browser

Pseudo-Browsers

A pseudo-browser is a native application marketed as a web browser that, instead of providing its own rendering and execution engines, uses the native web views.

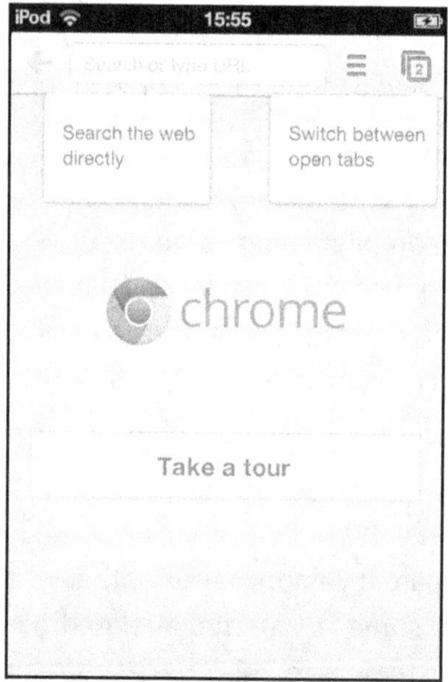

Fig. 2.5: Chrome for iOS

From a user's point of view, it's a browser. From a developer's point of view, it's just the web view with a particular UI. Therefore, we have the same rendering engine as in the preinstalled browser, but with a different UI. These pseudo-browsers are mostly available for iOS and Android, and they offer the same service as the native browser but with different services on top of them.

Google Chrome for iOS (Fig. 2.5) is a key example of a pseudo-browser. Because of an App Store licensing limitation, Google cannot deliver its own rendering and execution engine with a native app. Therefore, Google decided to deliver a Chrome experience application with the default iOS web view engine. This means Chrome for iOS does not have the same HTML5 compatibility or features as Chrome for Android or desktop Chrome, but it does have the same features as the iOS web view.

Chrome for iOS is an example of a pseudo-browser: the rendering and execution engines are provided by the iOS web view, not by the Chrome team, so only updates to iOS will enable more developer features for this "browser."

2.4.1.3 Native Web Apps

Also known as a hybrid application, a native web application is a compiled native application that usually uses a full-screen web view as the whole application container. One approach is that the whole application is developed using web technologies HTML, CSS, JavaScript, but it is packaged and compiled as a native application so we can distribute it in native application stores. Another approach is to use some native layers and some web layers at the same time, such as native UI components with only some parts in a web view, with JavaScript logic.

We can also use web views ourselves if we have native know-how, such as Objective-Con iOS or Java on Android. We just need to add the web view and connect the component to some local or generated HTML code.

If we don't have any native know-how or just want to make it work fast and across multiple platforms, we can use a framework that will help us with the process. Some frameworks add a layer of JavaScript and native code, offering new APIs for web developers to use.

2.4.1.4 e-books

The latest e-book readers support some kind of HTML5 and web content based on different formats such as EPUB 3 or Kindle Format 8. These formats are based on HTML5, meaning that we can create interactive e-book experiences with HTML, CSS, and JavaScript.

2.4.2 Mobile Browsers

When browsing the Web on our mobile devices, we can use the preinstalled browser available by default on every device or we can install new browsers through the application stores. Let's review the most important browsers in both categories.

2.4.2.1 Preinstalled Browsers

Practically every mobile device on the market today has a preinstalled browser. One of the big features of these browsers is that the average user typically doesn't install a new web browser; therefore, on each device the preinstalled browser is the most-used one. One main disadvantage of preinstalled browsers is that usually there is no way to update the browser independently from the operating system. If your device doesn't get operating system updates, usually you will not get browser updates.

Safari on iOS

- Safari is a web browser developed by Apple based on the Web Kit engine that offers a great browsing experience and smart zoom options. First released in 2003 with Mac OS X Panther, a mobile version has been included in iOS devices since the introduction of the iPhone in 2007. It is the default browser on Apple devices.
- It is updated with every operating system change to include new features that allow us, as developers, to create better user experiences.
- Safari on iOS formerly known as Mobile Safari was the first mobile browser to support a range of new features, including those that allow us to create animations, transitions, 3D effects, and Flash-like experiences using HTML, JavaScript, and CSS but without Flash what we currently known as HTML5.
- This browser is designed for touch and multi-touch navigation. It can support focus navigation if the user is attaching an external keyboard, and it was also the first browser to support accessibility features such as a screen reader for people with visual disabilities. Most of the HTML5 APIs were first implemented in Safari on iOS.

Android Browser

- Up to and including Android 4.0 (Ice Cream Sandwich), the Android OS came with its own browser, based on WebKit. It is called the Android browser, sometimes referred to as Android WebKit. While many developers believe that it is similar to Google Chrome or even Safari on iOS, the truth is that the Android browser has always lagged behind other mobile browsers in terms of performance, HTML5 compatibility, and even bugs found.
- The browser has changed a lot between different versions of the operating system, to the extent that versions 2.2 and 4.0 can be considered two distinct browsers. Even in the same version of the operating system, we can find customized versions of the browser on devices from different vendors, such as Samsung or Sony.
- Google realized that the Android browser was not good enough for its platform, so it started a completely separate project, Google Chrome for Android, to replace this browser.
- The Android browser is considered a legacy browser after Android 4.1 from late 2012 and has been replaced by Google Chrome. However, the web view still executes the Android browser engine.
- Google Chrome for Android is now the default browser preinstalled on most new devices coming to the market with Android 4.1. However, devices that were upgraded to 4.1 from 4.0 still have the Android browser.

Google Chrome

- Google's Chrome for Android is an edition of Google Chrome released for the Android system. On February 7, 2012, Google launched Google Chrome Beta for Android 4 (Ice Cream Sandwich) devices, for selected countries. In 2012, Chrome appeared in the mobile world as a downloadable browser for Android 4.0, and since Android 4.1 (Jelly Bean) it has begun to replace the default browser. It shares most of its code with the desktop version of Google Chrome and is one of the most modern HTML5 browsers on the market.
- Unfortunately, only Android 4.0 or newer devices can install Chrome. However, one of the key features is that the browser is upgradeable through the Google Play Store without the need to wait for an operating system upgrade. That means that Chrome users will have new HTML5 features available sooner than users of other platforms.
- In mid-2012, Google also released Google Chrome for iOS, a pseudo-browser for iPhone, iPod, and iPad users that delivers the Chrome experience. It uses the same user agent name as Safari, adding a string called CriOS (presumably for "Chrome for iOS") so developers looking for the Chrome string inside that name will not be confused and decide to deliver Chrome-only code.

BlackBerry Browser

Every BlackBerry device comes with a mobile web browser with focus navigation and, more recently, touch navigation support. Many versions of the browser are available, depending on the device. There are devices with trackball and cursor navigation, older devices with focus navigation, and newer smartphones with touch support.

The first generation of the BlackBerry browser was included with Device Software version 4.5 and earlier. The second generation, available from versions 4.6 to 5.0, had are designed rendering engine but was still far behind other mobile browsers in terms of performance and compatibility.

BlackBerry devices running OS 6.0, 7.0, and 7.1 have a WebKit-based browser that was completely redesigned for the tablet PlayBook and the new BlackBerry 10 platform.

Internet Explorer

Microsoft's browser can be considered to have been one of the first mobile browsers on the market. The first version was released in 1996, for Windows CE 1.0: it was first known as Pocket Internet Explorer (PIE), then Internet Explorer Mobile, and is now just called Internet Explorer.

The new operating system from Microsoft, launched in 2010 as Windows Phone 7, came with a new version of Internet Explorer Mobile that was based on the IE7 engine, with some IE8 features mixed in. It offers similar behavior to Internet Explorer 7, and multi touch support.

Older Windows Mobile devices supported an IE4 or IE6 engine. Browser from Microsoft: Internet Explorer 9, using the same code base as IE9 for desktops with some special mobile additions. This was the start of a new way of Microsoft seeing the mobile web browser.

Nokia Browser

Nokia Browser is a generic name for different real products available for different platforms inside the Nokia world.

1. Nokia Browser for Series 40

Every Nokia Series 40 device comes with a built-in web browser created by Nokia. In 2010, Nokia acquired a browser company called Novarra that offers cloud-based web support. Nokia has since created a new Java-based browser called the Nokia Xpress browser formerly Ovi Browser that offers a new experience for feature phones and social devices. This browser was originally available as a free download from the Nokia Store and is now being preinstalled in newer Series 40 devices, such as the Asha series devices.

The new browser renders websites on the server and delivers a compressed, already rendered version to the phone, giving users a fast browsing experience. This browser works with touch and focus-based devices, and it adds the ability to create installed web apps for Nokia Store distribution with HTML5 support all rendered from the Nokia servers.

2. Nokia Browser for Symbian

In 2005, Nokia created the first open source WebKit-based mobile browser for Symbian devices known for many years as the S60 OSS browser. Depending on the device, it supports focus, cursor, and multi touch navigation. Many devices support more than one navigation type; for instance, the Nokia E7 supports touch (finger and stylus) navigation and cursor navigation when the keyboard is opened.

2.4.2.2 User-Installable Browsers

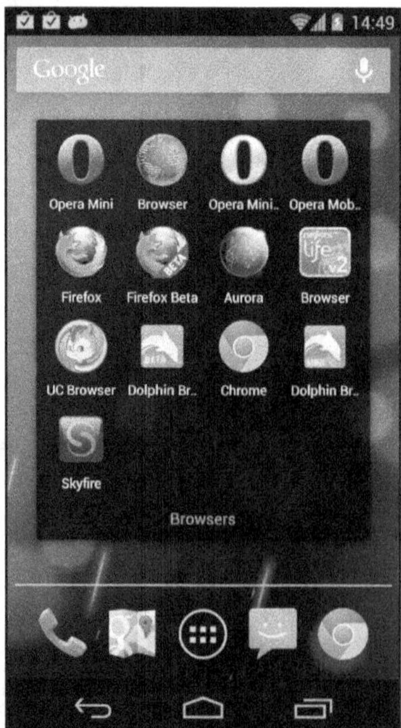

Fig. 2.6: Browsers that can be installed on Android devices

These are free and commercial web browsers that users can install after they buy a device. Sometimes they are included on the device by the vendor or the operator in a particular country or region.

On iOS there is no way to replace the default browser Apple's policies do not allow anything but the default rendering or execution engine, and the OS does not support the ability to change the default browser. Even if we install apps using the web view, such as Chrome for iOS, the operating system will always open Safari when we click on links in any app. On Android we can find several browsers with their own rendering engines that can replace the default browser (see Fig. 2.6).

Opera Mobile

Opera has lost the desktop browser war, but it took its experience in browser creation and entered the mobile world in 2000. Opera Mobile is a full browser supporting tab and cursor navigation that comes factory preinstalled on some devices and is sometimes preinstalled by the carrier, replacing the default device browser.

Opera Mobile is also available for download by users of Android, MeeGo, and Symbian devices. Usually, users can download the latest version and a beta of the next version, known as the Opera Mobile Labs build.

Opera Mini

Opera Mini remains one of the best Java ME application sever produced for feature phones. It is a free browser that works on almost any device, including feature phones from Nokia, LG, Samsung, and Sony, and smartphones such as Android and iOS devices like iPhone, iPod, iPad.

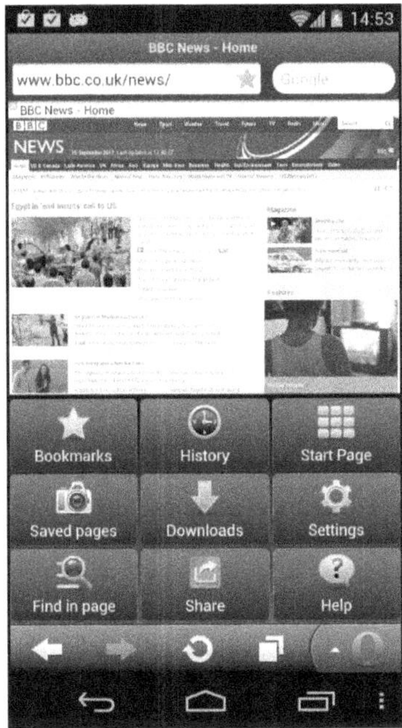

Fig. 2.7: Opera mini

It supports "the full web". This means that if you browse using Opera Mini, you won't be accessing websites directly. Instead, the application will contact an Opera Mini server that will compress and pre-render the websites. This allows very quick full web navigation for every device, whether low-end or smartphone.

It is an excellent option for low-end and mid-range devices. The same browser is available for smartphones.

From version 4, it supports video playback, Ajax, offline reading, and smart zooming, even in low-end devices (see Fig. 2.7). From version 5, it also supports tabbed browsing, a password manager, and touch navigation in devices with touch support. Versions 6 and 7 include new rendering engines, more CSS3 support, and performance improvements. Opera offers a beta version of future versions of the browser known as Opera Mini Next.

Firefox Browser

Firefox for mobile is the build of the Mozilla Firefox web browser for devices such as smartphones and tablet computers. The Mozilla Foundation arrived a bit late to the mobile browser world. Mozilla offers a downloadable Firefox version for Android and MeeGo (the Nokia N9) and a working version for the Windows 8 Metro UI optimized for tablets, and it has been updated in sync with the desktop version. It uses the same Gecko engine as the Firefox desktop browser and it works on smartphones and tablets.

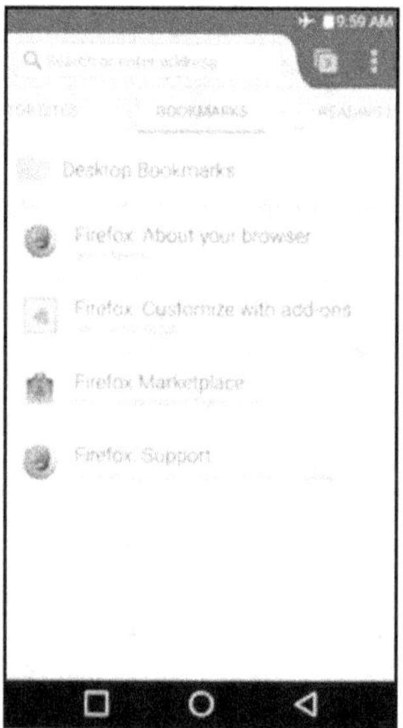

Fig. 2.8: Firefox browser on android device

Dolphin Browser

Dolphin Browser formerly Tunny Browser is a mobile browser for the operating systems Android and iOS developed by Mobotap. It was one of the first alternative browsers for the Android platform that introduced support for multi-touch gestures. Dolphin Browser uses the Webkit engine and the native platform rendering abilities, which allows for a small disk footprint. It can run Adobe Flash on Android.

Fig. 2.9: Dolphin browser

The latest versions of this application for Android replace the web view with their own WebKit-based engine, which has one of the top scores in terms of HTML5 compatibility and performance. You can download Dolphin from Apple's App Store, the Google Play Store, or the Dolphin website.

UC Browser

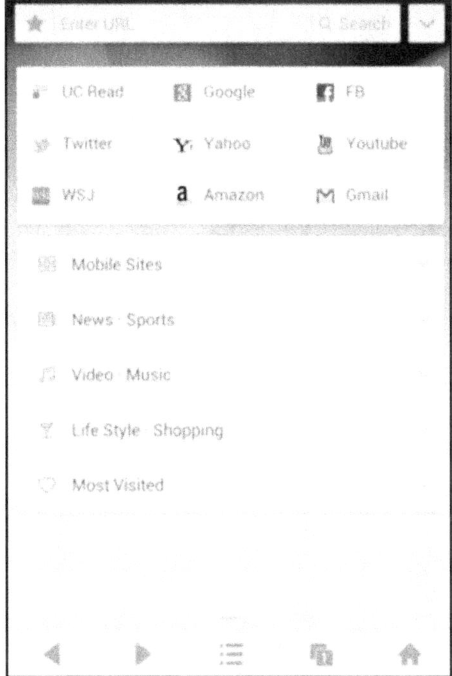

Fig. 2.10: UC browser

- UC Browser is a mobile browser developed by Chinese mobile Internet Company UCWeb also known as UC Mobile. Originally launched in April 2004 as a J2 me-only application, it is available on platforms including Android, iOS, Windows Phone, Symbian, Java ME, and BlackBerry. It is a cloud-based browser supporting full HTML and Java-Script, multiple windows, and many advanced features.
- The UC Browser formerly known as UCWEB is the number one browser in the Chinese market and number two in the Indian market and is now available in English for other markets as a downloadable browser.
- The browser uses cloud acceleration and data compression technology. UC Browser's servers act as a proxy which compresses the data of web pages before sending it to users. This process helps load web content faster. The browser can adapt to different network environments and support multi-file format downloading. In addition, UC Browser has HTML5 web app and cloud syncing features.

2.5 TOOLS FOR MOBILE WEB DEVELOPMENT

Unlike desktop web development, where you're likely to create and test your work on the same device, mobile development generally requires setting up and managing several development environments.

2.5.1 Working with Code

We can use almost any web tool available on the market, including Adobe Dream weaver, Microsoft Visual Studio, Eclipse, Aptana Studio, and also any good text editor, such as Sublime Text, Textmate, WebStorm, or Notepad++. It is often easier and cleaner to work directly with the code rather than using a visual tool or IDE in mobile web development.

Adobe Dreamweaver

Since the CS 5.5 version, Dreamweaver has worked better with mobile markup and allows us to validate against mobile web standards. In this editor, when we create a new document we can choose HTML5 as the document type, as shown in Fig. 2.11.

Version CS6 includes several improvements that support mobile web design and development, such as:

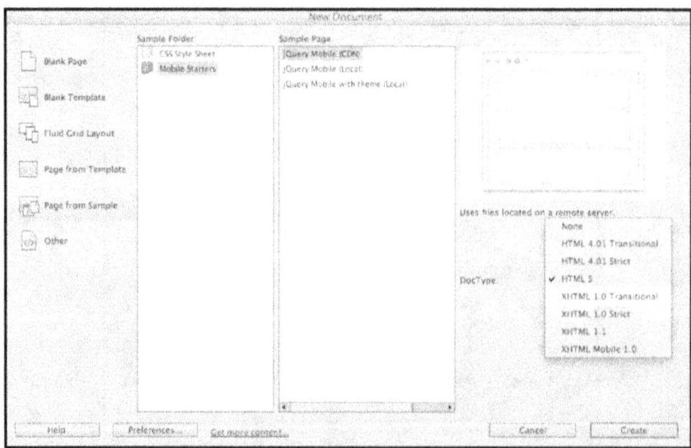

Fig. 2.11: HTML5 as document type

- HTML5 support and code hinting
- Multiple screen previews
- jQuery Mobile integration
- PhoneGap Build integration for native web app compilation from the IDE

Dreamweaver allows us to define new files as HTML5 or XHTML Mobile Profile documents, as well as giving us the ability to start with a jQuery Mobile template.

Adobe Edge Tools

Adobe offers a group of tools under the name of Edge that help designers and developers to create HTML5 applications. They include:

Edge Code

A complete HTML5 editor based on web technologies, this tool is based on the open source editor Brackets and it includes several interesting ideas on how to code HTML, CSS, and JavaScript quickly and easily.

Edge Reflow

A tool that helps designers to create responsive web design solutions

Edge Inspect

A tool for mobile HTML5 testing

Edge Animate

A tool to design HTML5 animations visually

You can download these tools from Adobe's website.

Microsoft Visual Studio and WebMatrix

Microsoft IDEs have supported HTML5 syntax and IntelliSense since version 2010 SP1.

Users can also use WebMatrix for mobile web development; it's available for free.

WebMatrix has supported mobile websites since version 2, including:

- Mobile friendly templates
- Connection with the Windows Phone emulator and iOS simulation
- Code completion for HTML5 and the jQuery Mobile UI framework

Eclipse

If users would like to use Eclipse as thier development environment, there are several plug-ins they can use to create mobile HTML5 apps. Suggested are Aptana from Titanium, a free Eclipse-based IDE for HTML5 and mobile development.

Native Web IDEs

If users are going to target native web or hybrid apps, some platforms offer tools and IDEs they can use to develop, test, and build their final packages. The most important products include:

Nokia Web Tools

For testing and compilation of S40 web apps. A legacy 1.2 version that will help with the legacy WRT Symbian format is still available.

Tizen IDE

For the creation of Tizen apps based on HTML5

Intel XDK

A nonofficial for creating tool for creating Apache Cordova HTML5 native apps

Titanium Studio

An Eclipse plug-in to create Appcelerator Titanium JavaScript mobile apps

2.5.2 Testing

Mobile browsers are really different, and we need to test our mobile apps using tools that are as accurate as possible.

If it doesn't work in the emulator, it probably will not work on the real device, and if it works in the emulator, it probably will work on the real device yes, again "probably"!

There are some problems with this testing approach, though. For one thing, there are hundreds of differences between real devices, and hundreds of bugs. Furthermore, there are several platforms without emulation. That is why real device testing is mandatory. Let's first review emulators and simulators. The most useful tools for testing will be emulators and simulators.

Emulators

- An emulator is a piece of software that translates compiled code from an original architecture to the platform where it is running.
- It allows us to run an operating system and its native applications on another operating system. In the mobile development world, an emulator is a desktop application that emulates mobile device hardware and a mobile operating system, allowing us to test and debug our applications and see how they are working.
- The browser, and even the operating system, is not aware that it is running on an emulator, so we can execute the same code that we would execute on the real device. Emulators are created by manufacturers and offered to developers for free, either standalone or bundled with the Software Development Kit (SDK) for native development.
- There are also operating system emulators that don't represent any real device hardware, but rather the operating system as a whole. These exist for Windows Phone and Android.

Simulators

- Simulator is a less complex application that simulates some of the behavior of a device, but does not emulate hardware and does not work over the real operating system. These tools are simpler and less useful than emulators.
- Simulator may be created by the device manufacturer or by some other company offering a simulation environment for developers. In mobile browsing, there are

simulators with pixel-level simulation, and others that neither create a skin over a typical desktop browser such as Firefox, Chrome, or Safari with real typography nor simulate these browser's rendering engines.

- Emulators and simulators don't replace real device testing, but they are useful for UI testing, JavaScript debugging, and testing different scenarios. These tools are useless to test performance, touch interaction, and some hardware scenarios, such as the accelerometer and lighting conditions.
- As the emulators have the same operating system and applications as the real devices, you'll need to wait for the OS to load before opening a web page.

Android Emulator

- The Android emulator is available in conjunction with the SDK to create native Java applications for Android. You can download it for free from the Android Developer page; the base SDK and the different Android OS versions are available separately.
- The Android emulator is available for Windows, Mac OS X, and Linux. Once you've download edit, create a folder for the contents on your hard drive and unzip the package. On Windows, there is an installer version that will do the work for you.
- In the folder where you extracted the package, there is an android terminal command on Mac OS X/Linux and an SDK Setup.exe application for Windows that opens the Android SDK Manager shown in Fig. 2.12, where you can download and configure Android platforms known as packages or targets after installing the base SDK.
- You can download as many packages as you want, one per operating system version; you can even download vendor-specific emulators, such as for the Motorola Xoom 2, LG Optimus 3D, or Galaxy Tab. Try to download the latest releases of every Android version, such as Android 2.3.3, Android 4.0, and Android 4.1.

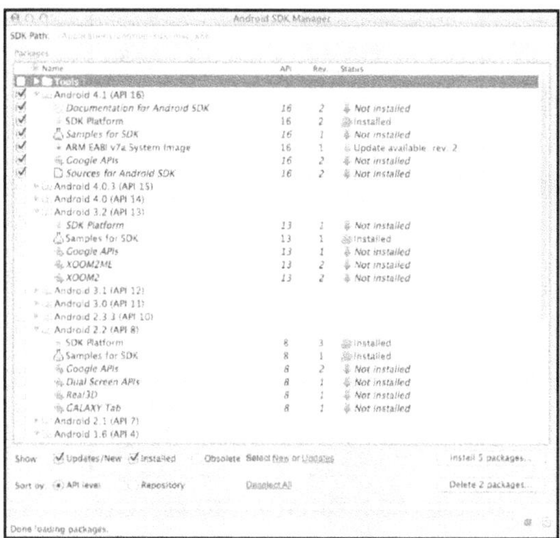

Fig. 2.12: Android SDK Manager

- One you've created the device, you can select it and click Start to reach a result like the one shown in Fig. 2.13.

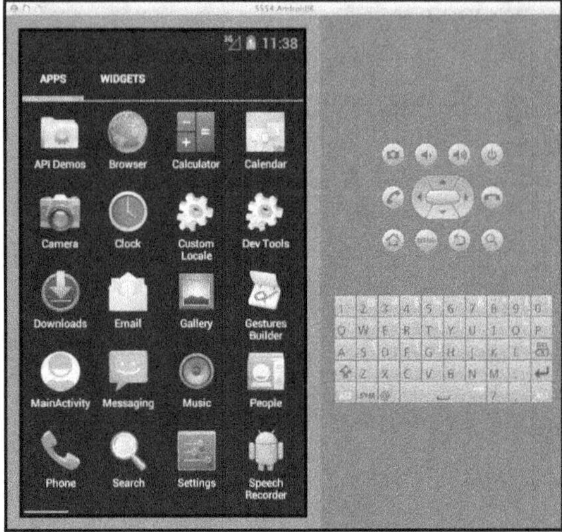

Fig. 2.13: Android device emulator's screen

- When you start the Android Virtual Device (AVD), you will be prompted with an opening configuration window, as seen in Fig. 2.14. In this Launch Options window you can scale the emulator if it's bigger than your own computer screen a possible situation when opening tablet emulators using the "Scale display to real size" option. If you want to delete all the settings and applications installed on that emulator, you can use the option "Wipe user data".

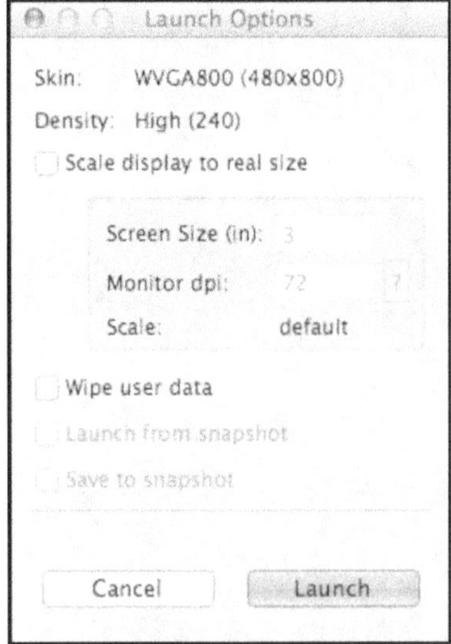

Fig. 2.14: Launch AVD screen

- When using the Android emulator, you can use the shortcuts Ctrl-F11 and Ctrl-F12 to change the emulator's orientation.

iOS Simulator

- Available for only Mac OS, the iOS Simulator shown in Fig. 2.15 offers a free simulation environment for the iPhone and iPad, including the mobile browser Safari. It is not an emulator, so it does not really provide a hardware emulation experience and is not a true performance indicator.
- However, it is perfectly suitable for seeing how your website is rendering and how your code is working. It's especially convenient for loading local or remote files by typing in the URL field using your desktop keyboard.

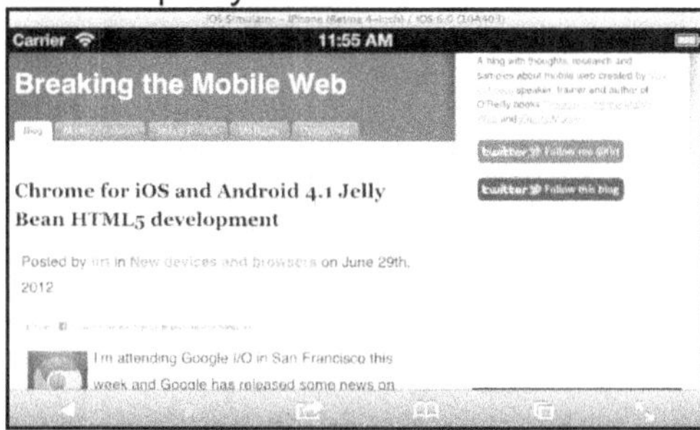

Fig. 2.15: The iOS Simulator

- The iOS Simulator is included with the SDK for native development, available for free at the Mac App Store (search for Xcode) or at from Apple's website. The SDK may take a while to download, because it's about 1.5 GB. You will always download the latest version of the operating system and can then add previous versions such as 6.0, in which case you can switch between versions using the Hardware → Version menu option.
- To download a previous version of the operating system to the simulator, you need to open the Xcode app, open Preferences, and select Downloads.
- Within the Simulator, you can also select what device you want to simulate using the Hardware → Device menu option.

Nokia Emulators

- Nokia has always had the better emulators, since the beginning of mobile web development. Instead of one emulator per device, you'll find one emulator for each version of each platform. You can download emulators for Series 40 devices (feature phones and social devices) and for Symbian smartphones at the Nokia forum.
- Nokia also has a tool called the Nokia Mobile Browser Simulator, developed in 2003 to test mobile websites for old WAP1.0 devices and the first WAP2.0 ones. Today, this tool is still available but deprecated; we don't need it.
- Unfortunately, Nokia emulators, like that shown in Fig. 2.16, are available only for the Windows operating system.
- If you need to emulate a Nokia device, first find the correct platform version for that device at Nokia's website and then download the emulator for that platform. Nokia guarantees (and it works almost all the time) that every device based on the same platform version has the same browser and rendering engine and even the same hardware features.

Fig. 2.16: A touch-based browser running in a Nokia S40 emulator

- Once you've launched the emulator, you can open the browser and type in the URL or use the shortcut File → Open, which allows you to type or paste a URL or browse for a file in your local file system. The emulator will open the browser automatically.
- Nokia S40 emulators support the use of localhost or 127.0.0.1 to connect with your desktop host computer.

BlackBerry Simulators

Research in Motion (RIM), vendor of the popular BlackBerry devices, has two different tools available for web developers: emulators and a simulator for web apps known as Ripple.

RIM has done a great job with emulators, with only one problem: it is very difficult to decide which one to download and use. Dozens of different installers are available at BlackBerry's developer site; you can download the proxy server and the emulators.

The BlackBerry Smartphone Simulators (for BlackBerry OS versions up to 7.1) are compatible only with the Windows operating system, but the emulators for BB10 and Play-Book are also available for the Mac and Linux platforms.

Ripple: Ripple is a free tool available as a Google Chrome for desktop plug-in that helps us test HTML5 web content and WebWorks native web applications in a simulation environment. It's available for free and it's compatible with Mac and Windows. There is also a standalone version that may be deprecated in the future, based on Chromium.

You can simulate different scenarios, from BlackBerry 7 to PlayBook and the newest BlackBerry 10 platform, and it includes mobile web support and WebWorks support (adding support for native web API testing). While Ripple is good for a first testing, remember that it is really the Chrome engine, not the real web engine running on BlackBerry devices. Also, Ripple requires an HTTP connection (local or external), so you cannot just open files from the local file system.

BlackBerry Smartphones: The first requirement for older emulators is to download the BlackBerry Email and MDS Services Simulator Package. This proxy allows any simulator to access the network and emulates email services and an enterprise server. Before opening a browser, you need to start this service on your computer.

The BlackBerry Smartphone Simulators are available. The first step is to select the smartphone you want to emulate (for example, the BlackBerry Tour 9630) and choose either the carrier you want (or Generic), or the OS version.

Once you've installed your emulator, you can launch it, open the browser, and type the URL you want to access.

Windows Emulators

If you want to test your applications on Windows Phone, you can download the free Windows Phone SDK or buy a license of Visual Studio. The Windows Phone emulator (Fig. 2.17) comes with the SDK and includes the current version of Internet Explorer to test web content.

The Windows Phone 7.x emulator needs a Windows 7 desktop environment and the Windows Phone 8 emulator needs a Windows 8 desktop environment.

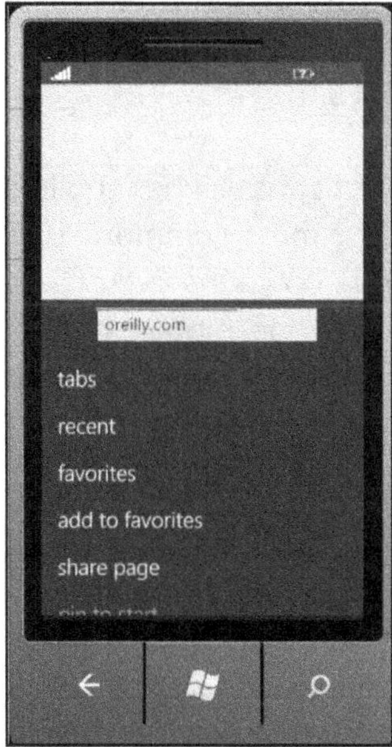

Fig. 2.17: Windows emulator

The Windows Phone emulator is compatible with only Windows VistaSP2, Windows 7, or Windows 8 and requires a graphic driver with WDDM 1.1 support. You can check your hardware specifications to verify whether your graphic driver is compatible. If not, you will see the emulator, but you will see only a white page when trying to load Internet Explorer.

If you want to emulate Windows 8 for tablets, you have two options:

- Use your own Windows 8 for desktop environment.
- Use the windows simulator included with Visual Studio for Windows 8 (even with Express, a free version of the IDE). It includes Internet Explorer 10.

The Windows Simulator works only on Windows 8 desktop machines; it emulates a tablet touch environment, where you can emulate touch gestures, geo location, and different screen sizes and orientations.

2.5.3 Production Environment

The mobile production environment, surprisingly, doesn't differ too much from a classic web environment. Although many web hosting companies used to offer a "premium WAP hosting" option (obviously, more expensive than the non-mobile options), there is no need for any such distinction.

Web Hosting

To get started, you will need a web server with your favorite platform installed. It should support either static or dynamic files on all platforms you plan to work with (PHP, ASP.NET, Java, Ruby, Python, and so on). Cloud hosting via a service like Amazon EC2, Google App Engine, Aptana Cloud, or Microsoft Azure will work well, too. You will need to have permissions to manage MIME types on the server.

Domain

Which domain alternative should you use? You can create a subdomain of your desktop website if you have one, like m.mydomain.com, or you can use the main entry point (mydomain.com or www.mydomain.com).

Error Management

You'll need to ensure that your error pages will be mobile compatible. You should be able to configure the default error pages for most common HTTP error codes, like 404 (Page Not Found) and 500 (Internal Server Error), on your server. These files must be mobile compatible. If you are providing both the desktop and mobile versions of your website from the same domain, you should create dynamic code to detect whether or not the device accessing your site is a mobile device. In the case of a 500 error, deliver a very simple HTML page for both desktop and mobile users.

QUESTIONS

1. What is WAP? Explain WAP1 and WAP2.0 standards.
2. Explain following terms associated with mobile device display:
   (i) Resolution
   (ii) Physical dimensions
   (ii) Pixel density ratio
   (iv) Aspect ratio
3. State and explain the web platforms that are not browser.
4. Explain preinstalled and user installable mobile browsers in detail.
5. Which tools are available for the mobile testing? Give the steps to use android emulator.

✠ ✠ ✠

Unit III

APPLICATION ARCHITECTURES AND DESIGNS

3.1 MOBILE STRATEGY

- When creating mobile web applications, we need to remember that we can create browser-based apps, full-screen web apps, or native web apps. All the types have some architectural rules in common, but there are also some practices that are useful only for a particular type.
- Many websites even from big companies showing messages like "You can only browse this site with iOS or Android" or providing a good experience only for WebKit-based browsers. If you browse such websites with modern non-WebKit browsers, such as IE10, Firefox, or Opera, you get an awful outdated version that may even be not touch optimized when browsing with touch devices.
- With mobile web we can create full-screen web apps and native apps. Determining when to get out of the browser depends on your particular case:
- With full-screen web apps you gain more space, as well as an icon in the device's Home screen or applications menu. That can help the user to remember web app in the future; they will not need to type in the URL again.
- You get the same visibility advantage with a native app, but you also have the ability to run native code and extend what the browser can give you in terms of API support, and you win some discoverability, as the user will find your app when searching or browsing inside the application store.
- If you are providing a full-screen web app or a native app, every platform will have a way to invite the user to install it while browsing your website. On some platforms you can even send parameters from the website to the native app so the user can continue the experience on the native side using the same context as the website: for example, continuing to read the same article.

3.1.1 Context

Remember that a mobile user has a different context than a desktop user. You should think about and define your user's possible contexts:

- Where is the user?
- Why is the user accessing your mobile website?
- What is the user looking for?
- What can you offer from a mobile perspective to help solve the user's problem?
- Where will the user be when accessing your website? Walking on the street, using public transportation, at the office, traveling as a tourist?

The context will tell many things about navigation, use cases, and the usability needs for mobile site.

3.1.2 Server-Side Adaptation

A different approach is to create 'n' different versions of site and redirect the user to the appropriate one depending on the device detected. The main problem with this approach is that you need to maintain 'n' different versions of the same documents.

With this strategy minimum of four versions are required for a successful mobile website, with an optional fifth. If you create fewer versions, some users will probably have a bad experience with your site.

Using a server-side adaptation mechanism, you can reduce the number of required versions to two: one for low-end and mid-range devices and one for high-end devices and smartphones. In the high-end and smartphone world it will be better to use an adaptation strategy for the many features that are not compatible with all devices. Broadly, here are the features need to consider for each device category:

Low-End Devices

Basic XHTML markup, maximum screen width of 176 pixels, basic CSS support (text color, background color, font size), no JavaScript.

Mid-Range Devices

Basic XHTML markup, average screen width of 320 pixels, medium CSS support (box model, images), basic JavaScript support (validation, redirection, dialog windows).

High-End Devices

XHTML or HTML 4 markup, average screen width of 240 pixels, advanced CSS support similar to desktops, Ajax and DOM support, optional touch support, optional orientation change support for an average screen width of 320 pixels.

Smartphones

HTML5, large screen size and high resolution, touch support, support for CSS3 (animations, effects) and Ajax, local storage, geo location.

Web App for Smartphones

Same as smartphones, plus offline support, full-screen and icon installation, native integration, and device APIs.

3.1.3 Progressive Enhancement

Progressive enhancement is a simple but very powerful technique used in web design that defines layers of compatibility that allow any user to access the basic content, services, and functionality of a website and provide an enhanced experience for browsers with better support of standards.

Progressive enhancement has the following core principles:

- Basic content is accessible to all browsers.
- Basic functionality is accessible to all browsers.

- Semantic markup contains all content.
- Enhanced layout is provided by externally linked CSS.
- Enhanced behavior is provided by unremarkable, externally linked JavaScript.
- End user browser preferences are respected.

In the mobile web, a progressive enhancement approach will also include some server side detection and adaptation that will be mandatory for some specific mobile markup e.g. sending an SMS.

3.1.4 Responsive Web Design

It follows the progressive enhancement idea, as the same document will provide the best experience on every device using the same URL.

It's a simple and powerful idea to provide one HTML document that will automatically adapt or respond on the client side to different scenarios, usually meaning available screen size or current orientation (landscape versus portrait). RWD is implemented using CSS3 media queries, which allow the same HTML to automatically change the layout and design in different conditions, so it can be used to separate between:

- Feature phones
- Smartphones
- Tablets
- Desktop browsers
- Smart TVs

A different CSS style-sheet or a portion of one will be executed in every scenario, so the layout and full design can be different on each type of device.

While in a desktop browser we can resize a window, that is not possible on mobile devices or even on smart TVs so the magic of RWD is only useful for different orientations(portrait or landscape) or some special behaviors, such as the full-screen versus in-browser experience.

In RWD, the HTML file served is exactly the same, while the CSS may vary based on the device specifics. For example, screen width, screen height, pixel density, or orientation. Unfortunately, there is no way yet to recognize touch versus non-touch devices or other mobile-specific features using CSS3 standards.

3.1.5 RESS

- Responsive Web Design + Server Side Components (RESS) incorporates the best of two worlds: RWD and server-side adaptation. With this technique, we can decide on the best version and/or compatible experience on the server side, and then RWD on the client side will make the final adjustments, such as having a fluid layout and reacting to different orientations.
- While the concept has been around for a while the RESS involves the idea of having one version of the HTML on the server and changing some portions on the server side before delivering it to the client.

- RESS solves some of the problems of Responsive Web Design, such as ensuring high-performance HTML for mobile devices and serving mobile-specific code, responsive images, and compatible ads.
- For example, we can have a template that will change the header and the footer for feature phones, smartphones, tablets, and desktops, while the main section of the HTML remains the same. The same URL will deliver the current device version, which RWD will then adapt as the context changes.

3.2 NAVIGATION

When creating mobile web concept, developer should define what will be in the navigation tree for the user. To do that, developer need to understand what services and information will be available for the mobile user. Always remember the 80/20 law: 80% of desktop site will not be useful to mobile users. Therefore, developer need to research the 20% should be focusing on.

Some Tips to Follow:

- Define the use cases for example, find a product price.
- Order the use cases by the most frequent for a mobile user.
- If you have a desktop website, try to maintain visual consistency with it.
- Define no more than five main sections below the home page. If you need more, separate services into more mobile pages.
- Always offer a link to the desktop website, sometimes called the "classic version."
- Determine whether locating the user is useful for your services.
- Avoid startup or welcome screens in browser-based apps.
- In full-screen web apps or native web apps, always provide navigation mechanisms such as back buttons, because in those cases there will be no browser toolbar or UI.

3.3 DESIGN AND USER EXPERIENCE

Designing a mobile website or mobile app can be a challenge at the beginning. Mobile website will look different on every device it's viewedon; developer need to keeping it in mind should develop a strategy to create the best web design.

A mobile website ideally consists of vertically scrollable documents. The typical two or three column design is not suitable for mobile web pages, unless the target devices are tablets or devices with a landscape orientation mode. Every mobile web document has a few identified zones:

- Header
- Main navigation
- Content modules
- Second-level navigation
- Footer

These sections will be created one after the other in a vertical scope. Only for devices with a landscape orientation and smartphones is it suitable to create an alternative organization, where you can move the main navigation section to a right-side column.

On high-end smartphones, main navigation can become a top or bottom tab bar, and the content modules can shrink with an accordion or master-detail design.

When creating a mobile version of an existing desktop website, developer need to understand that they are mobilizing the website, not minimizing it. Minimizing a desktop website simply involves displaying the same content on a smaller screen. Mobilizing is more than that; it requires understanding the context and offering services and content in a manner that is useful and allows for quick access by the user.

Best Practices Include:

- Avoid horizontal scrolling.
- Maintain visual consistency with your desktop site, if you have one.
- Reduce the amount of text.
- Use fonts that will be readable on every screen.
- Use background colors to separate sections.
- For low-end and mid-range devices, do not insert more than one link per line.
- Provide a "Go to Top" link in the footer.
- Provide a Back button in the footer
- Provide the most-used features at the top.
- Minimize the amount of user text input required if you have multiple fields.
- Save the user's history and settings for future predictive usage.
- Provide different styling for touch devices.
- Use lists rather than tables.
- Provide the best possible experience to every mobile device.
- Use high-quality color images and fancier features for smartphones.

If you are providing a shortcut, a native app, or an offline version of your mobile website, create an alert at the top of the design alerting the user to download it.

3.3.1 Touch Design Patterns

Touch devices have unique features in terms of design and usability. With the same amount of effort, the user can access every pixel on the screen; this encourages a different way of thinking about a design. Another difference is that the user will use her finger for touch selection unless it is a stylus-based device. A finger is big compared to a mouse pointer, and the hit zone should reflect this.

Useful Design Tips for Touch Devices:

- Provide a reasonable amount of space between clickable elements.
- For frequently used buttons and links, provide a big clickable area.

- For less frequently used buttons, you can use a smaller area.
- Use finger gestures on compatible devices.
- Hide the URL bar so you can have more space available for your app.
- Do not create touch gestures on the borders of your page (top, bottom, left, or right), as some mobile browsers will capture those gestures for their own actions.
- When using touch gestures, make them obvious such as swipe right or left for picture gallery navigation; if they are not obvious, provide alternative buttons and/or an example tutorial at the first load.

3.3.2 Tablet Patterns

Designing tablet a website leads us to a big question: should we base it on the desktop version or on the mobile version? The answer may differ, depending on factors such as tablet size (7" or 10") and how the content is structured.

If you are not providing a specific layout for tablets, starting from the desktop version is frequently the preferred way, as the screen size allows the display of more content. However, tablets may be using cellular networks or not-so-fast WLAN networks, such as a public WiFi connection.

Providing smartphone-optimized experiences for landscape tablets does not seem that good idea, as too much space is being wasted.

3.4 WML

- WML stands for Wireless Markup Language. It was incorporated into the WAP 1.1 standard and was the first standard of the mobile web.
- A WML file is an XML file, normally using the **.wml** extension. It is similar to HTML in some ways and very different in others. Essentially, WML is a subset of HTML, but has its roots in XML. It describes how content is presented to the wireless device, allowing you to display information, present input options and tell the user how to respond once an option has been selected using the keyboard.
- The current WML standard is 1.3, although many mobile devices in use today support only the WML 1.1 standard. Therefore it's practical to stay away from 1.3-specific features, unless you know that your target market's devices are 1.3-ready.

Key Differences between WML and Standard HTML, Including the Following:

- WML is highly structured and very particular about syntax. Several current HTML browsers allow for "messy" code such as missing tags. Such mistakes are not allowed in WML; the mobile browser will complain and generally would not display the page.
- WML is case sensitive. The tags <b> and <B> are treated as different tags, although they accomplish the same purpose (bold text). Therefore, you must be careful to match the case of your opening tags with your closing tags (for example, <b>This is bold</B> will not work as expected).

- Many tags have required attributes. Developers familiar to HTML may be used to including only attributes they need-in some WML tags, you must include a few attributes, even if they are blank or default.
- WML pages are structured in "decks", allowing for multiple pages to be defined in each WML file.
- WML also has a client-side scripting language, WML Script, to help automate particular tasks, validate input, and so on.

Let's take a look at a typical WML file:

```
<?xml version="1.0"?>
<!DOCTYPEwml PUBLIC "-//WAPFORUM//DTD WML 1.1//EN"
"http://www.wapforum.org/DTD/wml_1.1.xml" >
<wml>
<card id="home" title="Welcome to Old Mobile">
<p mode="wrap">This is a <b>typical</b> paragraph in WML</p>
<p mode="wrap">It can include images,
<a href="http://wap.yahoo.com">External Links</a> and
<a href="#two">Internal Links</a>.
</p>
</card>
<card id="two" title="Second screen">
<p>This is like a second page in the same document</p>
</card>
</wml>
```

We can recognize many tags found in HTML here, like p, b, and a, and they have the same functionality. Other tags the two standards have in common include img, br, and input.

The WML specification was developed by the WAP forum and defines the syntax, variables, and elements to be used in a valid WML file. The WML1.1 Document Type Definition (DTD) is available from www.wapforum.org/DTD/wml_1.1.xml and all WML applications must correspond to it.

Understanding Decks

A WML document is called a "deck" which is comparable to an HTML page. Unlike the flat structure of HTML content, WML document or decks are divided into separate units of user interaction. Each unit is called a card. WML pages are structured within decks, allowing several pages ("cards") to be defined in each WML file.

WML was conceived for mobile devices. Consequently, we will find tags and attributes supporting mobile device functionality such as voice calls, keyboard support, adding contacts to the phone book, and accessing the SIM card in the standard. We can use the well-known anchor tag to create an absolute link, a link to a relative document, or a link to another card in the same document using the #card_name URL.

Advantages of WML

Like HTML, WML is easy to use. However, compared to HTML, WML has the following advantages in the context of wireless:

- WML is part of the WAP standard and its use is required.
- Transmission of WML (WMLC) documents requires less bandwidth compared to HTML documents because WML documents are simpler and WML is compressed before it is sent to the WAP device.
- Compared to HTML documents, displaying WML documents requires less processing power and memory. Consequently, a WAP device can work with a less powerful (cheaper) CPU and the use of less power means that the battery can operate longer without recharging.
- WML provides support for limited graphics with a limited gray scale.

Limitations of WML

- Like HTML, WML does specify how the content is to be displayed. Thus micro browsers on different WAP devices are likely to display the WML content differently.
- WAP devices such as WAP phones will not accept large decks.
- There are many variations between WAP phones, for example Screen sizes, keypads, and soft keys can be different.

Current Standards

In terms of the mobile web today, our real work will be directly related to the following standards and pseudo-standards:

- HTML5 and other sub-standards
- XHTML Mobile Profile 1.0, 1.1, and 1.2
- XHTML Basic 1.0 and 1.1
- HTML 4.01
- De facto standard mobile HTML extensions
- WAP CSS
- CSS Mobile Profile (CSS MP)
- CSS 2.1
- CSS 3.0 and other sub-standards, such as CSS3 transitions and CSS3 columns

We can distinguish two main types of standards: HTML-based and CSS-based.

3.5 XHTML MOBILE PROFILE AND BASIC

3.5.1 XHTML Basic

The XHTML Basic document type is defined as a set of XHTML modules.

Structure Module*: body, head, html, title

Text Module*: abbr, acronym, address, blockquote, br, cite, code, dfn, div, em, h1, h2, h3, h4, h5, h6, kbd, p, pre, q, samp, span, strong, var

Hypertext Module*: a

List Module*: dl, dt, dd, ol, ul, li

Basic Forms Module: form, input, label, select, option, text area

Basic Tables Module: caption, table, td, th, tr

Image Module: img

Object Module: object, param

Meta information Module: meta

Link Module: link

Base Module: base

(*) = This module is a required XHTML Host Language module.

Although XHTML Basic can be used as it is - a simple XHTML language with text, links, and images - the intention of its simple design is for use as a host language. A host language can contain a mix of vocabularies all rolled into one document type. It is natural that XHTML is the host language, since that is what most Web developers are used to.

When markup from other languages is added to XHTML Basic, the resulting document type will be an extension of XHTML Basic. Content developers can develop for XHTML Basic or take advantage of the extensions. The goal of XHTML Basic is to serve as a common language supported by various kinds of user agents.

3.5.2 XHTML MP (XHTML Mobile Profile)

XHTML MP (eXtensibleHyperText Markup Language Mobile Profile) is the markup language defined in WAP2.0. WAP2.0 is the most recent mobile services specification created by the WAP Forum (now the Open Mobile Alliance [OMA]). The specification of WAP CSS (WAP Cascading Style Sheet or WCSS) is also defined in WAP2.0. WAP CSS is the companion of XHTML Mobile Profile and they are used together.

XHTML Mobile Profile is a subset of XHTML, which is the stricter version of HTML. XHTML Mobile Profile is XHTML Basic plus some additional elements and attributes from the full version of XHTML. The goal of XHTML Mobile Profile is to bring together the technologies for mobile Internet browsing and that for the World Wide Web.

The differences compared with working with HTML5:

The file must have a root element (html tag).

- Every tag name and tag attribute must be in lowercase.
- Every attribute must have a value, and it must be enclosed in quotes.

For example,

```
<option selected> is invalid; you must use <option selected="selected">.
```

- Every tag must be closed. This may seem obvious, but it is not; tags like <img>,<input>, and <br> do not need to be closed in HTML, but they do need to be closed in XHTML. The general rule is to use self-closed tags, like <br />.
- The tags need to be closed in reverse order. If you open a paragraph and then a link, you must close the link before closing the paragraph.
- XHTML entities must be well formed. A mandatory space should be   and an ampersand character should be &
- The DOCTYPE declaration is mandatory, and the XML opening tag is optional. Infact, for mobile browsers we should not insert the XML opening tag.

Available Tags

XHTML MP, as a subset of XHTML derived from HTML, will look familiar to most web developers.

The tags available in both XHTML Mobile Profile 1.2 and XHTML Basic 1.1 (the two standards are almost at the same level) are listed in Table 3.1. Some features, like scripting support, were added in XHTML MP 1.1 and others, like object support, in the last standard (1.2).

Tag Types Tags Available

Table 3.1: HTML Tags Available in XHTML MP 1.2 and Basic 1.1

Tag Types	Tags Available
Structure	body, head, html, title
Text	abbr, acronym, address, blockquote, br, cite, code, dfn, div, em, h1, h2, h3, h4, h5, h6, kbd, p, pre, q, samp, span, strong, var
Links	a
Presentation	b, big, hr, i, small
Stylesheet	style
Lists	dl, dt, dd, ol, ul, li
Forms	form, input, label, select, option, textarea, fieldset, optgroup
Basic	tables caption, table, td, th, tr
Other	img, object, param, meta, link, base, script, noscript

Advantages of XHTML MP

The greatest advantage brought by XHTML MP is that developers can now use the same technologies for the development of both web sites and WAP sites.

Benefits WAP Application Development

- The same development tools can be used to develop both web sites and WAP sites. You can stick to your web development tools to build your mobile Internet browsing application. These results in a lower development cost (no need to buy new development tools) and a lower time investment.

- Ordinary web browsers can be used to view your WAP site during the development process.
- HTML / XHTML pages on your web site can be converted to XHTML MP documents with minor changes or even without any changes.

Advantages of XHTML MP

- XHTML MP supports WAP CSS, which enables the separation of content and presentation in different files. Mobile devices have very different characteristics such as screen sizes. The separation of the content and the presentation means you can write the content once, and change the style and layout to suit different mobile devices with various WAP CSS files.
- With XHTML MP and WAP CSS, you have more control over the presentation. For example, you can control borders, backgrounds, margins, padding, etc. You can also specify the font sizes, font families and font colors. Such features are not available in WML 1.x.

XHTML MP Document Structure

Here is our first XHTML MP example. It shows the structure of a typical XHTML MP document.

```
helloWorld.xhtml
<?xml version="1.0"?>
<!DOCTYPE html PUBLIC "-//WAPFORUM//DTD XHTML Mobile 1.0//EN"
"http://www.wapforum.org/DTD/xhtml-mobile10.dtd">


<html xmlns="http://www.xyz.org/1999/xhtml">

 <head>
  <title>XHTML MP Test</title>
 </head>

<body>
  <p>Hello world. Welcome to our XHTML MP test.</p>
 </body>
</html>
```

XHTML MP documents start with the prolog, which contains the XML declaration and DOCTYPE declaration

```
<?xml version="1.0"?>
<!DOCTYPE html PUBLIC "-//WAPFORUM//DTD XHTML Mobile 1.0//EN"
"http://www.wapforum.org/DTD/xhtml-mobile10.dtd">
```

The prolog components are not XHTML MP elements and they should not be closed, i.e. you should not give them an end tag or finish them with />.

The rest of the document is the same as an ordinary HTML document, except that there should be no xmlns attribute for the <html> tag in HTML.

XHTML MP Documents must contain the <html>, <head>, <title>, and <body> elements.

3.6 MOBILE HTML5

Mobile HTML5 is just creating HTML5 documents for the mobile web. Originally called Web Applications 1.0 before HTML5, the new standard began as a couple of tags and JavaScript APIs that modern browsers should implement. Apple was one of the first companies to apply these ideas (in Safari for iPhone).

HTML5 is a markup language, has been come into existence around January 2008. The two measure organization is involving in developing of HTML5 since its initiating time. One is W3C (World Wide Web Consortium) and the one is WHATWG (Web Hypertext Application Technology Working Group).

In HTML previous version there was need of a DTD declaration with DOCTYPE assuming like (<!DOCTYPE html PUBLIC "-//W3C//DTD XHTML1.0 Transitional//EN" "http://www.w3.org/TR/xhtml1/DTD/xhtml1-transitional.dtd">), which was a little bit complex to remember even and slightly mistakes may have occur during writing such a long DOCTYPE element. So with the development of HTML5 this feature of HTML has been enhanced.

<!DOCTYPE html>

DOCTYPE is such an element, which tells the browser about the html version, DOCTYPE is not a HTML tag, but for the Proper SEO purpose and introducing the version of HTML to the browser the tag is very useful. There is no need to declaration of DTD with the DOCTYPE tag. DOCTYPE tag is defined at the top of the page.

Here is the Syntax for DOCTYPE

```
<!DOCTYPE html>
```

Below is complete syntax along with example

```
<!DOCTYPE html>
<html>
    <head>
        <title>
            Page title will go here
        </title>
    </head>
    <body>
        This is test page
    </body>
</html>
```

Creating Our First HTML5 Template

HTML5 does not follow XML rules, so it's less strict in terms of syntax. The minimum HTML5 template looks like this:

```
<!DOCTYPE html>
<title>My title</title>
```

The html, body, and head are all optional tags in HTML5. Even if you open them, you do not need to close them, so the following code is also valid HTML5:

```
<!DOCTYPE html>
<title>My title</title>
<html>
<head>
<body>
```

Usually, a mobile HTML5 template also includes some important meta tags.

Syntax Rules

Being a non-XML language, HTML5 has its own rules.

- The html, body, and head tags are optional.
- There are elements that must always be closed, such as ul, script, select, or div.
- There are elements that you can close, self-close, or not close at all, such as p, li, option, input, head, body, img, br, or link. For example,
</br>, <br />, and <br> are equivalent.
- Element and attribute names are not case-sensitive.
- Boolean attributes exist. In those cases, you do not need to provide a value. The mere presence of the attribute (as in <input required>) indicates a true value.

New Elements in HTML5

- **Semantic Block Elements:** Header, footer, article, section, nav, aside
- **Semantic Inline Elements:** Time, output, progress, mark
- **Text Elements:** wbr, ruby
- **Multimedia Elements:** Video, audio, canvas

3.7 CSS FOR MOBILE

Web (and mobile) browsers have a great feature that makes our lives much easier in the CSS world. If we use any selector or attribute that the browser does not understand, the browser will just ignore it. This will be very helpful in the following pages. Usage of CSS2.1, CSS 3.0, CSS Mobile Profile, and WAP CSS is the same.

WCSS, or WAP CSS (the OMA standard that comes with XHTML MP), is a CSS 2.0 subset, like CSS MP (the W3C standard that comes with XHTML Basic).

3.7.1 WCSS Extensions

WCSS (WAP Cascading Style Sheet or WAP CSS) is the mobile version of cascading style sheet. It is a subset of CSS2 (the cascading style sheet language of the World Wide Web) plus some WAP specific extensions. CSS2 features and properties that are not useful for mobile Internet applications are not included in WAP CSS. WAP CSS is the companion of XHTML Mobile Profile (XHTML MP). Both of them are defined in the WAP2.0 specification, which was created by the former WAP Forum (now the Open Mobile Alliance [OMA]). There are lots of WAP2.0- enabled cell phones on the market currently.

WAP Specific Extensions to CSS

WAP CSS includes some WAP specific extensions to web CSS2, which means some properties are defined in WAP CSS but not in web CSS2. These WAP specific extensions are very useful for mobile Internet browsing applications. The WCSS properties in the extensions can be grouped into the following three categories:

Access Key: This category contains only one WCSS property: -wap-accesskey. This WCSS property is used to specify a shortcut key for an XHTML MP element.

Input: The WCSS properties in this category are used to specify whether a text field can be left empty and what type and how many characters can be entered in a text field.

Marquee: The WCSS properties in the marquee category are used to scroll some content across the screen. For example, if you have a line of text that is wider than the screen width, you can make use of the WCSS properties in the marquee category to generate a text scrolling effect instead of displaying the text on multiple lines.

WCSS Access Key Extension

Specifying Keypad Shortcuts for Elements (-wap-accesskey Property)

Only one WCSS property, -wap-accesskey, is included in the access key extension. The -wap-accesskey property is used to specify a keypad shortcut for an XHTML MP element. Valid property values are *, #, 0, 1, 2, 3, 4, 5, 6, 7, 8, and 9.

WAP CSS examples

- a.wcss_class_1 {-wap-accesskey: 1}
- input.wcss_class_1 {-wap-accesskey: 4}
- a.wcss_class_2 {-wap-accesskey: *}
- input.wcss_class_2 {-wap-accesskey: #}

WCSS Input Extension

The input extension is consisted of two WCSS properties: -wap-input-format and -wap-input-required. The <input> WML element contains the format attribute and the 'emptyok' attribute. The format attribute defines the type and number of characters that a user can enter in an input field, and the 'emptyok' attribute defines whether an input field can be left empty.

In XHTML MP, the format attribute and the emptyok attribute are not included in the <input> element any more and their corresponding function has been moved to WAP CSS. The -wap-input-format and -wap-input-required properties are used to replace the format attribute and the emptyok attribute respectively.

If you want to ensure that your XHTML MP page functions correctly in the WAP browser of most mobile devices, you may want to include both the WCSS property and the WML attribute in the same element.

For example,

```
<input type="text" format="N" style='-wap-input-format: "N"'/>
```

If both the -wap-input-format WCSS property and the format attribute (or the -wap-input-required WCSS property and the emptyok attribute) are specified in the same XHTML MP element and their values are different, the WCSS property takes precedence.

WCSS Marquee Extension

The properties in the marquee extension of WCSS enable the scrolling of some content across the screen of a mobile device. The content can be a line of text, an image, an anchor link, etc (Note: some WAP browsers [from Sony Ericsson, for example] only support scrolling text). This feature is very useful for displaying a line of text or an image that is wider than the screen. The WCSS marquee extension consists of four properties and one property value. An overview of their functions is given below:

- **-wap-marquee property value** : It is used with the display property. The XHTML MP element that is applied with the WAP CSS style rule "display: -wap-marquee" will scroll across the screen of a mobile device.
- **-wap-marquee-dir property** : It is used to specify the direction of a marquee animation.
- **-wap-marquee-loop property** : It is used to specify the number of times that a marquee animation should repeat.
- **-wap-marquee-speed property** : It is used to specify the speed of a marquee animation.
- **-wap-marquee-style property** : It is used to specify how a marquee animation should scroll across the screen. Three styles are available: scroll, slide and alternate.

3.7.2 CSS3

The first working draft of CSS3 was come in 19-01-2001. And since the first introduction still it is under construction. There were some certain shortcomings in CSS2 and due to its unlikeness the developer introduced CSS3. It is divided into different modules according to its specifications.

We have basic CSS3 support and a group of other sub-standards in the W3C, such as:

- CSS Background and Borders
- CSS 2D and 3D Transforms
- CSS Transitions
- CSS Animations

- CSS Columns
- CSS Flexible Box Layout
- CSS Fonts
- CSS Device Adaptation
- CSS Regions

3.8 CSS FOR MOBILE BROWSER

Where to Insert the CSS ?

The first question to answer is: where should we tell the browser what styles to apply?

We have many options:

- <style>tags inside the XHTML or HTML markup
- External stylesheets (.cssfiles)
- style attributes inside the tags

The third option might seem like the most efficient approach, but it is not the best one. That said, there are times when it is useful. It is easiest to insert inline styles to avoid defining IDs and ID selectors for each control:

```
<input type="text" name="name" style="-wap-input-format: A*a">
```

If the website you are creating is a one-page document, it will be faster to include the CSS in the <style>HTML tag to avoid a request and a rendering delay. The other ideal situation for this technique is if your home page is very different from the other pages in your site.

Media Queries

If we decide to use only one HTML site for both desktop and mobile devices, our only option for changing the design and layout is the CSS file, unless we do not want any mobile design adaptation. This situation is a good fit for the media attribute.

The CSS standard allows us to define more than one stylesheet for the same document, or one stylesheet with different definitions on different types of media. The media attribute was part of the CSS 2.1 standard, and the most-used values for media attributes are screen (for desktops), print (to be applied when the user prints the document), and handheld (for... yes, mobile devices). There are also other values, like tv and braille, but no browsers currently support these.

We can just define two style sheets, one for screen and one for handheld, and all our problems will be solved. The two style sheets can define different properties for the same elements, and we can even use display: none to prevent some elements from being shown on mobile devices:

```
<link rel="stylesheet" type="text/css" media="screen"
href="desktop.css" />
<link rel="stylesheet" type="text/css" media="handheld"
href="mobile.css" />
```

CSS3 Media Queries

These complex media definitions include conditions about different properties, such as screen size or current orientation.

For example, we can say: "Apply this stylesheet for devices with a maximum screen width of 480 pixels." This will apply to an iPhone, because in landscape mode it has a screen width of 480 px and it does not support print, handheld, or any other media type. Here is an example to write this as a conditional media query:

```
<link rel="stylesheet" media="screen and (max-device-width: 480px)"href="mobile.css">
```

We can also define CSS media queries inside the same stylesheet file. For example, the following code will change the background color displayed on a mobile device:

```
@media screen and (max-device-width: 480px) {
body {
background-color: red;
}
}
```

Media queries accept expressions and some operators. Parentheses are required around expressions. The possible types of conditional expressions are:

Boolean Attributes

Such as color or monochrome

Attribute Value Equal to

The syntax is <attribute>:<value>and it is always evaluated as "equal to," such as width: 500 px or density: 326 dpi. The values can accept CSS units and constants.

Attribute Greater Than or Equal to

The syntax is min-<attribute>:<value>, such as min-width: 500 px (meaning "if the width is equal to or greater than 500 CSS pixels").

Attribute Less Than or Equal to

The syntax is max-<attribute>:<value>, such as max-width: 1024 px (meaning "if the width is no greater than 1,024 CSS pixels").

The possible operators between expressions are:

NOT Operator

Using the NOT keyword before a conditional. 'NOT' has a low precedence, meaning that it will always be applied to the whole expression unless we segment it using parentheses.

ONLY Operator

Using the ONLY keyword before a conditional. This means exclusivity. For example, only screen evaluates as true only on devices that do not support any other type, such as print. Usually it's a way to separate mobile devices from desktops, as desktop browsers support the print scheme.

AND Operator

Using the and keyword between two conditions, such as only screen and width: 320 px. We can use parentheses in conditions to avoid possible logical problems.

OR Operator

There is no OR keyword available; however, using a comma, we can emulate an OR operation, such as for orientation: all and (orientation: landscape), all and (min-width: 700 px).

Media Features

The following are the standard CSS media query features that we can use on mobile devices:

aspect-ratio

Defines the aspect ratio of the display area, the value must be two integers separated by a slash (horizontal/vertical), such as aspect-ratio: 3/4. This defines the relation between width and height, and it changes as the dimensions change. In mobile browsers, changing the device's orientation usually changes aspect-ratio.

device-aspect-ratio

Defines the aspect ratio of the device, the value must be two integers separated by a slash (horizontal/vertical), such as aspect-ratio: 4/3. This defines the relation between device-width and device-height. On mobile devices it is the aspect ratio in portrait orientation.

device-width and device-height

Define the width or height of the device in the default orientation (portrait on mobile devices). The value is expressed in CSS pixels.

Width and height

Define the width or height of the current view port. The value is expressed in CSS pixels. If we do not provide a view port definition, the available width will be the default one (from 800 to 1,024 px.

Orientation

Defines the current device orientation, such as landscape or portrait; This is reevaluated automatically when the user changes the orientation.

Resolution

Defines the current resolution (pixel density) of the device's screen, it accepts values in dots per inch (dpi) and dots per cm (dpcm). This feature will accept dots per CSS pixel (dppx) in the near future. For today's devices, using the prefixed device-pixel-ratio is the solution.

Browser Extensions

Mozilla accepts the -moz-touch-enabled Boolean attribute, which will be evaluated only on touch devices, and the -moz-device-pixel-ratio extension. WebKit based browsers support -webkit-device-pixel-ratio and Opera supports-o-device-pixel-ratio.

3.9 HTML5 COMPATIBILITY LEVELS

HTML5 in mobile devices is usually thought of as a mix of W3C standards, drafts, and defacto practices, including HTML, CSS, and JavaScript APIs. The W3C maintains the Mobile Web Initiative, where you can find some useful links, discussions, and best practices.

Testing Your Browser

One of the biggest problems with HTML5 is that every browser has different compatibility in terms of the standards supported. While there is no standard to define how "HTML5 compatible" a browser is? there are some initiatives in the community to solve this problem.

HTML5 Test

The most-used resource today to measure HTML5 support is **html5test.com**. This website will execute a test suite on your browser and give you a score based on the APIs/features supported, plus a bonus score for any optional features supported (such as video codecs).

This website is primarily useful for comparing different versions of the same browser, as in Fig. 3.1; if you compare two different browsers the temptation is to interpret a higher score as indicating better compatibility, but the problem is that this algorithm does not consider which APIs are most useful, maybe Browser A has a better score than Browser B, but only Browser B supports the API you are looking for.

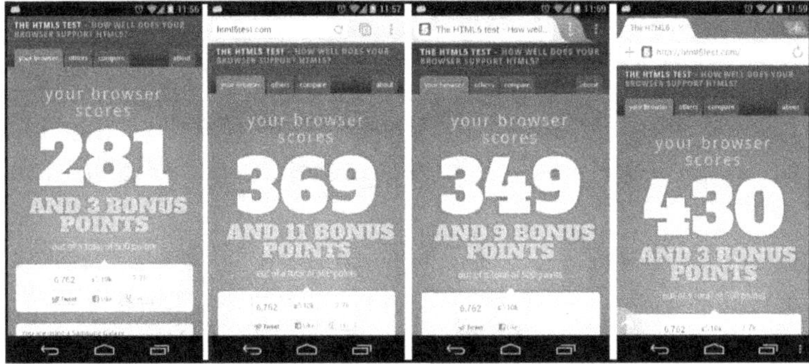

Fig. 3.1: HTML5 test for different Android browsers on the same device

Ringmark

Ringmark is an open source mobile browser testing suite that will give you not an exact score, but a compatibility level (a ring) regarding your current support. The test has three different rings covering several standards and features that a browser may support.

If one feature on one ring fails, the suite will not execute the next ring's tests. Ringmark will identify a browser as being Ring 0, Ring 1, or Ring 2 compatible. Therefore, if you are creating an app or a game, you can say that it is compatible only with Ring 1 browsers, for example, so you will know which APIs and features will work properly.

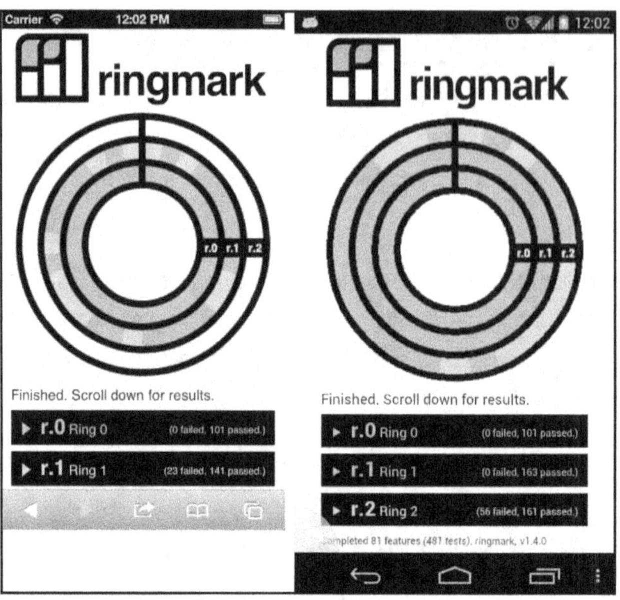

Fig. 3.2: Safari on iOS and Dolphin for Android

The first Ring 1 compatible browser was Dolphin for Android, released in August 2012, as seen in Fig. 3.2. The prize for the first Ring 1 compatible default installed browser was claimed by BlackBerry with the new BlackBerry 10 platform at the beginning of 2013.

3.10 BASICS OF MOBILE HTML5

3.10.1 The Document Head

The head part of a mobile web document will be very similar to that in a desktop web document, with the addition of some new metatags useful only in mobile browsers.

Title

First we will define a title, as for any other web page. The space available for the title in a mobile browser is small compared with a desktop browser (Table 3.2 gives the average lengths of the titles displayed on the different phone-factor platforms). The page title is used as the heading at the top of the screen on some devices; other devices also use the title as the default text for bookmarks and the history list.

Table 3.2: Average Characters Used in Titles on Smartphone Platforms

Browser/Platform	Average Number of Charts Used in Titles
Safari on iOS	40 chars in portrait and 60 in landscape (75 on 4.5" devices). Hidden after the user scrolls the page. Hidden in full-screen web apps.
Android browser	After 2.0, titles are not displayed on the screen.
Chrome for Android	Titles are not displayed on the screen. You can see the first 15 chars on the window list, or tabs on tablets.
Internet Explorer	No usages.

Browser/Platform	Average Number of Charts Used in Titles
Symbian/$60	35 chars in portrait, 20 in landscape.
Nokia Series 40	20 chars in third edition.
	No usage in fifth and sixth editions.
Firefox	15 chars in portrait and 50 in landscape, replacing the URL when the page loads.
BlackBerry	15–30 chars, depending on screen width.
webOS	No usage upto webOS 1.3. In webOS 1.4, the title appears only if the user scrolls down from the top.
NetFront	No usage.
UC browser	10 chars in portrait and 30 in landscape, replacing the URL when the page loads.
Opera Mobile	Depends on the screen, between 20 and 60 chars.
Opera Mini	Depends on the screen, between 20 and 60 chars.

HTML Head Elements

Tag	Description
<head>	Defines information about the document.
<title>	Defines the title of a document.
<base>	Defines a default address or a default target for all links on a page.
<link>	Defines the relationship between a document and an external resource.
<meta>	Defines metadata about an HTML document.
<script>	Defines a client-side script.
<style>	Defines style information for a document.

The HTML <head> Element

The <head> element is a container for metadata (data about data). HTML metadata is data about the HTML document. Metadata is not displayed. Metadata typically define document title, styles, links, scripts, and other meta information. The following tags describe metadata: <title>, <style>, <meta>, <link>, <script>, and <base>.

The HTML <title> Element

The <title> element defines the title of the document. The <title> element is required in all HTML/XHTML documents.

The <title> element:

- Defines a title in the browser tab.
- Provides a title for the page when it is added to favorites.

- Displays a title for the page in search engine results.

A simplified HTML document:

```
<!DOCTYPE html>
<html>
<title>Page Title</title>
<body>
The content of the document......
</body>
</html>
```

The HTML <style> Element

The <style> element is used to define style information for an HTML document. Inside the <style> element you specify how HTML elements should render in a browser:

```
<style>
body {background-color:yellow;}
p {color:blue;}
</style>
```

The HTML <link> Element

The <link> element defines the page relationship to an external resource. The <link> element is most often used to link to stylesheets:

```
<link rel="stylesheet" href="mystyle.css">
```

The HTML <meta> Element

The <meta> element is used to specify page description, keywords, author, and other metadata. Metadata is used by browsers (how to display content), by search engines (keywords), and other web services.

Define keywords for search engines:

```
<meta name="keywords" content="HTML, CSS, XML, XHTML, JavaScript">
```

Refresh document every 30 seconds:

```
<meta http-equiv="refresh" content="30">
```

The HTML <script> Element

The <script> element is used to define client-side JavaScripts. The script below writes Hello JavaScript! into an HTML element with id="demo":

```
<script>
function myFunction {
  document.getElementById("demo").innerHTML = "Hello JavaScript!";
}
</script>
```

The HTML <base> Element

The <base> element specifies the base URL and base target for all relative URLs in a page:

```
<basehref="http://www.google.com/images/"target="_blank">
```

3.10.2 The Document Body

The body is the most important section of the document, as it defines the content that the user will see. This is what you see on your computer screen when you go to a web page, and most of the work you do is on code found between the opening and closing body tag.

Key Best Practices Include:

- Avoid formatting tags such as big, format, and center.
- Use semantically correct, clean XHTML or HTML5; we will define styles later with CSS.
- Do not create a large document. Larger documents cause problems on old browsers(and caching problems even on some modern ones).
- If you have a lot of text to show, for feature phones, separate the content into many pages.
- Do not use tables for layout.

HTML <body> Tag

A simple HTML document, with the minimum of required tags:

```
<html>
<head>
<title>Title of the document</title>
</head>

<body>
The content of the document......
</body>

</html>
```

The <body> tag defines the document's body. The <body> element contains all the contents of an HTML document, such as text, hyperlinks, images, tables, lists, etc.

3.11 HTML5 MOBILE BOILERPLATE

Boilerplate is the term used to describe sections of code that have to be included in many places with little or no alteration. It is more often used when referring to languages which are considered verbose, i.e. the programmer must write a lot of code for minimal functionality. The need for boilerplate can be reduced through high-level mechanisms.

When creating a new website, it is helpful to have a template (boilerplate) with all the well-known hacks, solutions, and best practices already implemented to use as a starting point, rather than having to start from scratch. HTML5 boilerplate is starting to emerge: a mobile-specific version is maintained by the community as an open source project.

The Template Includes:

- Meta tags, such as view port and icon references.
- normalize.css, an alternative to CSS reset (a way to normalize defaults on different browsers).
- Some JavaScript libraries, such as Zepto.js and Modernizr (two libraries we will cover later in this book).
- A JavaScript helper class useful for some JavaScript-based hacks, such as the iOS viewport bug fix.
- High-performance and mobile-specific configuration files for Apache.

3.12 THE CONTENT

If we focus our content semantically, we will not have big problems adapting our design to different mobile scenarios. By "semantically," means using the well-known paragraph, structure, and list HTML5 elements. Be sure to understand and make proper use of every HTML element, such as header, footer, article, abbr, and address.

Block Elements

If we define a viewport allowing user scaling, most browsers support a way to zoom into a block element (such as a paragraph), using a double-tap gesture, for example. To make this work properly we should not use paragraphs that are forced to be wider than the screen (because we have defined the width and the font-size as fixed); this will force the browser to zoom out and the paragraph will be unreadable.

Lists

Using standard lists will help us a lot in defining our designs later with CSS and for semantic search engine optimization. For the mobile web, we should use the following list types:

Ordered Lists (ol tag)

For navigation link menus.

Unordered Lists (ul tag)

To present lists of similar objects.

Definition Lists (dl tag)

To show key/value details.

If we are showing a product detail page, in many browsers it's better to use a definition list rather than a table for attributes:

```
<h2>iPhone 5</h2>
<dl>
<dt>Price</dt>
<dd>300 EUR</dd>
```

```
<dt>Memory</dt>
<dd>32Gb</dd>
<dt>Network</dt>
<dd>LTE, 3G, WiFi, Bluetooth</dd>
</dl>
```

The dt tag is used for the key (definition term) and the dd tag for the value (definition description). This is very useful, semantically correct, and clearer than using a table. Later, with CSS, we can rearrange the elements.

Tables

Using tables for document layout is bad in desktop web development. Mobile browsing is more a one-column experience, unless we are working with tablets. If you do want or need to use a table, you should limit it to at most five columns of tabular data (preferably with short column headings and data values). We can define the table title (caption), the header (thead), the body (tbody), the footer(tfoot), and the columns (colgroup, col), and finally the rows (tr), the header cells(th), and the data cells (td). Cells can be merged using the rowspan and colspan attributes, and the design should be defined in CSS.

Links

Hyperlinks are the heart of the Web, and this holds for the mobile web, too. Every link in a mobile website should have the well-known href attribute, set to the URL of the desired resource, and the most important links on the page can have an accesskey attribute assigned for easy access via keyboard shortcuts, on devices that support access keys. The target attribute should be avoided for feature or social phones because those browsers do not have tab or multi page support.

Accessibility

The accessibility of a mobile website should be as important as the graphic design, the performance, or the user experience. Some mobile operating systems, such as iOS, support accessibility features such as screen voice readers, gesture helpers, or contrast color utilities. Your mobile website or app is accessible it means that anyone can use it, with any device.

3.13 HTML5 FORMS

The forms section of HTML5 was originally a specification titled Web Forms 2.0 that added new types of controls for forms. The work was initially carried out under the W3C. It was then combined with the Web Applications 1.0 specification to create the basis of the breakaway Web Hypertext Application Technology Working Group (WHATWG) HTML5 specification.

One of the best things about HTML5 forms is that you can use almost all of these new input types and attributes right now.

3.13.1 Design

Avoid using tables for form layout. The best solution is to use definition lists, labels, and input controls. Using CSS you can enhance the form and even with different layouts for different devices and orientations. If you start your design with a fixed-layout from the HTML, such as using tables, you will not have the ability to modify it from CSS.

A typical key/value form should look like the following code:

```
<form action="formAction" method="post">
<dl>
<dt><label for="name">Name</label></dt>
<dd><input type="text" name="name"></dd>
</dl>
</form>
```

The usage of the label tag is very important for mobile input controls, and especially for touch devices. For example, if you insert a checkbox without a label tag, the user will need to tap (click) over the tiny checkbox to select it, which can be fiddly. Using a label allows the user to tap anywhere in the text assigned to the checkbox to select it.

So, a form with a checkbox should look something like the following:

```
<form action="formAction" method="post">
<input type="checkbox" name="accept" id="accept" value="yes">
<label for="accept">I accept terms and conditions</label>
</form>
```

We can also assign access keys to the form controls (using the accesskey attribute in the input tags) and show which keys are assigned in the labels, with a CSS class. This method is very useful in devices with QWERTY keyboards, where you can assign a letter to each field instead of numeric values:

```
<form action="formAction" method="post">
<input type="checkbox" name="accept" id="accept" value="yes"
accesskey="a">
<label for="accept">I <span class="accesskey">A</span>ccept terms
and conditions</label>
</form>
```

A typical form should include one or more fieldset tags, each with a legend inside. The fieldset is just a container for form controls, and the legend is a child tag that defines the title or legend for its parent:

```
<fieldset>
<legend>Personal Information</legend>
<!-- controls here -->
</fieldset>
```

Some mobile browsers will add navigation between all interactive form elements, such as Previous or Next buttons on virtual keyboards that will jump between elements in the current order, or tab index declarations, as if it were tabbed navigation on a desktop. Therefore, it's important to define a coherent order for the elements.

3.13.2 Elements

An HTML5 mobile form can contain the following form elements:

- Single-line text boxes for different types of input
- Password boxes
- Multiline text boxes
- Date and time selectors
- Select lists for single selection
- Select lists for multiple selection
- Checkboxes
- Radio buttons
- File selectors
- Range selectors
- Non interactive elements, such as hidden input fields and keygen elements.

HTML5 added the following form elements:

```
<datalist>
<keygen>
<output>
```

HTML5 <datalist> Element

The **<datalist>** element specifies a list of pre-defined options for an <input> element. Users will see a drop-down list of pre-defined options as they input data. The **list** attribute of the <input> element, must refer to the **id** attribute of the <datalist> element.

Example

An <input> element with pre-defined values in a <datalist>:

```
<form action="action_page.php">
  <input list="browsers">
  <datalist id="browsers">
    <option value="Internet Explorer">
    <option value="Firefox">
    <option value="Chrome">
    <option value="Opera">
    <option value="Safari">
  </datalist>
</form>
```

HTML5 <keygen> Element

The purpose of the **<keygen>** element is to provide a secure way to authenticate users. The <keygen> element specifies a key-pair generator field in a form. When the form is submitted, two keys are generated, one private and one public. The private key is stored locally, and the public key is sent to the server. The public key could be used to generate a client certificate to authenticate the user in the future.

Example

A form with a keygen field:

```
<form action="action_page.php">
  Username: <input type="text" name="user">
  Encryption: <keygen name="security">
  <input type="submit">
</form>
```

HTML5 <output> Element

The <output> element represents the result of a calculation (like one performed by a script).

Example

Perform a calculation and show the result in an <output> element:

```
<form action="action_page.asp"
  oninput="x.value=parseInt(a.value)+parseInt(b.value)">
  0
  <input type="range"  id="a" name="a" value="50">
  100 +
  <input type="number" id="b" name="b" value="50">
  =
  <output name="x" for="a b"></output>
  <br><br>
  <input type="submit">
</form>
```

New Elements in HTML5

Below is a list of the new HTML5 elements, and a description of what they are used for.

HTML5 offers new elements for better document structure:

Tag	Description
<article>	Defines an article in the document
<aside>	Defines content aside from the page content
<bdi>	Defines a part of text that might be formatted in a different direction from other text

Tag	Description
<details>	Defines additional details that the user can view or hide
<dialog>	Defines a dialog box or window
<figcaption>	Defines a caption for a <figure> element
<figure>	Defines self-contained content, like illustrations, diagrams, photos, code listings, etc.
<footer>	Defines a footer for the document or a section
<header>	Defines a header for the document or a section
<main>	Defines the main content of a document
<mark>	Defines marked or highlighted text
<menuitem>	Defines a command/menu item that the user can invoke from a popup menu
<meter>	Defines a scalar measurement within a known range (a gauge)
<nav>	Defines navigation links in the document
<progress>	Defines the progress of a task
<rp>	Defines what to show in browsers that do not support ruby annotations
<rt>	Defines an explanation/pronunciation of characters (for East Asian typography)
<ruby>	Defines a ruby annotation (for East Asian typography)
<section>	Defines a section in the document
<summary>	Defines a visible heading for a <details> element
<time>	Defines a date/time
<wbr>	Defines a possible line-break

New Input Types: color, date, datetime, datetime-local, email, month, number, range, search, tel, time, url, week.

3.13.3 Form Attributes

HTML5 includes new attributes that can be applied to almost every form element, including input, textarea, and select. Some of the attributes are semantic flags, and some others provide new behavior.

Placeholder

A placeholder is a hint that is shown inside a text box until the user inserts text in that field. When the user starts typing, the placeholder is hidden, as shown in Fig. 3.3. This feature is very useful in mobile designs because of the lack of space to add more information or hints about what the field should contain.

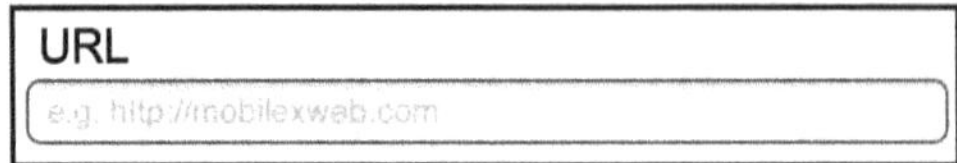

Fig. 3.3: Placeholder

The placeholder is the gray descriptive text inside the text box that is automatically deleted when the user begins typing a value in the box. The placeholder attribute is available in HTML5, and for non compatible browsers we can create a little script to give this functionality, even using the standard placeholder attribute as the source:

```
<input type="text" name="zip" placeholder="Your ZIP Code">
```

We can customize the appearance of the placeholder using some nonstandard CSShacks, such as:: -webkit-input-placeholder for WebKit-based browsers,:-msinput-placeholder for Internet Explorer 10, and: moz-placeholder for Firefox:

```
input::-webkit-input-placeholder, input:-ms-input-placeholder,
input:moz-placeholder {
color: #AFEFAF;
}
```

autofocus

Adding the autofocus Boolean attribute to a control tells the browser to focus on that element once the page is loaded, so we do not need to rely on JavaScript hacks to support that feature. For example, if we are working on a search engine, we can focus on the main search field using:

```
<input type="search" autofocus>
```

autocomplete

The autocomplete attribute accepts an on or off value, and it can be applied to the form element as a whole or to individual input elements. This allows us to enable or disable the autocompletion or autosuggestion features that the browser may use in forms.

readonly

If for some reason we do not want the user to interact with a form element, we can disable it with disabled or make it readonly. Both attributes are Boolean:

```
<select disabled></select>
<input readonly type="tel">
```

required

The required attribute does not need much introduction; like autofocus, it does exactly what you'd expect. By adding it to a form field, the browser requires the user to enter data into that field before submitting the form. This replaces the basic form validation currently implemented with JavaScript, making things a little more usable and saving us a little more development time. required is a Boolean attribute, like autofocus. Let's see it in action.

```
<input type="text" id="given-name" name="given-name"required>
```

required is currently implemented only in Opera 9.5+, Firefox 4+, Safari 5+, Internet Explorer 10 and Chrome 5+, so for the time being you need to continue writing a script to check that fields are completed on the client side in other browsers (*cough* IE!). Opera, Chrome, and Firefox show the user an error message (see Fig. 3.4) upon form submission. In most browsers, the errors are then localized based on the declared language. Safari does not show an error message on submit, but instead places focus on that field.

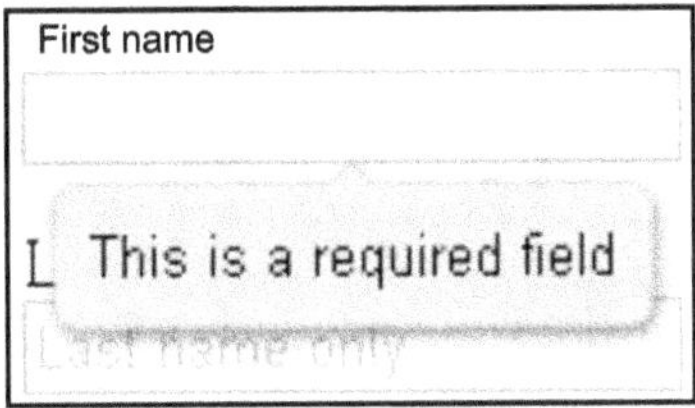

Fig. 3.4: Form field

Input Validation Attributes

HTML5 includes a validation feature that can be used by JavaScript or CSS. In this category, we can find the following new attributes:

required

A Boolean attribute that can be applied to any input type.

min

Specifies the minimum valid value; can be applied to numeric (number or range)or date input types.

max

Specifies the maximum valid value; can be applied to numeric (number or range) or date input types.

pattern

Specifies a regular expression against which the input value should be validated.

step

Used for numeric (number or range) input types; specifies the legal number intervals

form

The form attribute is used to associate an input, select, or text area element with a form (known as its *form owner*). Using form means that the element does not need to be a child of the associated form and can be moved away from it in the source. The primary use case for this is that input buttons that are placed within tables can now be associated with a form.

```
<input type="button"name="sort-l-h"form="sort">
```

formaction, formenctype, formmethod, and formtarget

The formaction, formenctype, formmethod, and formtarget attributes each have a corresponding attribute on the form element. These new attributes have been introduced primarily because you may require alternative actions for different submit buttons, as opposed to having several forms in a document.

formaction

formaction specifies the file or application that will submit the form. It has the same effect as the action attribute on the form element and can only be used with a submit or image button (type="submit" ortype="image"). When the form is submitted, the browser first checks for a formaction attribute; if that is not present, it proceeds to look for an action attribute on the form.

```
<input type="submit"
value="Submit"formaction="process.php">
```

formenctype

formenctype details how the form data is encoded with the POST method type. It has the same effect as the enctype attribute on the form element and can only be used with a submit or image button (type="submit" or type="image"). The default value if not included is application/x-www-formurlencoded.

```
<input type="submit"
value="Submit"formenctype="application/x-www-form-urlencoded">
```

formmethod

formmethod specifies which HTTP method (GET, POST, PUT, DELETE) will be used to submit the form data. It has the same effect as the method attribute on the form element and can only be used with a submit or image button (type="submit" or type="image").

```
<input type="submit" value="Submit" formmethod="POST">
```

formtarget

formtarget specifies the target window for the form results. It has the same effect as the target attribute on the form element and can only be used with a submit or image button (type="submit" ortype="image").

```
<input type="submit" value="Submit" formtarget="_self">
```

3.13.4 Form Validation

- To reduce the number of client-side scripts and server-side trips required for validation and to improve the usability of our forms, we should provide as many input validation properties as we can.
- The first typical option is to define the maximum size accepted for the text input using the max length property, expressed as a number of characters. Many platforms automatically add a character counter while the user is typing. A second popular option is to define the right input type for input elements, such as number or date. That will definitely improve usability and validation.
- To add more layers of validation without our own custom algorithms, HTML5 and WAPCSS (from XHTML MP) offer us some solutions.

HTML5 Validation

As we saw earlier, HTML5 adds some validation attributes, such as required, pattern, min, and max. The question is, what happens if a required input field is left without content? or if a numeric input field has a value greater than the max definition? What happens if the user does not type a valid email address in an <input type="email"> field?

The behavior changes per mobile browser there are some of the things that may happen:

- A validation bubble appears if the control does not validate against the rules.
- The form ca not be submitted until the whole form validates against the rules.
- The JavaScript API is used to validate the input. We can use the new CSS validation pseudo classes to show the validation process dynamically.

On desktops, most browsers add a validation bubble or halt the submission if validation rules are not met. However, most mobile browsers ignore that and leave it up to our CSS or JavaScript code to enforce the validation rules.

Example

Input Text Field Validation

Top of Form

Input Text Field Validation

First Name *

Last Name *

Submit

```
<fieldset>
 <legend>Input Text Field Validation</legend>
 <ol>
  <li>
   <labelfor="firstname">First Name *</label>
  <inputtype="text"id="firstname"name="firstname"placeholder="First Name"required />
  </li>
  <li>
   <labelfor="lastname">Last Name *</label>
   <inputtype="text"id="lastname"name="lastname"placeholder="Last Name"required />
  </li>
 </ol>
</fieldset>
```

```
<inputtype="submit"value="Sign up"/>
```

QUESTIONS

1. Which are the different mobile strategies to provide the best possible experience to every mobile device? Explain any one in detail.
2. What is WML? Explain with example. Give advantages and limitations of WML.
3. Explain XHTML MP (XHTML Mobile Profile) document structure with example. What are the advantages of XHTML MP?
4. Explain following WCSS extensions:
   (i) WCSS access key extension
   (ii) WCSS input extension
   (iii) WCSS marquee extension
5. Explain different types of conditional expressions of CSS3 media queries.
6. Explain different tests to check HTML5 compatibility levels.
7. Write and explain HTML5 Head and Body structure with example. What do you mean by HTML5 boilerplate?
8. Explain datalist, keygen and output elements og HTML5 form.
9. Explain following form attributes of HTML5:
   (i) placeholder
   (ii) autofocus
   (iii) autocomplete
   (iv) required
   (v) form
   (vi) formaction
   (vii) formenctype
   (viii) formmethod
   (ix) formtarget
10. Explain HTML5 form validation with example.

✠ ✠ ✠

DEVICES, IMAGES, MULTI-MEDIA

4.1 DEVICES

Before moving on with more HTML5, CSS, and JavaScript code that we can use on mobile devices, we need to pause and talk about feature and device detection. As know not every browser supports exactly the same features and even different versions of the same browser.

For that reason, we need to design and develop our code that makes it as future-proof as possible. So we are going to look at some techniques that will be useful for feature, device detection, and fallback mechanisms.

4.1.1 Device Detection

Some techniques useful for feature detection, device detection, and fallback mechanisms.

Possible Problems

To find the right solutions, first we need to identify all the possible problems we may need to deal with. We can summarize the possible problems with regard to features as follows:

- An HTML feature we want to use it but are not available, such as the progress element.
- A CSS feature we want to use it but not available, such as CSS animations.
- A JavaScript API we want to use it but not available or only partially available.
- We have to contract with different contexts: different input modes, screen resolutions, pixel densities, and screen sizes.
- A feature may not work correctly even when it is officially implemented.

Possible Solutions

Different types of solutions are available to solve problems we detect.

For Example

- Use internal HTML, CSS, or JavaScript mechanisms to provide a fallback, so if A is not available, B will automatically be executed.
- Use a polyfill, so if A is not available, some code is being executed on top of the Browser that emulates A compatibility.
- Use a client-side feature detection framework, so if A is not available the framework will warn us somehow so we can use another solution.
- Use a client-side device detection mechanism, so if we already know that browser X does not support A, we can use another solution.
- Use a server-side feature library, so if A is not available, we change the code from the server or redirect the user to another page.

About Polyfills

Polyfill look like a good idea for classic web progress in some situations, when developing for the mobile web avoids them as much as possible.

It is a JavaScript framework that fills a gap for some feature that the browser does not recognize natively it offers compatibility by emulating the same behavior.

The problem on mobile browsers is performance. Like every JavaScript framework, a polyfill will take time and battery power to "fill the gap" and if a browser does not support a feature it may be because it's an old platform and old platforms mean less memory and slower performance. Therefore doing something that harms performance, may be a very bad idea. That's not always the case, but you should at least test what the possible performance impact may be before deciding to use a polyfill.

4.2 CLIENT-SIDE DETECTION

On the client side (in the browser), we can detect features, provide fallbacks, and issue queries about the current platform using a mix of technologies.

Basically, all browsers will make the following assumptions without notice an error or stopping the rendering:

- If an element is unknown, the browser will ignore the open element, such as <progress> with all its attributes, and its closing element, such as </progress>.
- If an element is known but one or more of its attributes are unknown, the element will be rendered properly and the unknown attributes will just be ignored.
- If a CSS selector or CSS at-rule is unknown, the whole declaration will be ignored.
- If a CSS selector is valid but a style is unknown, only that definition will be ignored.
- If a CSS selector and a style are valid, but the value for the style is unknown, only that definition will be ignored.
- If the same CSS style on the same element is declared more than once, the last valid declaration will be used.

HTML Fallbacks

Providing fallbacks for new HTML elements is really easy. Hopefully, browsers will provide the fallback mechanism by default. Let's carry on with the progress example:

```
<progress max="100" value="8">
<img src='loading.gif'>
Progress 8%
</progress>
```

Browsers supporting the progress element will completely ignore all the child elements: that is, the img element and the progress 8% text. Browsers that do not support the progress element will just ignore it, and they will parse the img and the text properly.

When it comes to attributes, it's even easier, we just use any attribute we want, and non compatible browsers will ignore it or take a default action. Therefore, <input required> will render properly on all browsers (with some ignoring the required), and <input type="date"> will fall back to a type="text" input field on browsers that do not support date input controls.

CSS Fallbacks

In CSS style declarations, if a browser does not understand a style it will just ignore it, without affecting any other declarations.

For Example

```
#logo
{
background-image: url('logo.png');
background-size: 50%;
}
```

The background-size style is new in CSS3; non compatible browsers will just ignore it and use only the background-image style. When we want to use a style value that may not be compatible with all browsers, we should use a multiple declaration, with the first value being the most widely compatible and the last one the most specific.

Vendor Prefixes

- According to the CSS standard, when a browser is implementing a feature that is experimental, proprietary, or not yet mature enough for general usage, or if the discussion of how to implement it is not yet finished, the implementation must use a prefix so developers know that the final standard may change.
- Today's browsers can change a lot in just a few months, and because of their nature, they are hungry for more and more features.
- Therefore, today we use more prefixed features than we really want to, and the prefix system seems somewhat obsolete and nonsensical.
- The problem with prefixes is that we need to clone our code to define every possible prefix available today, such as webkit for Web Kitbased browsers, moz for Firefox, -o- for Opera or -ms- for Internet Explorer.
- Some values are not compatible between browsers, so we need to use different ones for each prefix.
- Vendor prefixes have created a new problem on the Web for mobile devices. As Safari on iOS and Android the top browsers when the mobile HTML5 started are WebKit-based, many developers just used the -webkit- prefix.

JavaScript Fallbacks

If we use JavaScript APIs everything looks simpler, as we can use simple conditionals to verify whether an API, attribute, or feature is available.

JavaScript APIs are usually Implemented as:

- Constructor functions, such as new WebSocket()
- Functions on standard elements, such as window.openDatabase()
- Properties or styles on standard elements, such as DOMElement.style.transform
- Event names, such as touchstart.

Modernizr

- Modernizr is a free and open source JavaScript library that will detect whether certain HTML5 and CSS3 features are available in the user's browser and expose the results as Boolean JavaScript flags and CSS classes. When you download the framework you can select one by one all the features that you want to detect, so you get a customized build (Fig. 4.1).

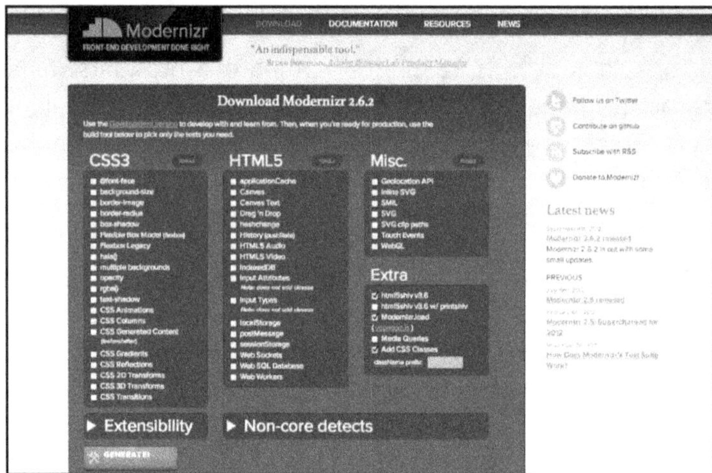

Fig. 4.1: Modernizr customization

- On the desktop side, Modernizr adds support for semantic HTML5 elements, such as section in IE6. When you include the framework, after the page loads you will receive a Modernizr global object with Boolean flags for every feature checked. For example, if you want to know if CSS columns are available you can use the Boolean attribute Modernizr.csscol umns. Besides the JavaScript flags, the framework adds classes to the body element for each selected feature.

- If the feature is available, the JavaScript property name is added as a class name. If the feature is not available, a no-<*name*> class is added. For example, for CSS columns, the class name added would be either csscolumns or no-csscolumns. Besides all the Modernizr CSS classes, the framework adds the no-js class to the body when JavaScript is not enabled in the current context.

- As all the website content is inside the body element, we can make use of cascade selectors in the same stylesheet to define different styles, as in:

```
// This style will be applied to columns-compatible browsers
.csscolumns article
{
column-count: 2;
padding: 10px;
}
// This style will be applied to non-columns-compatible browsers
no-csscolumns article
{
padding: 5px 50px;
}
```

- Modernizr does not remove the need to prefix features. However, there is an optional feature that you can add to your build, which will give you a tool, that will prefix an attribute for you.

For Example

var propertyName = Modernizr.prefixed('column-count');

It can also look for a prefixed object in a container, as in:

var raf = Modernizr.prefixed('requestAnimationFrame', window);

Conditional loading Modernizr adds (as an optional feature) a conditional resource loader that will help you load JavaScript files based on current compatibility.

The Basic Syntax is:

```
Modernizr.load({test: Modernizr.feature,
yep : 'feature-yes.js',
nope: 'feature-no.js'
});
```

With this tool you can load different JavaScript files based on feature compatibility. The feature can be any Boolean attribute, so we can mix more than one feature, as in test: Modernizr.geolocation and Modernizr.touch. The yep and nope attributes accept one string or an array of strings to load multiple files. Besides yep and nope, we can also define scripts with both that will always be loaded, and a complete callback that will be executed after all scripts have been loaded and parsed.

Platform Detection

JavaScript has a native navigator object that represents the client browser on which the code is running. The navigator object has many properties.

- appName (the browser's name this is most useful),
- appVersion (the browser's version),
- userAgent (a long string identifying the browser),
- plugin (an array of supported plug-ins for the object tag),
- platform (the operating system), and
- userLanguage.

Generally, we will use the string function indexOf to verify whether some of these attributes have the values, we can also use these for values match and a regular expression.

For Example

```
// Detects if it is an Android device
var isAndroid = navigator.platform.indexOf("android")>=0;
// Detects if it is an iOS device
var isIOS = navigator.userAgent.match(/iPhone|iPad|iPod/);
```

Detect Mobile Browsers

If you want to detect whether your code is running on a mobile browser or not, the simple way is to look for some keywords in the User Agent, such as mobile or well known mobile OS's names. There is a free open source framework that can help you with this available as JavaScript code and many server-side scripts from Modernizer.

4.3 SERVER-SIDE DETECTION

Before we get into detection of mobile devices and services on the server, we need to go back a bit and consider an old friend: the HyperText Transfer Protocol, also known as HTTP. Knowing a bit about its internals will help us determine what we can do in terms of mobile web development. There are no special server requirements for mobile websites; you can just use the same Apache, Internet Information Server (IIS), or other server you are currently using for desktop websites.

HTTP

HTTP is a protocol originally defined in 1991 for document transportation over TCP/ IP networks. It has two main versions: 1.0 and 1.1 (the last and current version of the protocol, defined in 1996). This same protocol is the one that we need to use from the server side in mobile web development. If we consider WAP1.1, where the device communicates with the WAP gateway and the WAP gateway is the one connecting to our server via HTTP. A similar approach is used in proxied browsers, like Opera Mini and the Nokia Xpress browser (see Fig. 4.2). However, from the server's point of view the requests coming in will always be HTTP requests.

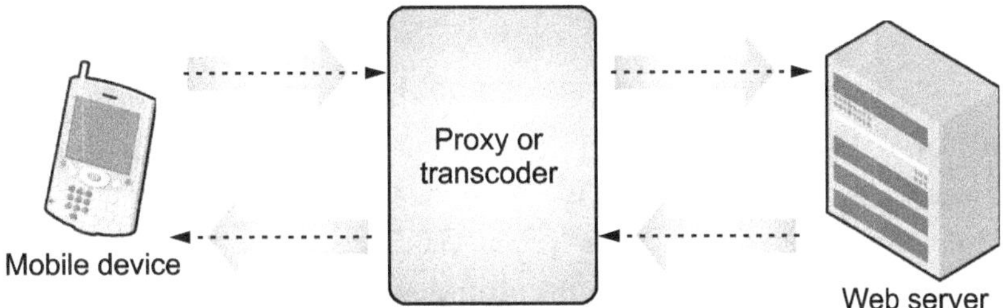

Fig. 4.2: Cloud-based browser

The request An HTTP request involves a client (the browser) sending a request to a server using its IP address (previously converted from a domain name). That request has a header and an optional body. The body is generally sent when we are doing a POST request.

The most common request type is a GET, requesting a document or a file from the server. The server responds with a response status code (hopefully not the famous 404), a header, and an optional (but generally sent) body. The body is the requested file.

SPDY and HTTP 2.0

Because HTTP 1.1 was created in 1996 and the Web has evolved enormously over the past few years, Google has developed an open network protocol to replace HTTP, with the particular objectives of reducing page loading latency and improving performance and security. SPDY (pronounced "speedy") multiplexes and prioritizes all the resources loading through only one connection, maximizing performance without the need of hacks or tricks.

SPDY is based on HTTP, so any HTTP server can work with SPDY if we add a translation layer in between.

Google has released an Apache module to add support for this protocol. As performance is a key issue in mobile browsing, mobile platforms have been among the earliest adopters, with some offering SPDY support from late 2011. The Android browser (from version 3.0), Google Chrome for Android, Amazon Silk, Opera Mobile from 12.1, and Firefox from version 15 support SPDY.

The Request Header

The request header has many fields that are defined by the browser and sent to the server (if no proxy, gateway, or transcoder is in the middle). Every mobile browser supports HTTP authentication, showing a modal window for username and password entry so the user can log in to a website.

The User Agent

The user-agent string identifies the browser. Microsoft also added other information to the user-agent string, like the operating system and details on the plug-ins and languages supported. The end result was a very complex user agent syntax with no standards.

What we can Identify

The mobile browser does not send information about:

- The International Mobile Equipment Identity (IMEI) or serial number to identify the device uniquely.
- The type of network used (WiFi, 3G, GPRS, EDGE, CDMA).
- The carrier (operator) providing service to the device.
- The country of the user.
- If the user is roaming.
- The phone number of the user.
- The device's brand and model number (at least, not directly).

Some of this information (carrier, brand, and model number) can be inferred, but the other identification data will not be available. That is why we cannot identify users automatically without a login, as in desktop web applications. If you are working closely with the carrier for your mobile website, you may be able to have yourself added to the WAP gateway's URL white list. You will then be able to receive a customer ID or phone number in a new, nonstandard header.

Here's what we can get from the device headers:

- The carrier and country, from the IP address of the request (if it is using a wireless network, such as 3G or 4G).
- The country (and maybe city or even exact location), from the IP address of the request (if it is using a WiFi network).
- The brand and model number, inferred from the User-Agent header.
- The language in which the operating system is defined.
- What markups and document types are accepted, if the header is not defined as */*.

The iOS Detection Problem

The user-agent string on iOS devices includes the operating system version (such as 5.1 or 6.0) and the device type (such as iPod, iPhone, or iPad), but it does not include any reference to the current device hardware or generation.

Therefore, there is no way of using HTTP headers to determine if the user is browsing with an iPhone 3GS, an iPhone 4, or an iPhone 5. Likewise, you can not tell if the user has a first- or third-generation iPad. Anyway, on the server side there is no way to tell if the user is on a larger screen device.

The User Agent Profile

The UAProf (User Agent Profile) is a voluntary standard defined by the Open Mobile Alliance (formerly WAP Forum). It takes the form of an XML file defining the abilities of the device, including its screen size, download features, and markup support. The XML is defined by the manufacturer or the carrier, and a link to the XML is defined in a header (typically x-wap-profile).

User Agent Tricks

There are different versions of Firefox available for Android, and Firefox OS. However, while the user-agent strings for Firefox reveal which platform the user is on, they do not identify the brand and model of device the user is using to browse the Web. Opera Mobile had a similar problem, but starting with version 12.1 it includes a Device- Stock-UA header whose value is that of the user agent of the default browser on the current device, so we can detect which device it is regardless of which Opera version the user has. The User-Agent header does not include any reference to the device hardware.

How to Read a Header

The specifics depend on the language, but all server-side platforms offer a way to read the request's header. Some languages use the parameter name as the header name (for example, Accept-Charset), and others use a longer version with the syntax HTTP_*X*, where *X* is the header name in all uppercase and with the dashes (-) replaced by underscores

For Example

HTTP_ACCEPT_CHARSET

How to Read the IP Address

The IP address from which the request originated can be read with the following code:

```
        // In Java
String address = req.getRemoteAddr();
        // In PHP
$address = $_SERVER["REMOTE_ADDR"];
```

4.4 DEVICE INTERACTION

Mobile browsers have the useful facility of being able to interact with the device both the operating system and the hardware. Communication can be driven by URIs used in links or JavaScript APIs. Some specific platforms support both an API and a URI scheme for the same feature; in that case the API usually is the preferred way as it's more flexible and less error-prone.

Mobile-Specific URIs

There are some URI schemes that many mobile browsers understand that enable us to communicate with some phone features. We can use these URIs in typical a elements, and in some browsers we can use JavaScript to force the URI using location href. Usually we are talking about using a protocol name, a colon, and parameters, such as *tel:2222*:

```
<a href="protocol:parameters"></a>
<script>
location.href = "protocol:parameters";
</script>
```

Making a Call

The first standard defined by the Internet Assigned Numbers Authority, or IANA is to use the *tel:<phone number>* scheme. It's a good idea to provide the phone number in the international format a plus sign (+), the country code, the local area code, and the local number as we do not really know where our visitors will be located. For example:

```
<a href="tel:+1800229933">Call us free!</a>
```

Some devices also allow sending DMTF tones after the call has been answered by the destination. This is useful for accessing tone-controlled services, help desk systems, or voicemail; you can say to the link, "call this phone number and, when the call is answered, press 2, wait 2 seconds, and then press 913#." You do this using the *postd* parameter after the number: the syntax is *; postd=<numbers>*. You can use numbers, *, and # (using the URL-encoded *%23* value), as well as *p* for a one-second pause and *w* for a wait-fortone pause. For example:

```
<a href="tel:+1800229933;postd=4">Call us free!</a>
```

This function does not work on all mobile devices, but on devices that do not understand it, the primary telephone number should at least be called. The compatibility list for this feature is complex, if the user activates a call link, she will receive a confirmation alert asking whether to place the call, showing the full number so she can decide. As shown in Fig. 4.3, some non-phone devices offer a contextual menu allowing the user to copy or save the phone number instead (the same functionality can be achieved on phone devices after a long-press gesture over a link).

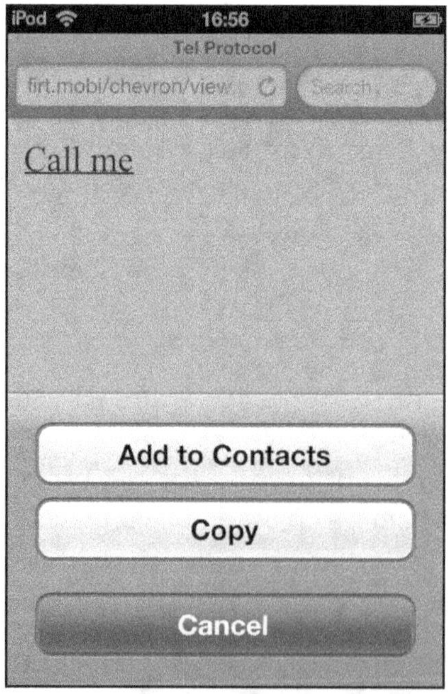

Fig. 4.3: Context menu of iPod

Not as well supported today as *tel:*, the other way to originate a call is using the WTAI standard, via the *wp* public library and the *mc* (make call) function.

Sending Email

Some modern devices with browsers also have mail applications that can react to the classic web mailto: protocol.

The syntax is:

```
mailto:<email_destination>[?parameters].
```

The detected parameters can change from device to device but generally include cc, bcc, subject, and body. The parameters are defined in a URL format (key=value&key=value), and the values must be URI-encoded.

For Example

```
<a href="mailto:info@mobilexweb.com">Mail us</a>
<a href="mailto:info@mobilexweb.com?subject=Contact%20from%20mobile">
Mail us
</a>
<a href="mailto:info@mobilexweb.com?subject=Contact&
body=This%20is%20the%20body">
Mail us
</a>
```

Sending an SMS

To implement SMS, there are two possible URI schemes, sms:// and smsto://.

The syntax is:

sms[to]://[<destination number>][?parameters].

The destination number is optional, so you can open the SMS composer from the device without any parameters defined. The parameters usually define the body, but this property is not compatible with all phones for security reasons (to avoid a website sending premium SMS texts, for example). As with an email, an SMS is not automatically sent when the user presses the link. The link only opens the SMS composer window; the user must finish the process manually.

Here are Some Samples:

```
<a href="sms://">Send an SMS</a>
<a href="sms://?body=Visit%20us%20at%20http://mobilexweb.com">
Invite a friend by SMS
<a>
```

```
<a href="sms://+3490322111">Contact us by SMS</a>
<a href="sms://+3490322111?body=Interested%20in%20Product%20AA2">
More info for product AA2
</a>
```

Other Communication Apps are Listed Below:

- **Adding a Contact to the Phonebook:** It might be useful to invite users to add your company's contact information (only the phone number, or full details) to their phonebooks for future communication.
- **Integrating with Other Applications:** Some devices allow us to integrate our websites with other native installed applications. This is dramatically nonstandard, though, and it depends very much on the device and the applications that the user has installed.

4.5 IMAGES

We need to find a balance with regard to the number of images and media elements in a document. Every image or resource adds to the network traffic, number of requests, and load time, unless we use best practices and techniques to optimize performance

With HTML5 we can render images with Scalable Vector Graphics (SVG), the canvas element, and Cascading Style Sheets (CSS). With CSS3 we can replace images for a lot of use cases, such as gradients, rounded corners, shadows, and other effects.

Image Formats

Almost every mobile browser understands standard static web image formats: GIF, JPEG, and PNG. On tablets and modern smart phones, all of these formats will work without any major issues.

Image Size and Memory Consumption

- When you load an image in a web application, the original file size matters only in the data- transfer. Once the file is on the browser, it is decoded in memory and it is always treated as a bitmap. Therefore, the size in memory can be calculated as width × height × bits per pixel.
- We should be careful, therefore, about loading big image files even if they are small in terms of bytes. Just to give an example, a full-screen image on a third generation iPad will typically use around 12 MB of RAM.
- Using more RAM will impact website performance when loading, scrolling, and returning from a frozen state (for example, when changing tabs). A new format that is compatible with some mobile browsers is *WebP* (read it as "weppy"). WebP is an open format created by Google, based on the VP8 video codec; it is intended to replace the JPEG and PNG formats as it has a better compression algorithm for both lossy and lossless images.

- For example, an image of the same image quality will have a file size in WebP that is, on average, 25%–45% smaller than in JPEG. WebP is also smaller for lossless images (on average, a WebP image is 26% smaller than the same image in PNG format). Therefore, it's a good candidate for the mobile web, as it is likely to enhance performance (less traffic, less time).

Animation Formats

- For animation, the standard in mobile web development is the *animated GIF*. As Flash support is not included in many browsers (as you'll see later in this chapter), and even when it is included it can be slow, banners and animations will be most widely compatible using this classic format, until SVG or other solutions become more widely supported.
- The polyfill *APNG-canvas* should make APNG work with Safari on iOS, the Android browser, and Chrome. Browsers that do not support APNG will just render the first frame of the animation.
- Modernizr has an extension attribute, APNG that will give us current compatibility information. APNG-canvas is a polyfill, that is compatible with mobile browsers that use the Canvas API to run the animation.
- The advantage of APNG over animated GIFs is the ability to use alpha channels and 32-bit images. A quick way to create APNG files is using APNG Edit, a free Firefox for desktop plug-in available from Mozilla's Add-Ons.
- An SVG element can also be animated, and it can be packaged as an *.svg* file or as a full URL that we can load as an iframe with all the contents inside. Older devices had support for XHTML+SMIL animation format. It is an obsolete standard today.

3D Formats

- As some mobile devices such as the Evo 3D and LG Optimus 3D have 3D screens, we can use some 3D image formats. However, having a 3D screen does not mean that those devices browse the Web in 3D.
- The most often used format is the JPS (JPEG Stereoscopic) format, which is basically just two JPEG images side by side (one for each eye). If you use the JPEG extension, viewers will just see two images, one beside the other. Special 3D software will understand it better if the JPS extension is used; this tells it to load the image in the right way.

Inline Images

- A data URL or data URI is a mechanism for defining a URL with embedded content such as an inline image defined in 1998. For example, we can define an img tag with the image itself inside it, without using an external file. This can be done using a base64 encoding of the image file basically, storing the binary file as a set of visible ASCII characters in a string.

- For small images, icons, backgrounds, separators, and anything else that does not merit a new request to the server. All modern mobile browsers are compatible with this feature. The size of an image (or any other binary file) will increase by about 30% when it's converted to a base64 string for a data URI, but its size will be reduced again if we are serving the document using GZIP from the server.

Responsive Images

- When developing for the mobile web, we need to adapt to different contexts, and when using Responsive Web Design we need a way to have adaptive images, or images that are available in different sizes for different contexts. The ability of a web app to adapt images involves a technique called responsive images.
- When using Responsive Web Design techniques and background images, we can make it work with background-size and background-position to change the image's clip based on the current available screen size or orientation.

Providing One Single Image

To provide one Single Image, a simple approach is to provide a single file (say, 200×80 pixels, 400×160 pixels, or something in between) that will be rendered at different sizes on different devices. The problems with that solution are:

- If we provide an image smaller than the current density (for example, a 100×100 image on a device with a pixel ratio of 2 that is expecting a 200×200 image), the browser will resize the image, and that means we will lose quality. Even if the result is not so bad and there are no visual glitches or problems, the user may realize that the image does not have "good resolution" and is not as sharp as it could be.
- If we provide an image larger than the current density, the browser will again resize the image. Usually resizing down does not cause problems in terms of visual quality. The problem is that we are delivering a big file (from 2 to 4 times bigger than necessary), meaning more bandwidth, a longer download time, and more memory consumption. And usually devices with lower density are older or cheaper, meaning they have less power and less memory.

Using img Elements

If we decide to provide an img image with a resolution higher than the medium standard one, it's important to explicitly define the width, height, or both. If not, we may have a problem.

For Example if we use img as follows

```
<img src="logo.png">
```

and we expect the logo to be 200 CSS pixels wide. If we provide a 400-pixel-wide image (ultra-high density), the browser will use 400 px as the width value, so it will render at double the size. Even worse, on ultra-high-density screens it will be rendered as 800 device pixels wide (400 multiplied by the pixel ratio of 2).

SVG

Standard Vector Graphics is an open XML specification describing 2D vector graphics. An SVG document can be static (declared in an XML file or tag) or dynamically generated from a JavaScript script using the DOM API. As a vector-rendering engine, a great feature is the adaptation to different screen sizes and resolutions without loss of quality.

SVG is a W3C standard for desktop platforms, with two subsets prepared for mobile platforms: *SVG Basic* and *SVG Tiny*. Thanks to this standards fight (as with XHTML mobile versions), we can use either SVG Basic or SVG Tiny with the same code and results.

SVG can be used in different ways:

- As an external file using img
- As an external file using object
- As a CSS background
- As a CSS effect
- As a font
- As inline SVG

4.6 VIDEO

Serving video content to mobile devices is very important for many portals and content providers.

We can provide multimedia content in three formats:

- Downloadable content
- On-demand streaming content
- Live streaming content.

Containers and Codecs:

Video and audio files come with two technologies: a container format and one or more codecs inside. The container is what you usually see more frequently: the file extension, such as *.mov* or *.mpeg*. The codec is the algorithm that encodes and decodes the media; these are usually divided into video and audio codecs. MPEG-4 containers are the most common. For these containers, AAC is the typical audio option, and the most compatible video codecs are H.263 and H.264; of the two, H.264 is preferred because of its compression algorithm (you get a smaller file for the same quality).

There are devices with support for containers, such as Flash Video (FLV), Audio Video Interleave (AVI), Real Video (RV), QuickTime Movie (MOV), and Windows Media Video (WMV) containers, H.264, also known as AVC, is one of the most used codecs and is commonly distributed inside MPEG-4 files. Its power is defined by its ability to provide high quality with smaller sizes.

The MPEG-4/H.264 alternatives include:

- The Ogg container, which usually comes with a Theora free video codec and a Vorbis audio codec (sometimes known as Ogg/Theora/Vorbis). On desktop, it's compatible with Firefox, Opera, and Google Chrome but on mobile it's right now only on Firefox.
- The WebM container, open and free project created by Google for HTML5 era. This container uses a VP8 video codec and Vorbis for audio. On desktop, Firefox, Opera, and Google Chrome support it, and on mobile only Android Browser from 2.3 and Google Chrome for Android.
- The 3GP and 3GP2 containers, created by the 3GPP organization. These are based on MPEG-4 and optimized for mobile devices; they are still well distributed on mobile devices, but MPEG-4 is a much more modern solution and is referred today. Handbrake is a free and open source video transcoder for Mac OS, Linux, and Windows that will help us with video conversions for mobile devices.

Reference Movies for iOS

Safari on iOS also supports "reference movies," created with QuickTime Pro or a similar tool. A reference movie provides a list of movie URLs with different bit rates (for example, for WiFi, 3G, or EDGE), so QuickTime can select the correct one for the device. You can find an Objective-C Mac tool provided by Apple to generate iOS reference movie files from the command line.

Delivering Video

We can deliver files using HTTP or a multimedia-streaming server, such as Adobe Flash Media Server. Unfortunately, most mobile browsers only support HTTP as the transport layer. Multimedia files are generally large. If we deliver non compatible files, the user will be paying for useless traffic and will not be happy with us. Check your server configuration, because using HTTP 1.1 we can support partial downloads and the ability to seek to any part of the file. For the best HTTP streaming technique, we need the server to support partial downloads. If your server does not support that, there is a great PHP script available.

Linking to Video Files

Usually, if MIME types are well defined on the server side, the user clicking on a link to a video file will start a video download automatically. On modern devices, instead of downloading the file, the browser will open the default video player application, which (if both client and server are compatible) will start playing your file using HTTP streaming. Only older feature phones will not play the video until the complete file has been downloaded. WURFL and Modernizr provide capabilities to help you understand video container and codec compatibility on both the server and the client side.

The HTML5 Video Element

HTML5 includes a new video element that can be used to embed and/or play videos in full-screen mode. We must specify a width, a height, and one or more video files to play. We can define one source video file using the src attribute, as in:

```
<video width="300" height="200" src="video.mp4"></video>
```

Because of the codec hell discussed earlier, the video element accepts a multiple-video definition using child source elements. That is, we can define different videos using different containers and codecs, and the browser will take the first one that is compatible with the current environment:

```
<video width="300" height="200">
<source src="video.mp4" type="video/mp4">
<source src="video.ogg" type="video/ogg">
<source src="video.webm" type="video/webm">
</video>
```

The type attribute can contain just the MIME type for the container (such as video/ mp4), or it can also include codec version declarations, such as:

```
<source src='video.mp4' type='video/mp4; codecs="avc1.58A01E,mp4a.40.2"'>
```

The video element typically acts as a video player in a rectangular area on the HTML page. However, on most smartphones it simply acts as a placeholder on the page; when we start playing the video, it always moves to a full-screen mode managed by the media player app, such as QuickTime on iOS. We can see this in action in Fig. 4.4.

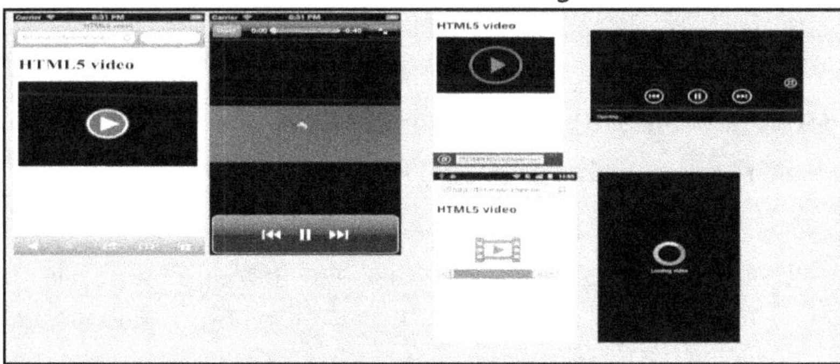

Fig. 4.4: QuickTime on iOS

A video element is shown as a placeholder that will open a full-screen player on some mobile browsers (in this case, Safari on iOS 6, Internet Explorer 9, and Android browser 2.3) in some cases, the playing is in landscape mode.

Advanced Declarations

The video element supports more attributes that we can define. However, support on mobile browsers is quite rare, as the browser or the media player application will take control of the player, and not our HTML code. These attributes are:

autoplay

- A Boolean attribute that, if present, will start the video playing automatically. On mobile browsers it's usually disabled as the playing action will be triggered only by a user action.

loop

- A Boolean attribute that, if present, will start playing the video from the beginning again when it reaches the end.

muted

- A Boolean attribute that, if present, will start the video in silent mode.

Preload

- Preload defines how to buffer or preload the video. It accepts the values none, metadata, or auto. On desktop browsers we can apply any CSS attribute to the video player, such as transformations, shadows, or transitions, and we can also use a video player as a canvas context image. However, because of the nature of video playing on mobile browsers (only full-screen or as a plug-in), these browsers do not support these features.

Providing Fallbacks

Anything inside the video element, apart from the source elements, will be ignored by HTML5-compatible browsers but used by non compatible browsers, so we can, for example, add a message, a link to the video, or an alternative embedded system, such as object, embed, or Flash:

```
<video width="300" height="200" src="video.mp4">
<!-- Fallback HTML code -->
```

Embedding video is not compatible with your browser.

```
<a href="video.mp4">Download the video</a>
</video>
```

Flash Lite (from version 3.0) supports only Flash Video format (FLV), while the major Flash Player supports FLV and MPEG-4. We can use the Flash Player as a fallback if HTML5 video is not available.

Video Player API

HTML5 browsers include a video player API that we can use to manage video playing from JavaScript. This API usually involves events that we can bind to so we can detect video download errors, codec errors, and video playing time events (such as onplay and onpause). With this API we can also use JavaScript to provide our own video playing controls, as any video DOM element has play() and pause() methods and properties such as volume and current Time. Safari on iOS will ignore any volume definition, as the user can change it using the hardware keys:

```
var player = document.getElementById("player");
player.volume = 0.5;
player.play();
```

The problem with mobile browsers is again the full-screen playing experience. With that problem, our website is frozen while the video is playing, so we have no option to customize the experience unless the user's device is a tablet. There are a few open source video player solutions available on the market, such as HTML5 VideoJS and jPlayer. On most mobile browsers, such as Safari on iOS, we can only execute the play() method after a user action, such as a click event. Other solutions, such as using load events of timers, will be ignored.

Streaming

Streaming audio or video is a difficult solution if we want to be compatible with all devices, because different platforms support different streaming technologies. Some devices, including Symbian, Windows, and BlackBerry devices, support the Real Time Streaming Protocol (RTSP). When a link with this protocol is used (such as in rtsp://server/content), the default media player Real Player or Windows Media is opened. The content can be a file to be streamed (a prerecorded audio or video file) or a live event (such as radio or TV show, sports event).

Modern smartphones, such as Android and iOS devices, do not support these streaming standards, which were created for the desktop world and direct connections. Consequently, different streaming solutions have appeared on the market over the last year to use HTTP as a streaming transport protocol.

These standards are:

- Apple HTTP Live Streaming (HLS)
- Adobe HTTP Dynamic Streaming
- Microsoft Smooth Streaming
- Dynamic Adaptive Streaming over HTTP (DASH).

Today, the Apple solution seems to be the most compatible with at least some mobile browsers.

HTTP Live Streaming

Apple has created a new way to deliver live streaming using HTTP, called HTTP Live Streaming, which it has presented to the IETF as a proposed Internet standard. HTTP Live Streaming supports the H.264 codec for video and AAC or MP3 for live audio streaming, as well as a bandwidth switcher for different qualities. However, the best feature is that it passes any firewall or proxy because it is HTTP-based. The implementation involves an extended M3U file (*.m3u8*) including links to different streaming segments, supporting different bandwidths.

The video element will point to that file:

```
<video width="300" height="200" controls src="live.m3u8"></video>
```

Embedding with Object

Before HTML5 appeared on the market, the way to embed a video without any Flash support was to use the object tag:

```
<object data="video.mp4" type="video/mp4" width="300" height="300" />
```

The previous example worked on Symbian devices for many years. The HTML fallback mechanism allows us to use the video element as the first option, with a fallback to a Flash Player, a fallback to the object element, and finally a fallback to a link to the video file. An alternative solution was the embed tag, preferred for iOS 1 and 2.x (but completely replaced by the video tag on newer iOS devices):

```
<embed src="poster.jpg" href="video.m4v" type="video/x-m4v" />
```

4.7 AUDIO

Audio is another media element that we can use in our mobile websites. HTML5 includes a new audio element that is almost the same as the video element in terms of attributes and compatibility. While some mobile browsers support WAV and Vorbis audio files, they all work well with the MP3 audio format. Therefore, we can usually use only one source definition with the MP3 audio file, such as:

```
<audio width="300" height="50" controls src="audio.mp3">
```

Audio playing not available.

```
<a href="audio.mp3">Download the file</a>
</audio>
```

Before iOS 4, all audio elements played as a full-screen blank page following the video player action. From version 4, audio playing is embedded in the HTML page. If you want the user to have audio controls on the page, as in Fig 4.5, you should always define the controls attribute.

Fig. 4.5 Audio Control

The Safari on iOS and Chrome UIs for the audio element when using audio we need to use the controls attribute if we want something to render on the screen.

Invisible Audio Player

When it comes to audio, we do not need any visual element on the HTML page in most situations we just want to play a song or a sound effect for a game. To avoid the onscreen controls, we can create a full audio player from JavaScript without using HTML code. The JavaScript API is the same as for the video element. To load an audio file and play it, we can use the following code:

```
var player = document.createElement("audio");
player.src = "audio.mp3";
player.load(); // You can call play() directly or load it first
```

```
player.addEventListener("load", function() {
player.play();
}, true);
SoundJS—part of the CreateJS family—is a cross-platform audio Java.
```

Web Audio API

The Web Audio API made its debut in the mobile web space with Safari on iOS 6. It's a pretty new API created by Google and at the time of this writing is in early draft with the W3C. As a low-level API, we can use it to play binary audio files, create our own sounds dynamically, or apply audio effects in our web apps. To use this API completely, you need some advanced technical knowledge of audio management. The API is available through an AudioContext global constructor or a prefixed version, as shown here:

```
var context = false;
if (window.AudioContext || window.webkitAudioContext)
{
context = window.AudioContext ? new AudioContext() :
new webkitAudioContext();
}
else
{
// API not available;
}
```

For simple audio playing purposes, the following code will bring an audio file by binary Ajax request and play it:

```
var request = new XMLHttpRequest();
var audioBuffer;
request.open("GET", "myaudio.mp3", true);
request.responseType = "arraybuffer"; // Defines binary file
request.onload = function() {
context.decodeAudioData(request.response, function(buffer) {
var audioSource = context.createBufferSource();
audioSource.buffer = buffer;
// We connect the audio with speakers
```

```
audioSource.connect(context.destination);
audioSource.noteOn(0); // Play without delay
});
};
request.send();
```

We can also create much more complex effects with the Web Audio API, such as mixing two audio files, cross-fading them, applying audio filters, and much more.

Audio Compatibility

Following Table shows audio compatibility for the main mobile web platforms.

Browser/ Platform	Preferred Delivery	Playing UI	Invisible Audio Support	Web Audio API
Safari on iOS	Audio element	Embedded from 4.0 Full-screen before 4.0	Yes	Yes from 6.0
Android browser	Audio element	Embedded	Yes	No
Chrome for Android	Audio element	Embedded	Yes	No (until 18)
Nokia Browser for Symbian	Audio element from Anna object before Anna	Embedded	No	No
Nokia Xpress browser	File link (no audio element)	N/A	No	No
BlackBerry browser	Audio element	Embeded	Yes	No
Internet Explorer	Audio element	Embeded	Yes	No
Firefox Mobile	Audio element	Embeded	No	No
Opera Mobile	Audio element	Embeded	Yes	No
Opera Mini	File link (no audio elelemt)	N/A	No	No
Amazon Silk	audio element	Embedded	No	No
UC browser	Audio element	Embedded	No	No

4.8 DEBUGGING AND PERFORMANCE

Debugging and performance optimization are the two scariest activities in the mobile web development.

4.8.1 Debugging

Developers need more tools for debugging and performance measurement, and the tools catalog available today is growing.

Server-Side Debugging

To debug server-side detection, adaptation, or content delivery scripts, we can use some HTTP tools before turning to the real devices.

User Agent Spoofing

User agent spoofing tools allow us to fool the server about the browser that is currently requesting the web page by changing how the client identifies itself to the server.

For example, using a desktop browser, we can say it is a mobile browser and the server will fall into the trap. We can use these tools to debug mobile redirects and detection frameworks, without the need of real devices or even emulators.

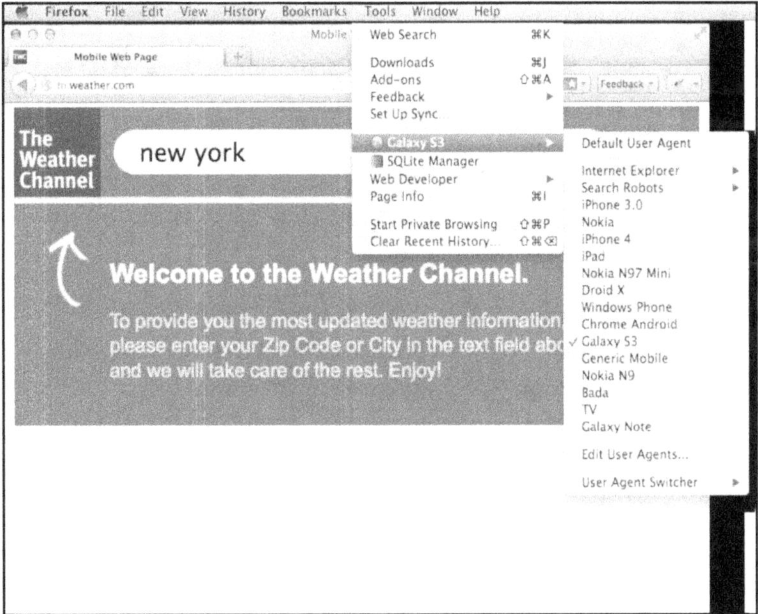

Fig. 4.6: Debugging tool

With User Agent Switcher you can test websites using any mobile user agent and render them with Firefox for desktop.

User agent tools do not emulate all the headers of a mobile device, including the accepted MIME types, so you should not rely on this plugin for testing this kind of detection. You can use other plug-ins to change HTTP headers. The latest versions of the desktop browser also include some tools for mobile web debugging, including a user agent cheating mechanism.

Markup Debugging

There is no automatic way to debug HTML. This is a manual operation on every emulator, device, or remote device you can access. Some browsers include a remote debugger that we can check for markup errors, but before for mobile markup.

HTML5 Validators

If you want to validate your HTML5 code, you can find some beta tools such as W3C's Nu Markup Validation Service and the Markup Validation Service. However, remember that HTML5 is not finished yet, and there are some extensions outside of the specific standards-therefore, these tools will be useful primarily for getting a big picture of errors and warnings.

W3C mobileOK Checker

The W3C offers a mobile markup checker that you can use for free. You can upload a file, copy and paste the code, or use a URL if you already have your mobile site on your server. This markup checker is based on best practices published in the Mobile Web Best Practices standard. It does not guarantee that your code will work perfectly on all mobile devices if it passes; it is just intended to help you find possible problems in your code and areas that do not conform to best practices. This tool is intended for XHTML, XHTML MP, and XHTML Basic websites, rather than modern HTML5 websites; however, it will still give us some hints about good practices to follow and potential errors we should investigate.

ready.mobi

The dotMobi team has created a free validator that includes the W3C mobileOK Checker tests and some others, plus some emulators and detailed error reports with suggestions. The validator is available at mobiReady. You can use it for a single document by providing a URL or copying and pasting the code, or to report on an entire site, including site-wide testing (registration is required for this last function). After analyzing your document, ready.mobi will assign you a score on a scale of 1 (very bad) to 5 (excellent). It will also report on the size of your document and resources and the estimated time and download costs for the user. This report is only suitable today for feature or social phone websites, not for HTML5 web apps.

Client-Side Debugging

Client-side debugging is one of the most painful activities in mobile web development. Every browser has a different rendering and JavaScript engine, and sometimes code that works on one device and does not work on another. This includes using the developer tools included with Chrome, Safari, or Internet Explorer, or the classic Firebug for Firefox. But just because everything works in a desktop browser does not mean that it will work in a mobile browser. The debugging solutions in this area include different kinds of tools:

Remote Debuggers

These open a debug session on the device that we can access remotely from a desktop computer, through WiFi or a USB cable. These tools can also be divided into official browser debuggers and injected debuggers, with the latter being a JavaScript file we need to inject in our HTML to provide the debugging session.

On-Device Debuggers

Using on–device debugger the debug session is seen on the device itself, in a separate window or pop-up.

Console Output Viewers

These are used only to see console output messages and errors from the browser. One problem we will have is that if a JavaScript error is encountered, many devices do not show any notice and the code simply ends its execution.

Firefox Remote Debugging

In Firefox 15 and later, the desktop browser has the ability to connect to a mobile version of the same browser. To use this feature, you need to have Firefox installed on both your desktop and a mobile device. Then, follow these instructions:

1. Open about:config in Firefox for desktop and define devtools.debugger.remote enabled as true.
2. Open about:config in Firefox for mobile and define devtools.debugger.forcelocal as false and devtools.debugger.remote-enabled as true.
3. Restart Firefox on the desktop and the mobile device.
4. Connect your mobile device (using WiFi) to the same network as your desktop computer.
5. Find your current mobile device's IP address (go to Settings → WiFi and tap on your current WiFi session.
6. Browse to the desired page on your mobile.
7. In Firefox for desktop, open the Remote Debugger from the Web Developer menu.
8. Replace localhost in the new window with your mobile IP address.

BlackBerry Remote Web Inspector

The BlackBerry browser for smartphones (7.x), PlayBook, and the newest BB10 platform supports a remote Web Inspector through WiFi. You can enable it through the browser's settings, where you will receive the URL to use on your desktop to open the Web Inspector session.

When enabling remote sessions using WiFi, as with the BlackBerry browser or Firefox, there is a security risk, as everyone on your own LAN can access the content, cookies, and storages on your mobile browser.

Opera Dragonfly

From Opera Mobile 9.5, we can debug mobile web applications using the remote debugging tool Dragonfly. To use this tool you will need Opera 9.5 or later (with Presto engine) on your desktop. You can open Dragonfly by going to Tools → Advanced → Developer Tools and checking the Remote Debug option. When you're done, enter *opera:debug* in the address bar of your Opera Mobile browser and specify your desktop IP address (public or private, if you are connected using WiFi to the same LAN). You will then have access to the same debugging features (DOM, CSS, and JavaScript) that you would if you were debugging a local desktop file.

Android Debug Bridge

While the Android browser does not have a remote debugger (at least, as of Android 4.2), we can still read the console errors and even use the same console object using the Android Debug Bridge (ADB). ADB is a command-line application available in the tools folder of your SDK.

4.8.2 Performance Optimization

Performance is the key to mobile web success. People want high-performance websites. We hate to wait on our desktops, and the situation is far worse on mobile devices, with their constrained resources.

HTTP Proxies

If you are using an emulator or a real device with WiFi capabilities, you can use any HTTP sniffer proxy, configuring the emulator and your device with your desktop IP address and port as the proxy for navigation. If you have a dedicated server (or even your own development computer with full inbound access to port 80), you can install one of these proxies and a web server and browse your website from any phone on any network to analyze how it is rendering and requesting resources.

Measurement

The first thing we need to do is to measure. If we cannot measure, we cannot optimize. However, measuring mobile websites is not easy. Typical desktop measurement and profiling tools do not work for mobile devices, and HTTP sniffers are difficult to implement for mobile browsers on 3G networks.

Performance APIs

The W3C's Web Performance Group is working on different APIs for accurate performance measurement on the browser. The Navigation Timing API is already available in some mobile browsers at the time of this writing, including the Android browser from 4.0, Google Chrome, the BlackBerry browser for BB10, Firefox, and Internet Explorer.

The Navigation Timing API allows us to measure times in an accurate way without affecting the measurement. It exposes a series of timestamps for performance hits, such as navigation start, request fetch start, request end, DOM loading, etc.

Therefore, to calculate how much time has passed from the navigation start point, we can use:

```
var now = new Date().getTime();
var page_load_time = now - performance.timing.navigationStart;
alert("User-perceived page loading time: " + page_load_time);
```

4.9 CONTENT DELIVERY

For any content you are serving in your mobile website, you can offer a *Share* service to publish the URL via Twitter, Facebook, and other social networks. We have to use some specific meta tags defining the information to share so the sharing mechanism works better. Some browsers, such as Safari on iOS and Internet Explorer 10 on Windows 8, have a sharing ability built in.

For most social networks, you should use the same URL you would use for the desktop website. On the server, the social network scripts will redirect mobile users to the mobile website.

For Twitter, you can use a link like this:

http://twitter.com/home?status=<*your message here*>

Twitter has a limit of 140 characters, including an optional URL using *http://*, which should be URL-encoded in the status variable. For long URLs, you should use a shortener service API.

For Facebook, you can share a link using:http://m.facebook.com/sharer.php?u=<*url to share*>&t=<*title of content*>

4.10 NATIVE AND INSTALLED WEB APPS

With HTML5, JavaScript supports some new APIs for client scripting and document work. Mobile browsers are already adopting some of these new APIs, even though all the standards are still in discussion.

Native Web App APIs

There are other extensions available for native web applications on some devices and many other JavaScript APIs are supported in installed applications.

These JavaScript APIs can include support for:

- Messaging
- Address book management
- Gallery
- Camera
- Calendar
- Device status information
- Native menus.

Also known as a hybrid application, a native web application is a compiled native application that usually uses a full-screen web view as the whole application container. In one approach, the whole application is developed using web technologies (HTML, CSS, JavaScript), but it is packaged and compiled as a native application so we can distribute it in native application stores. Another approach is to use some native layers and some web layers at the same time, such as native UI components with only some parts in a web view, with JavaScript logic.

Apache Cordova is an open source native web application framework for multiple platforms that is well known in the market because of one of its implementations: PhoneGap from Adobe.

QUESTIONS

1. What is device detection? Explain possible problems and solution.
2. Explain client side detection in detail.
3. Explain Server side detection in detail.
4. What is device Interaction? Explain specific platforms support both an API and a URI scheme.
5. List all Communication Apps and explain in detail.
6. Write short note on image format.
7. Write short note on Standard Vector Graphics.
8. What are the HTML5 video Element? explain.
9. Write short note on Video player API and HTTP Live Streaming.
10. List out the new audio element and explain any one in detail.
11. What is meant by Debugging? What are basic elements of server side debugging?
12. What is mean by Client-Side Debugging explain all debugging tool.
13. Write a note on Content Delivery.
14. Write a note on Native Web App APIs.

ADVANCED TOOLS, TECHNIQUES

5.1 J2ME PROGRAMMING BASICS

J2ME is the short form for Java 2 Micro Edition. J2ME is meant for tiny devices such as Mobile Phones, TV Set Top Boxes, Vehicle Telematics, Pagers and PDAs etc.

There are many differences between J2ME and other Editions of Java. The reason being the target devices of J2ME are very much different from the Computers. Some of the main differences between computers and the J2ME devices are:

- Limited processing power
- Limited system memory
- Limited storage capacity
- Small display
- Less Battery power
- Limited connectivity to internet.

J2ME was designed with all these above considerations. The J2ME compliant device manufacturers include the miniature version of the JVM in their devices, which is very light weight and suitable for these small devices. This JVM enables the execution of small Java programs which are called midlets. These midlets since they are nothing but Java programs (a little bit different) make these devices very powerful.

The J2ME applications can be used to do many useful things. A few of the capabilities of a J2ME program are:

- Making UDP connections back to the server or communication between two devices.
- Making HTTP connections back to a HTTP server to make rich applications.
- Making Socket connections.
- Bar Code scanning.
- Bluetooth programming.

5.1.1 Types of Configurations in J2ME

A configuration is a specification that defines the software environment for a range of devices defined by a set of characteristics that the specification relies on, usually such things as:

- The types and amount of memory available.
- The processor type and speed.
- The type of network connection available to the device.

A configuration is supposed to represent the minimum platform for its target device and is not permitted to define optional features. Vendors are required to implement the specification fully so that developers can rely on a consistent programming environment and, therefore, create applications that are as device-independent as possible.

5.1.2 J2ME Currently Defines Two Configurations

Connected Limited Device Configuration (CLDC)

- It is aimed at the low end of the consumer electronics range. Its platform is a cell phone or PDA with around 512 KB of available memory.
- For this reason, It is directly associated with wireless Java, which is concerned with cell phone users to purchase and download small Java applications known as MIDlets to their handsets.

Connected Device Configuration (CDC)

- CDC addresses the needs of devices that lie between those addressed by CLDC and the full desktop systems running J2SE.
- These devices have more memory (2 MB or additional) and more capable processors and they can support a much more complete Java S/W environment.
- CDC might be found on high-end PDAs and in smart phones, web telephones, residential gateways and set-top boxes.
- Each configuration consists of a Java virtual machine and a core collection of Java classes that provide the programming environment for application software.
- Processor and memory limitations, particularly in low-end devices, can make it impossible for a J2ME virtual machine to support all of the Java language features or instruction byte codes and software optimizations provided by a J2SE VM.
- The CLDC reference implementation is a source code and binary product for the Windows, Solaris and Linux platforms.

5.1.3 What is Profile in J2ME

A profile complements a configuration by adding additional classes that provide features appropriate to a particular type of device or to a specific vertical market segment. Both J2ME configurations have one or more associated profiles, some of which may themselves rely on other profiles.

These processes are described in the following list:

1. **Mobile Information Device Profile (MIDP)**
   It adds networking, user interface components and local storage to CLDC.
   It is primarily aimed at the limited display and storage facilities of mobile phones and it provides a relatively simple user interface and basic networking based on HTTP 1.1.

It is the best known of the J2ME profiles because it is the basis for Wireless Java and is currently the only profile available for Palm OS based handhelds.

MID Profile:

User Interface Package:

javax.microedition.lcdui: The UI API provides a set of features for implementation of user interfaces for MIDP applications.

Persistence Package:

javax.microedition.rms: The Mobile Information Device Profile provides a Mechanism for MID lets to persistently store data and later retrieve it.

Application Lifecycle Package:

javax.microedition.midlet: The MID let package defines Mobile Information.

Device Profile applications and the interactions between the application and the environment in which the application runs.

Networking Package:

javax.microedition.io: MID Profile includes networking support based on the Generic Connection framework from the Connected Limited Device Configuration.

Core Package:

java.io: Provides for system input and output through data streams.

java.lang: MID Profile Language Classes included from Java 2 Standard Edition.

java.util: MID Profile Utility Classes included from Java 2 Standard Edition.

2. **PDA Profile (PDAP)**

   It is similar to MIDP, but it is aimed at PDAs that have better screens and more memory than cell phones.
   The PDA profile, which is not complete at the time of writing, will offer a more sophisticated user interface and a Java-based library.

3. **Foundation Profile**

   It is extends the CDC to include almost all of the core Java 2 Version 1.3 core libraries. It is intended to be used as the basis for most of the other CDC profiles.

4. **Personal Basis and Personal Profiles**

   It basic user interface functionality to the Foundation Profile.
   It is intended to be used on devices that have an unsophisticated user interface capability and it therefore does not allow more than one window to be active at any time.
   Platforms that can support a more complex user interface will use the Personal Profile instead.

5. **RMI Profile**

The RMI Profile adds the J2SE Remote Method Invocation libraries to the Foundation Profile. Only the client side of this API is supported.

6. **Game Profile**

The Game Profile, which is still in the process of being defined, will provide a platform for writing games software on CDC devices.

5.1.4 MIDP Networking Model in J2ME

In MIDP, as in J2SE, IO streams are the primary mechanism available to applications to read and write streams of data.

Both J2SE and J2ME have a java.io package that contains these stream classes.

MIDP defines the javax.microedition.io package, which supports networking and communications for MIDP applications.

This package is in contrast to the J2SE java.net package, which defines networking support on that platform.

MIDP applications use the javax.microedition.io types to create and manipulate various kinds of network connections.

Then read from these connections and write to them using the types in the MIDP java.io package, which contains a subset of the classes and interfaces in the J2SE java.io package.

Important goal of MIDP networking is to abstract the heterogeneous nature, complexity and implementation details of different wireless network environments.

MIDP Generic Connection Framework

The MIDP generic connection framework defines an infrastructure that abstracts the details of specific networking mechanisms, protocols and their implementations from the application.

In the generic connection model, an application makes a request to a connector to return a connection to the target resource.

To make a connection, you use a generically formed address to specify the target network resource.

The form of the address is the same, regardless of the type of connection desired. The connector represents the actual connection returned as a generic connection.

That is, it characterizes the connection as one that has the lowest common denominator of attributes and behavior of all connection types.

Applications make all such connection requests through the same connector, regardless of the type of connection desired.

The connector abstracts the details of setting up a specific type of connection.

The connector provides only a single interface for obtaining access to network resources, regardless of the nature of the resource or the protocol used for the communication.

The term generic connection thus refers to the generic mechanism used to obtain access to resources, not to the content or type of the established connection.

In the MIDP generic connection model, you identify the resource and get a connection to it in one step.

This contrasts with the J2SE model, where the application must involve two objects:

One that represents the target resource itself, with the other object being the stream or connection to it. For instance, to access a URL in J2SE, an application constructs a java.net.

- URL object, which represents the actual URL resource. Using this object, the application then explicitly opens a connection to the URL resource, which yields a URL Connection object.
- This object represents the actual connection between the application and the resource and provides the medium through which the application accesses the contents of the resource.

Now, the application can obtain an input stream from the connection that delivers the content of the resource.

In the MIDP model, streams behave the same as in the J2SE model; they still do not know anything about the actual physical network resource. They simply know how to manipulate the content given to them when they were instantiated. The connector, however, hides from the application the details of interfacing the stream with the actual network resource.

There are two main advantages to the generic connection framework model.

- It abstracts the details of connection establishment from the application.
- This abstraction makes the framework extensible.

By using a standard, extensible mechanism for referencing network resources, MIDP platform implementations can be enhanced to support additional protocols while maintaining a single mechanism for applications to access all kinds of resources. Moreover, application logic remains independent of networking mechanisms.

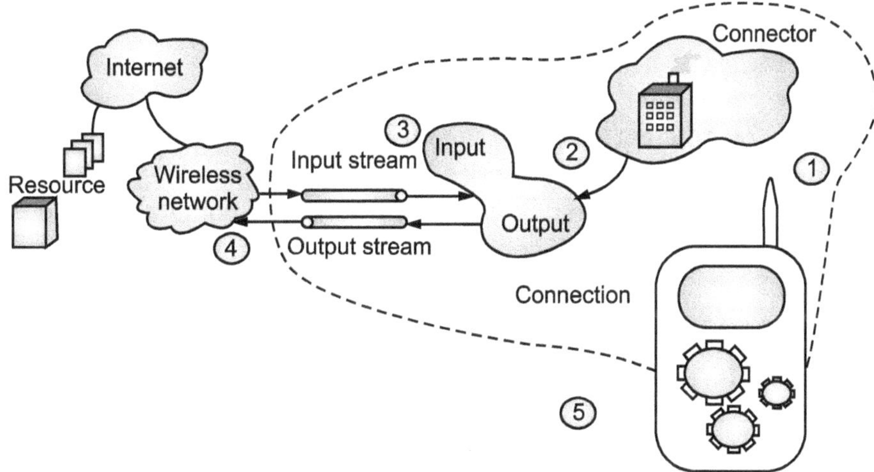

Fig. 5.1 Sematic representation of Connection Creation and Use

Above Fig. 5.1 shows a schematic representation of the steps involved in the creation and use of a connection. These steps, which we list next, correlate to the notation in the Figure.

- The application requests the Connector class to open and return a connection to a network resource.
- The Connector .open() factory method parses the URI and returns a Connection object. The returned Connection object holds references to input and output streams to the network resource.
- The application obtains the InputStream or the OutputStream object from the Connection object.
- The application reads from the InputStream or writes to the OutputStream as part of its processing.
- The application closes the Connection when finished.

A connection object contains an input stream and an output stream for reading and writing to the resource, respectively. Figure represents schematically the relationships between the connection and its two streams.

Once you have the connection, you use its two streams to interact with the network resource. There are two aspects to communicating with a network resource:

- Parsing the protocol message.
- Parsing the message payload the message content.

For example, if the client establishes an HTTP connection, the client must parse HTTP protocol syntax and semantics of the response message returned by the server. The HTTP message transports some kind of content and the client must also be able to parse the content appropriately. If, for example, the message content is HTML data, the client must properly parse HTML content. If the application does not know the format of the data delivered by the input stream, it cannot correctly interpret either the syntax or semantics of the stream content.

The MIDP generic connection framework defines a hierarchy of connection types that capture the nature of different kinds of stream connections. That is, the different types represent different protocols used by connections. Using the appropriate connection type makes it easier to parse and manipulate different kinds of content. For example, HTTP connections are a mainstay of MIDP networking communications. The generic connection framework defines a connection type whose interface supports constructing HTTP requests and parsing HTTP responses.

5.2 HTML5 SCRIPT EXTENSIONS

HTML5 is the latest and most enhanced version of HTML. Technically, HTML is not a programming language, but rather a markup language. This topic gives very good understanding on HTML5.

5.2.1 HTML5 Overview

HTML5 is the next major revision of the HTML standard superseding HTML4.01, XHTML1.0 and XHTML1.1. HTML5 is a standard for structuring and presenting content on the World Wide Web. HTML5 is cooperation between the World Wide Web Consortium (W3C) and the Web Hypertext Application Technology Working Group (WHATWG). The new standard incorporates features like video playback and drag-and-drop that have been previously dependent on third-party browser plug-ins such as Adobe Flash, Microsoft Silverlight and Google Gears.

5.2.2 Browser Support

The latest versions of Apple Safari, Google Chrome, Mozilla, Firefox and Opera all support many HTML5 features and Internet Explorer 9.0 will also have support for some HTML5 functionality. The mobile web browsers that come pre-installed on iPhones, iPads and Android phones all have excellent support for HTML5.

5.2.3 New Features

HTML5 introduces a number of new elements and attributes that helps in building a modern websites. Following are great features introduced in HTML5.

New Semantic Elements: These are like, <Header>, <Footer>and <section>.

Forms 2.0: Improvements to HTML web forms where new attributes have been introduced for<input> tag.

Persistent Local Storage: To achieve without resorting to third-party plugins.

WebSocket: A next generation bidirectional communication technology for web applications.

Server-Sent Events: HTML5 introduces events which flow from web server to the web browsers and they are called Server-Sent Events (SSE).

Canvas: This supports a two-dimensional drawing surface that you can program with JavaScript.

Audio and Video: You can embed audio or video on your web pages without resorting to third-party plugins.

Geolocation: Now visitors can choose to share their physical location with your web application.

Microdata: This lets you create your own vocabularies beyond HTML5 and extend your web pages with custom semantics.

Drag and Drop: Drag and drop the items from one location to another location on the same webpage.

5.2.4 HTML5 Syntax

The HTML5 language has a "custom" HTML syntax that is compatible with HTML4 and XHTML1 documents published on the Web, but is not compatible with the more esoteric SGML features of HTML4. HTML5 does not have the same syntax rules as XHTML where we needed lower case tag names, quoting our attributes; an attribute had to have a value and to close all empty elements. But HTML5 is coming with lots of flexibility and would support the followings:

- Uppercase tag names.
- Quotes are optional for attributes.
- Attribute values are optional.
- Closing empty elements are optional.

The DOCTYPE:

DOCTYPEs in older versions of HTML were longer because the HTML language was SGML based and therefore required a reference to a DTD. HTML5 authors would use simple syntax to specify DOCTYPE as follows:

```
<!DOCTYPE html>
```

Character Encoding:

HTML5 authors can use simple syntax to specify Character Encoding as follows:

```
<meta charset="UTF-8">
```

The <script> tag:

It's common practice to add a type attribute with a value of "text/javascript" to script elements as follows:

```
<script type="text/javascript" src="scriptfile.js"></script>
```

HTML5 removes extra information required and you can use simply following syntax:

```
<script src="scriptfile.js"></script>
```

The <link> tag:

So far you were writing <link> as follows:

```
<link rel="stylesheet" type="text/css" href="stylefile.css">
```

HTML5 removes extra information required and you can use simply following syntax:

```
<link rel="stylesheet" href="stylefile.css">
```

HTML5 Elements:

HTML5 elements are marked up using start tags and end tags. Tags are delimited using angle brackets with the tag name in between. The difference between start tags and end tags is that the latter includes a slash before the tag name.

Following is the example of an HTML5 element:

```
<p>...</p>
```

HTML5 tag names are case insensitive and may be written in all uppercase or mixed case, although the most common convention is to stick with lowercase. Most of the elements contain some content like <p>...</p> contains a paragraph. Some elements, however, are forbidden from containing any content at all and these are known as void elements. For example, br, hr, link and Meta etc.

HTML5 Attributes:

Elements may contain attributes that are used to set various properties of an element. Some attributes are defined globally and can be used on any element, while others are defined for specific elements only. All attributes have a name and a value and look like as shown below in the example. Following is the example of an HTML5 attributes which illustrates how to mark up a div element with an attribute named class using a value of "example":

```
<div class="example">...</div>
```

Attributes may only be specified within start tags and must never be used in end tags. HTML5 attributes are case insensitive and may be written in all uppercase or mixed case, although the most common convention is to stick with lowercase.

Standard Attributes:

The attributes listed below are supported by almost all the HTML5 tags.

Attribute	Options	Function
Access key	User Defined	Specifies a keyboard shortcut to access an element.
align	right, left, center	Horizontally aligns tags.
background	URL	Places a background image behind an element.
bgcolor	numeric, hexadecimal, RGB values	Places a background color behind an element.
class	User Defined	Classifies an element for use with Cascading Style Sheets.
Content editable	true, false	Specifies if the user can edit the element's content or not.
Context menu	Menu id	Specifies the context menu for an element.
data-XXXX	User Defined	Custom attributes. Authors of a HTML document can define their own attributes. Must start with "data".
draggable	true, false, auto	Specifies whether or not a user is allowed to drag an element.

Attribute	Options	Function
height	Numeric Value	Specifies the height of tables, images or table cells.
hidden	hidden	Specifies whether element should be visible or not.
id	User Defined	Names an element for use with Cascading Style Sheets.
item	List of elements	Used to group elements.
itemprop	List of items	Used to group items.
Spell check	true, false	Specifies if the element must have it's spelling or grammar checked.
style	CSS Style sheet	Specifies an inline style for an element.
subject	User define id	Specifies the element's corresponding item.
Tab index	Tab number	Specifies the tab order of an element.
title	User Defined	"Pop-up" title for your elements.
valign	top, middle, bottom	Vertically aligns tags within an HTML element.
width	Numeric Value	Specifies the width of tables, images or table cells.

HTML5 Document:

The following tags have been introduced for better structure:

section: This tag represents a generic document or application section. It can be used together with h1-h6 to indicate the document structure.

article: This tag represents an independent piece of content of a document, such as a blog entry or newspaper article.

aside: This tag represents a piece of content that is only slightly related to the rest of the page.

header: This tag represents the header of a section.

footer: This tag represents a footer for a section and can contain information about the author, copyright information, etc.

nav: This tag represents a section of the document intended for navigation.

dialog: This tag can be used to mark up a conversation.

figure: This tag can be used to associate a caption together with some embedded content, such as a graphic or video.

The markup for an HTML5 document would look like the following:

```
<!DOCTYPE html>
<html>
 <head>
   <meta charset="utf-8">
   <title>...</title>
</head>

<body>
   <header>...</header>
   <nav>...</nav>
<article>
     <section>
      ...
     </section>
  </article>
  <aside>...</aside>
  <footer>...</footer>
</body>
</html>
```

5.3 CODE EXECUTION

Execute JavaScript Code in Four Different Ways:

From a script tag

1. **The <script> Tag**

   The script tag has two purposes:

   - It identifies a block of script in the page.
   - It loads a script file.

   Which it does depends on the presence of the src attribute. A </script> close tag is required in either case.

A script tag can contain these attributes:

src="*url*"

The src attribute is optional. If it is present, then its value is a *url* which identifies a .js file. The loading and processing of the page pauses while the browser fetches, compiles and executes the file. The content between the <script src="*url*"> and the </script> should be blank.

If the src attribute is not present, then the content text between the <script> and the </script> is compiled and executed. The script should not contain the sequence because it could be confused with the </script>. Inserting a backslash between < and / in strings avoids the problem.

The backslash will be ignored by the JavaScript compiler.

Do not use the <! -- //--> hack with scripts. It was intended to prevent scripts from showing up as text on the first generation browsers Netscape 1 and Mosaic. It has not been necessary for many years. <! -- //--> is supposed to signal an HTML comment. Comments should be ignored, not compiled and executed. Also, HTML comments are not to include --, so a script that decrements has an HTML error.

language="javascript"

This attribute has been deprecated. It was used to select other programming languages and specific versions of JavaScript.

type="text/javascript"

This attribute is optional. Since Netscape 2, the default programming language in all browsers has been JavaScript. In XHTML, this attribute is required and unnecessary. In HTML, it is better to leave it out. The browser knows what to do.

defer

This attribute was intended to alter the timing of component loading in pages. It is not well supported and should not be used.

for="*name*" event="*name*"

This attribute is a Microsoft feature for declaring event handlers. It is not standard. Do not use it.

2. From an Event Handler

An event handler executes a segment of a code based on certain events occurring within the application, such as on Load, on Click. JavaScript event handlers can be divided into two parts: interactive event handlers and non-interactive event handlers. An interactive event handler is the one that depends on the user interactivity with the form or the document. For example, on Mouse Over is an interactive event handler because it depends on the user's action with the mouse. On the other hand non-interactive event handler would be on Load, because this event handler would automatically execute

JavaScript code without the user's interactivity. Here are all the event handlers available in JavaScript:

Event Handler	Used In
onAbort	image
onBlur	select, text, text area
onChange	select, text, textarea
onClick	button, checkbox, radio, link, reset, submit, area
onError	image
onFocus	select, text, testarea
on Load	windows, image
onMouseOver	link, area
onMouseOut	link, area
onSelect	text, textarea
onSubmit	form
onUnload	window

3. **From a Link, using the JavaScript: URL Protocol**

JavaScript can access the current URL in parts. For this URL:

http://css-tricks.com/example/index.html

- window.location.protocol = "http:"
- window.location.host = "css-tricks.com"
- window.location.pathname = "example/index.html"

So to Get the Full URL Path in JavaScript:

var newURL = window.location.protocol + "//" + window.location.host + "/" + window.location.pathname;

If you need to breath up the pathname, for example a URL like http://css-tricks.com/blah/blah/blah/index.html, you can split the string on "/" characters var pathArray = window.location.pathname.split('/');

Then access the different parts by the parts of the array, like

var secondLevelLocation = pathArray[0];

To put that pathname back together, you can stitch together the array and put the "/" back in:

```
var newPathname = "";
for (i = 0; i < pathArray.length; i++)
```

```
{
 newPathname += "/";
        newPathname += pathArray[i];
}
```

4. **From a Bookmarklet, Using the javascript:URL Protocol**

A bookmarklet is a bookmark in the browser containing some JavaScript code using the javascript: URL protocol. When the user activates the bookmark, the JavaScript code is executed over the current document. This allows us to execute a wide range of testing, debugging and other features over any web page.

There are bookmarklets on the Web that are large applications, encoded in a single line of JavaScript. The main problem with bookmarklets in mobile devices is how to add them. In the desktop web, the main way is to drag a link with the JavaScript code to the bookmarks area. This cannot be done in a mobile device, though, so bookmarklets are only useful if you can manage or synchronize them from a desktop (via iTunes for iPhone). There are a lot of bookmarklets for iPhone on the Web, including some that will show the source code of the page inside the mobile browser.

```
<a href="javascript:alert('Hi');">Click Me!</a>
```

Bookmarklets work in exactly the same way as this. The above can really be seen as one of the most primitive bookmarklets - add the link to your bookmarks and when selected, a basic pop-up will appear which greets you. Most bookmarklets are, however, more useful than this - typically they obtain information from or modify the current page in some way that is useful to the user.

5.4 CLOUD BASED BROWSERS

Cloud Browser is a fast Android browser. Cloud browser is inspired from iOS's Safari for its user interface. By using iOS Safari as an inspiration, we were able to develop a natural and modern user interface aimed at making our user's life easier.

Immersive mode on KitKat (4.4): Enter full screen mode from the setting menu and get into immersive mode.

Cloud Based Browser Characteristics:

Speed: Cloud Browser is without a doubt one of the fastest browsers on Android. By using our new CloudRenderEngine, we were able to achieve impressive performance results on our browser. This makes Cloud Browser usable on practically most devices to date, even on older devices.

Security: Cloud Browser has Icognito mode built in so if you need to browse the web anonymously, you know, you can do it with Cloud Browser. Also, our browser sports the latest in data encryption methods so you know, you are safe when browsing with Cloud Browser.

Productivity: Cloud Browser is very easy to understand and use, thus making migrating from other web browser an easy and painless process. You can even use the built in option to import bookmark.

Examples

1. **Opera Mini:** It is a cloud-based browser that takes very less space on your phone.
   - All you're browsing with Opera Mini goes through Opera servers.
   - These servers compress web pages, including text and images, down to 10% of their original size.
   - Because of this, Opera Mini is able to open websites even when you are on a congested/ fluctuating/ bad network area.
   - Opera Mini is the best companion when you travel. Outside the city, it can help reduce roaming or out-of-network charges.
   - It can help speed up the web and get you to your content faster.
2. **Opera Mobile**

   Key Features: Multiple tabs, Zoom-in
   Operating System: Windows Mobile, Symbian
3. **Skyfire**

   Key Features: Display rich websites with Flash or widgets like YouTube, customizable zoom feature.
   Operating System: Android, iPhone, Symbian, Windows Mobile
4. **Safari**

   Key Features: Display rich websites like YouTube, zoom feature, excellent touch-based user interface.
   Operating System: iPhone
5. **Google Android**

   Key Features: Display rich websites, zoom feature, touch screen interface
   Operating System: Google Android
6. **Microsoft IE for Mobile**

   Key Features: Standard browser features
   Operating System: Windows Mobile
7. **Firefox Mobile**

   Key Features: Mutiple tabs, Awesomebar, password manager, Add-on support, PC-syncing
   Operating System: Nokia Maemo, Windows Mobile 6.0 (alpha)

8. **Bolt**

   Key Features: Split screen mode, Widgets
   Operating System: Java MIDP 2.0

9. **Teashark**

   Key Features: Compressed downloads, Multiple tabs
   Operating System: Java MIDP 2.0

10. **Blazer**

    Key Features: Standard browser features
    Operating System: Palm OS

5.5 JS DEBUGGING AND PROFILING

What is JavaScript

- JavaScript is a dynamic computer programming language.
- It is lightweight and most commonly used as a part of web pages, whose implementations allow client-side script to interact with the user and make dynamic pages.
- It is an interpreted programming language with object-oriented capabilities.
- It was first known as **LiveScript,** but Netscape changed its name to JavaScript, possibly because of the excitement being generated by Java.
- It made its first appearance in Netscape 2.0 in 1995 with the name **LiveScript**.
- The general-purpose core of the language has been embedded in Netscape, Internet Explorer and other web browsers.
- JavaScript is the most popular programming language in the world.
- JavaScript is the programming language of HTML and the Web.
- Programming makes computers do what you want them to do.
- JavaScript is easy to learn.
- It is difficult to write JavaScript code without a debugger.
- Your code might contain syntax errors or logical errors, that are difficult to diagnose.
- When JavaScript code contains errors, nothing will happen. There are no error messages and you will get no indications where to search for errors.

5.5.1 JS Debugging

JavaScript Debuggers

- Searching for errors in programming code is called code debugging.
- Debugging is not easy. But fortunately, all modern browsers have a built-in debugger.

- Built-in debuggers can be turned on and off, forcing errors to be reported to the user.
- With a debugger, you can also set breakpoints and examine variables while the code is executing.
- Otherwise follow the steps at the bottom of this page, you activate debugging in your browser with the F12 key and select "Console" in the debugger menu.

There are Three Type of Debugging

1. Sever-Side Debugging.
2. Markup Debugging.
3. Client-Side Debugging.

1. Server-Side Debugging

To debug server-side detection, adaptation or content delivery scripts, we can use some HTTP tools before turning to the real devices.

There are Three Tools

User Agent Spoofing:

It allows us to fool the server about the browser that is currently requesting the web page by changing how the client identifies itself to the server. We can use these tools to debug mobile redirects and detection frameworks without the need of real devices or even emulators. The latest versions of the desktop browser also include some tools for mobile web debugging, including a user agent cheating mechanism. To use them, go to View→Developer→Developer Tools, access the Settings (the small gear icon at the bottom-right corner) and browse to the Overrides section, as seen in below Fig. 5.2.

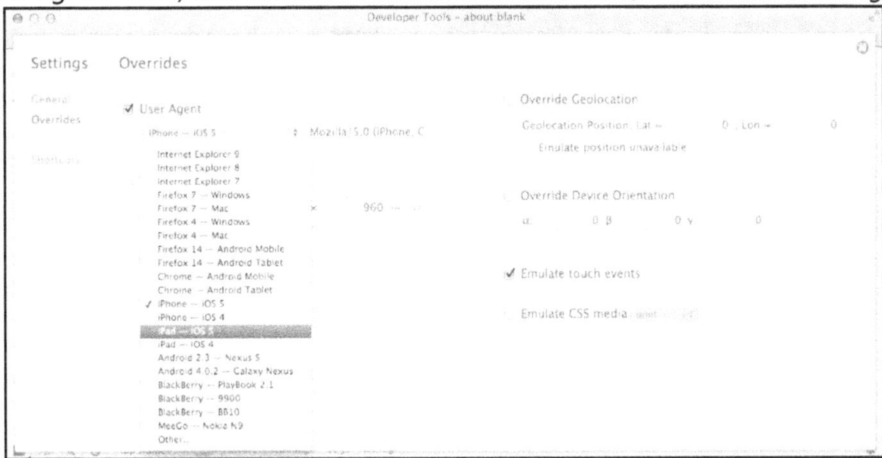

Fig. 5.2: Google Chrome for changing the current user agent and matching device metrics

HTTP Sniffing

When using real devices, it will be useful while debugging to store in some log all the request and response headers from the server-side code, so you can see the data the device is sending and receiving. Device anywhere includes a solution for this purpose for all devices or you can use any emulator that supports HTTP sniffing, like the Nokia and BlackBerry emulators. With other emulators and simulators, as well as with some real devices, we can use the typical desktop HTTP sniffing tools, such as Telerik Fiddler or Charles Web Debugging Proxy.

If you want Android browsers to browse the Web through a proxy (usually connected to a WiFi router and a proxy in the same LAN), you can define this behavior through the desired WiFi connection's "Modify network" contextual menu, activating Advanced Options and selecting Manual Proxy, as seen in Fig. 5.3. On iOS devices you need go to Settings → Wi-Fi, edit the hotspot using the blue edit action button and select Manual HTTP Proxy. On other operating systems, the process is similar.

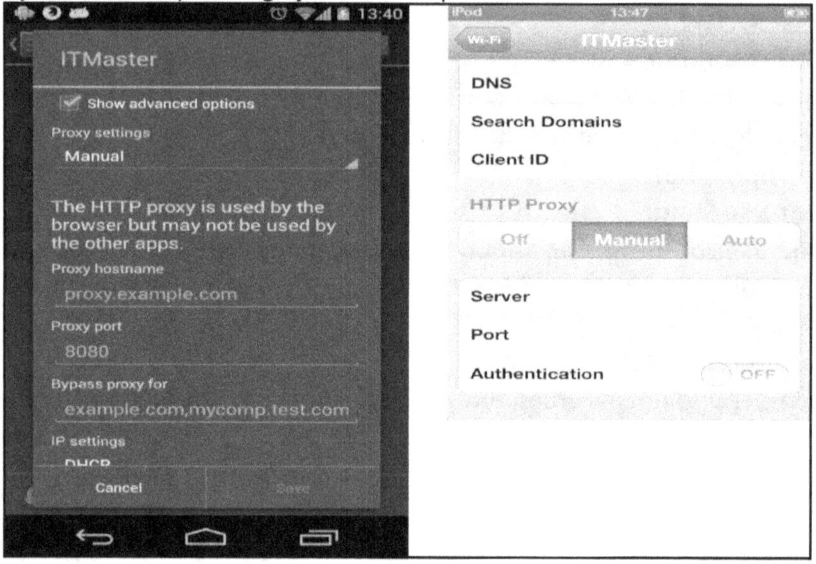

Fig. 5.3: iOS device: HTTP proxy for web browsers through the WiFi hotspot

Bandwidth Simulators

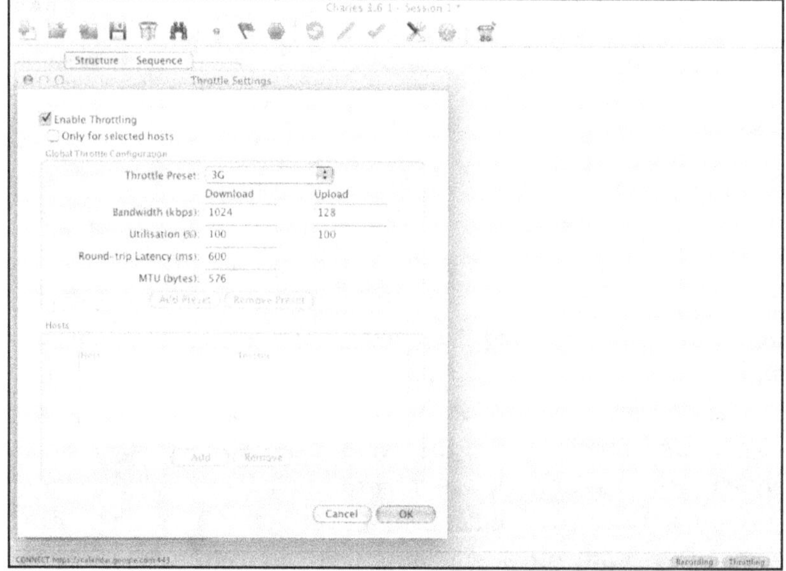

Fig. 5.4: The Charles Web Debugging Proxy : Proxy Throttling feature

With bandwidth simulators we can slow down our Internet connection and simulate a real 2G, 3G or 4G connection to get a better idea of performance and how our website is reacting. The Charles Web Debugging Proxy is an HTTP sniffing and proxy tool with a free version available that includes an HTTP throttling mechanism to simulate different bandwidths and latencies (as seen in Fig. 5.4). It is available for Windows, Mac and Linux.

2. Markup Debugging

There is no automatic way to debug HTML. This is a manual operation on every emulator, device or remote device you can access. Some browsers include a remote debugger that we can check for markup errors but before doing this it is a good practice to validate the code using one of the online tools available for mobile markup.

HTML5 Validators

If you want to validate your HTML5 code, you can find some beta tools such as W3C's Nu Markup Validation Service and the Markup Validation Service. HTML5 is not finished yet and there are some extensions outside of the specific standards therefore, these tools will be useful primarily for getting a big picture of errors and warnings.

W3C mobileOK Checker

The W3C offers a mobile markup checker that. This markup checker is based on best practices published in the Mobile Web Best Practices standard. It does not guarantee that your code will work perfectly on all mobile devices if it passes; it is just intended to help you find possible problems in your code and areas that do not conform to best practices. This tool is intended for XHTML, XHTML MP and XHTML Basic websites, rather than modern HTML5 websites; however, it will still give us some hints about good practices to follow and potential errors we should investigate.

ready.mobi

The dotMobi team has created a free validator that includes the W3C mobileOK Checker tests and some others, plus some emulators and detailed error reports with suggestions. The validator is available at mobiReady. You can use it for a single document by providing a URL or copying and pasting the code or to report on an entire site, including site-wide testing (registration is required for this last function). After analyzing your document, ready.mobi will assign you a score on a scale of 1 (very bad) to 5 (excellent). It will also report on the size of your document and resources and the estimated time and download costs for the user.

3. Client-Side Debugging

Client-side debugging is one of the most painful activities in mobile web development. Every browser has a different rendering and JavaScript engine and sometimes code that works on one device does not work on another. Typical desktop JavaScript techniques should be used first to debug logic problems in our code. This includes using the developer tools included with Chrome, Safari or Internet Explorer or the classic Firebug for Firefox. But just because everything works in a desktop browser does not mean that it will work in a mobile browser.

The Debugging Solutions in this Area include Different Kinds of Tools:

Remote Debuggers

- These open a debug session on the device that we can access remotely from a desktop computer, through WiFi or a USB cable. These tools can also be divided into official browser debuggers and injected debuggers, with the latter being a JavaScript file we need to inject in our HTML to provide the debugging session.

On-Device Debuggers

- Here the debug session is seen on the device itself, in a separate window or pop-up.

Console Output Viewers

- These are used only to see console output messages and errors from the browser.

Some other Client-Side Debugging Tools are Listed Below:

- iOS Remote Web Inspector.
- Connecting the session.
- Working with the session.
- Older iOS debugging tools.
- Older iOS debugging tools.
- Firefox remote debugging.

5.6 BACKGROUND EXECUTION

- When we see a mobile browser on a smart phone or a tablet, our first thinking is that it works in a similar way to a desktop browser. But, browser behavior can be really different and these differences impact our code's lifetime. Because of concerns about battery usage and general UI performance, most mobile operating systems, even on tablets, freeze all applications running in the background.
- Another important difference is that usually closing and minimizing are the same operation. Therefore, from a user's perspective, if she goes to a different app or to the Home screen, the browser (and all the open websites) will be frozen. That means no JavaScript code will be executed in the background.
- While some exceptions apply, this the expected behavior in most mobile browsers. A similar situation applies when the phone is in sleep mode or when the browser is still in the foreground but the user has switched to a different tab or window. Usually, the tabs or windows that are not in the foreground are not being executed and may not be in memory at all. Safari on iOS, Firefox, the Android browser and some other browsers freeze all Java-Script code when the user changes tabs/windows, locks the phone or minimizes the browser.

- Opera freezes our code when the user locks the phone or minimizes the browser, but it maintains execution if the user switches to a different tab. On the other hand, Google Chrome for Android keeps our website alive while the browser is still in memory, but if we are using timers the frequency slows down to one second.

Types of Background Execution

1. **Status Detection**

   Nearly all devices, timers are paused when the web page is sent to the background. There are different types of status detection.

   The Page Visibility API

   With this API we can check the document. Hidden property to see whether the document is actually hidden (true) or visible (false). It also exposes the new event visibility change that we can use to detect changes in visibility. The Page Visibility API is not available in every browser.

   Wakeup detection using timers.

   If the Page Visibility API is not available, such as in Safari on iOS up to version 6.0, we cannot detect when the user is hiding our website. However, we can detect when the user goes back to the website.

2. **Background Tab Notification Trick**

   While it can be an annoying behavior from a user's perspective when the page is active, an old HTML mechanism allows us to define a meta tag to reload a window automatically every *n* seconds. Some browsers, such as Safari on iOS, allow us to use this hack to automatically reload inactive tabs and keep them updated.

3. **Background Execution Compatibility**

   Some browser or platform like Safari on iOS Paused when device is locked, when window is not active or when browser is in background.

4. **Push Notifications**

   Android, BlackBerry and Windows Phone support push notification services for native installed apps. This kind of service is usually the way to alert the user of some update while the app is in the background or closed.

5.7 SUPPORTED TECHNOLOGY

There are several technologies (or APIs) that are bundled with JavaScript.

1. **The Document Object Model**

   It is a set of conventions for manipulating, browsing and editing XML and HTML documents using a set of API conventions that may be implemented in many languages. DOM APIs useful for PHP, .NET, Java and many other languages. It is a W3C specification with several versions available. By using DOM we can browse the HTML document structure and make changes and additions dynamically from JavaScript without refreshing the page.

2. The Selectors API

It is an extension to the DOM that allows us to use CSS selectors to retrieve an element result list from the DOM, *a la* jQuery. This method is very popular when using the jQuery JavaScript library and the API is included natively as part of most modern mobile browsers.

3. JSON

JavaScript Object Notation is a lightweight data interchange format known to be compatible with almost every language in common use. It is sometimes used in JavaScript as a replacement for other transport formats, like XML. It can be used in Ajax requests or to store and load information on the client side.

4. Binary Data

Because of the need for binary data in WebGL the 3D canvas modern browsers include a way to manage binary data efficiently, known as typed arrays. Even non-WebGL browsers, such as Safari on iOS, support these type extensions. The list of possible types includes DataView, Array Buffer, Float32Array, Int32Array and Uint8Array. Typed arrays work pretty much the same as normal JavaScript arrays, but their execution is much faster.

We can use these new data types with the Canvas, WebGL, XHR2, Workers, Sockets and File API.

5. Web Workers

It is a W3C specification that allows JavaScript to create working threads instead of executing all the code in the main UI thread, shared with the browser's rendering engine. Two kinds of workers: **workers** and **shared workers.**

- Worker allows a script to create an isolated thread that can communicate bi-directionally with the opener script and it has its own isolated context.
- Shared worker can be accessed by different scripts in the same domain that are working in different contexts, such as different tabs, windows.

6. HTML API's

With HTML5, JavaScript supports some new APIs for client scripting and document work. Mobile browsers are already adopting some of these new APIs, even though all the standards are still in discussion. We have already covered some of these APIs, such as Canvas.

7. Native Web App API's

There are other extensions available for native web applications on some devices and many other JavaScript APIs are supported in installed applications.

JavaScript APIs support the following Applications:

- Messaging
- Address book management
- Gallery
- Camera
- Calendar
- Device status information
- Native menus.

5.8 STANDARD JAVASCRIPT BEHAVIOR

JavaScript on the mobile web, we need to test compatibility and use some old-fashioned features.

1. Standard Dialogs

JavaScript supports a list of standard dialogs that are undervalued in modern desktop websites, often being replaced by Dynamic HTML or UI libraries. They make great standard dialogs for use in mobile websites.

The List of Available Dialogs is:

- Alert, for showing a message.
- Confirm, for receiving a Boolean response from the user.
- Prompt, for receiving a string from the user.
- Print, for sending the web page to the printer.
- Find, for invoking the find feature of the browser.

2. History and URL Management

JavaScript has a small number of standard mechanisms for browser history management: the location and history objects.

The location object has several properties regarding the address, like href for the whole URL and hash for the anchor part of the URL, if present (the # and everything to the right of it). Changing the location. href property will redirect the browser to another page, on compatible devices.

It has two useful methods: **reload(),** which refreshes the same page and replace(*url*), which sends the user to another page without creating a new history entry.

The history object has a few not-very-useful properties and three methods: **back (), go (*number*)** and **forward ().** The **back ()** method is the most commonly used, for emulating a back button.

3. **Manipulating Windows**

One of the most popular features of JavaScript in its early days was the usage of window. open to open the classic pop-up windows. For mobile browsers, the usage of this technique is not ideal, for many reasons. Many browsers can not open multiple windows and we cannot define any attributes for the pop-ups; they will just be full-sized, like the main window. Communication between the opener and the pop-up also often does not work well. Finally, closing pop-ups can be problematic on browsers that treat the new window as a normal page and not a pop-up, because window. Close works only on pop-ups.

4. **Focus and Scroll Management**

You can set the focus to a clickable element (such as a form input, link or button) using the focus function of every DOM element. The most helpful usage is for form input controls. The behavior varies in different mobile browsers. On some touch devices, focusing in a text box should automatically open the onscreen keyboard and in some cursor-based browsers it will position the cursor over the element.

On some devices, the global window object has a scrollTo() function that takes two parameters, xPosition and yPosition, specifying the position at the top-left corner of the screen to scrollTo. On some devices (like the iPhone), using scrollTo() emulates the user's scrolling and hides the browser's toolbars, as if the user were scrolling with her fingers. So, for some browsers it is common to use the following code, which automatically hides the toolbars after the onload event.

5. **Timers**

JavaScript offers three kinds of timers: the well-known **setTimeout()** and **setInterval()** and a new HTML5 timer, **requestAnimationFrame()**.

The first one is executed once and the second one is executed every *n* milliseconds until it is cancelled using clearInterval().

The latest is not yet supported in every browser and it's optimized for animations and games.

6. **Changing the Title**

In desktop web applications, it is common to change the title dynamically to alert the users of a change in the page, when updates are made in an Ajax application or simply as an animation (please, do not do this!).

In mobile browsers, this is not such a good idea, for the following reasons:

- Many browsers do not even display the title.
- If the user is working with many tabs at the same time, dynamically changing the title would not be useful because your web page will be frozen when it is in the background on most browsers.
- Animations in the title can be annoying in a mobile browser.

7. Cockie Management

Cookies are a great solution for the problem of statelessness in HTTP. They work in all devices and browsers. This is good. The bad thing is that the lifetime of a cookie can be shorter in the mobile ecosystem than in the desktop world, especially in low-end and mid-range devices because of the lack of memory storage.

Cookies are normally stored and read by the server, but JavaScript also allows us to read and write them as a client-side storage mechanism.

8. Event Handling

It is frequently used features of JavaScript is event handling, whether we define it inside the HTML document or by using code.

5.9 JAVA LIBRARIES

There are hundreds of Java libraries available today that cover every type of programming problem a Java developer is likely to come across.

The Java Class Library is a Set of Dynamically Loadable Libraries that Java Applications can Call at Run Time. The standard java library consists of a number of packages. Each package in turn consists of a number of classes .

Following are the java libraries that are bundled with JDK and used for almost any application developed in java.

1. Java.lang

The java.lang package contains the classes and interfaces that are fundamental to the core Java language. The most important classes of this package are Object, which is the root of class hierarchy and Class, instances of which represent classes at run time. Java depends directly on these two classes, making it indispensable for all java programs. Other classes from this package include: Boolean, Byte, Float, Math, Process and many more.

2. Java.util

This library provides users with generic java utilities like collections framework, formatted printing and scanning, array manipulation utilities, event model, date and time facilities, internationalization and miscellaneous utility classes. The classes and interfaces in java.util include: Hashtable, Vector, Enumeration, StringTokenizer, EventObject, Locale, Calendar and TimeZone and ResourceBundle.

3. Java.io

This library is very useful and contains the classes that handle fundamental input and output operations in Java. The I/O classes in this package can be grouped as follows:

- Classes for reading input from a stream of data.
- Classes for writing output to a stream of data.
- Classes that manipulate files on the local file system.
- Classes that handle object serialization.

4. **Java.net**

   The package java.net contains classes and interfaces that provide a powerful infrastructure for networking in Java. The java.net package can be roughly divided into two sections: a low level API and a high level API. Low level API has classes like InetAddress whereas high level API has classes like URL, URI, URLConnection and HttpURLConnection.

5. **Java.security**

   This package has several classes that allow users to encrypt a file using a user-provided key. It supports a cryptograph and digital signature.

6. **Java.sql**

   It contains all the SQL related classes and interfaces. This package provides the API for accessing and processing data stored in a data source.

7. **Java.swing**

   The UI library for developing desktop Java applications.

Most Widely Used Third Party Libraries

Below are some of the best and heavily used third party open source libraries in java. These libraries demonstrate the real power of java and make Java one of the most popular languages on planet.

Popular Utility Libraries

1. **Apache Commons Collections**

   This is a library that provides enhancements on core java collections. It provides additional collections and utility methods to manipulate collection objects easily and efficiently.

2. **Google Guava**

   Google Guava is an open-source set of common libraries for Java. It is designed by Google and was previously known as Google Collections. It's a useful source of miscellaneous utility functions and classes. It's basically a core library for immutable collections, string manipulation, caching, primitives support and easier I/O functions.

3. **Apache DBCP - Database Connection Pooling Library**

   This is a powerful library that provides feature of connection pooling to relational databases. This library has existed for long time and has been used in many applications including application servers.

4. **Apache IO - Input Output Utilities**

   Apache IO is a powerful library to do file and stream operations efficiently and quickly in java. Many utility methods from this library have been adopted in recent Java versions.

XML Manipulation Libraries

1. **JDOM**

   JDOM is a popular DOM parser library that is widely used in many java applications for parsing XML.

2. **DOM4J**

   It's a simple open source library for manipulation of XML, XSLT and XPath.

3. **XERCES**

   Yet another popular XML parser.

JSON Libraries

1. **Gson**

   JSON parsing library by Google

2. **Jackson**

   - A high performance JSON processor. Jackson is a multi-purpose Java library for processing JSON and XML data format.
   - It's a fast, lightweight and user-friendly library for developers.

3. **XStream**

   - XStream is a simple library to serialize objects to XML and JSON.

Graph Libraries

1. **JFreeChart**

   The JFreeChart is the easiest and most widely used graphical library for creating a wide variety of good looking charts. JFreeChart allows the users to generate pie chart, bar chart, timeseries chart, Gantt chart, histogram, X-Y charts and various specific charts.

2. **JasperReports**

   This is a full fledged feature rich library to create graph and charts. This is also available with enterprise support.

Logging Libraries

1. **Log4j**

   The most popular and oldest logging library.

2. **SLF4J**

   - Every Java programmer knows that logging is critical for any Java application, especially server side application.
   - Most of the programmers would be familiar with SLF4J as it is the most popular logging library.

- It provides Java API for various logging frameworks allowing users to plug in the desired logging framework at deployment time.

Document Manipulation

1. Docx4j

Docx4j is yet another document manipulation library for multiple types of document processing.

5.9.1 Mobile Libraries

The good news is that many developers have released alternative libraries that are geared for mobile devices and are lighter than the previous ones.

Zepto.js

It is a minimized JavaScript library optimized for performance. Its goal is to provide a 5–10 KB modular library that downloads and executes fast, with a jQuery-like syntax. With its addition with the HTML5 Mobile Boilerplate template, Zepto.js has become the most popular replacement for jQuery in mobile web development. As a jQuery-based library it uses the same $ query selector and most of the typical jQuery functions, such as the DOM, Ajax, forms and event methods.

baseJS

It is a lightweight library (8 KB) compatible with mobile Safari and other WebKitbased browsers. It has only been fully tested on Safari, from iOS 1.0 to 3.0. baseJS provides a selector similar to jQuery's, $(selector) and some similar methods, like each, addClass, hasClass, removeClass, toggleClass, getXY, fire and some Ajax methods.

XUI

It is a simple JavaScript framework for building mobile websites that takes up only 6.7 KB compressed. It has been fully tested on WebKit-based browsers and Opera Mobile. The developers are working on adding support for IE Mobile and BlackBerry. XUI is also similar to jQuery, but it is more powerful than baseJS. XUI uses x$ as the main selector object and includes the methods.

QuoJ

It is a micro JavaScript library (14 KB) optimized for mobile devices that includes DOM, event and Ajax functionality and a good quantity of touch gesture event handlers, such as pinch out, drag, rotate, hold, swipe and two-finger tap.

jQMobi

It is a query selector library optimized for mobile devices that takes 5 KB of JavaScript code using jQuery syntax. Based on Zepto and jQuery, this library focuses on ways to reduce the API to its most useful features and offers a fast version of a similar API. It includes basic DOM and Ajax management through the $ object and chained functions.

5.10 UI FRAMEWORKS

- These libraries enable Web developers to create great user experiences for their apps using technology and skills that they are familiar with. The best of these UI/UX frameworks include App Framework, Twitter Bootstrap 3, jQuery Mobile, Sencha Touch, Kendo UI and TopCoat. Each one provides a unique set of features to help Web developers make great apps.
- HTML5 Mobile User Interface Frameworks are libraries that will enable developers to easily create a professional grade user experience for their HTML5-powered app. All these platforms are appropriate for mobile Web apps as well as for native hybrid applications where a native wrapper allows the entire user experience be driven by HTML5. These hybrid applications are built using a wrapping technology like Cordova to give HTML5 applications access to native features of the device such as the camera through a JavaScript bridge API.
- These frameworks have a lot in common to help developers make great mobile apps. Most of these frameworks are based on jQuery or a jQuery style query selector JavaScript engine. A query selector is a JavaScript library that allows the framework to select elements make changes to the Document Object Model or DOM. Without a query selector those frameworks that require a query selector would not work appropriately or not work at all.
- These frameworks all include methods for loading data from the Web dynamically using asynchronous techniques to grab data in XML or JSON format. By providing access to resources on the Internet, these frameworks accelerate development and extend the capability of what is possible with HTML5 mobile apps.
- There are a variety of HTML5 user interface elements that all these libraries provide. Buttons, menus, forms, lists, toolbars, tabs, modal overlays and a variety of other controls are available from these frameworks. Most of these UI frameworks use font files to deliver icon images to the screen. Font files are a superior solution to flat files for icons because they consume less bandwidths are naturally resizable.
- All these frameworks take advantage of touch events as well as click events, allowing them to be used by mobile devices as well as desktop mouse-driven devices. Many frameworks make sure HTML elements are sized appropriately for touch activation as well.
- Many of these frameworks include a method of adding functionality through plugins or additional CSS or JavaScript library files. Developers only include what is necessary and nothing else. This progressive enhancement conserves as much speed and responsiveness, while providing options to add extra functionality as necessary.

5.10.1 Sencha Touch

- Built using lessons learned from Ext JS (an enterprise class desktop web framework), Sencha Touch (simply known as "Touch" in some circles) is a mature framework built to fit the most demanding app needs. Touch inherited the best of Ext JS, a versatile enterprise-level workhorse and took it to the next level by upgrading to utilize ECMAScript5, CSS3 and HTML5 best practices. That makes Touch different from Ext JS in the way that it no longer supports older browsers, but the functionality it offers is as good as it gets.
- Following the footsteps of its big brother, Sencha Touch will win your heart with plethora of widgets readily available out of the box.
- Responsive Web Design (RWD), while possible to some degree, is not advisable. However, Touch comes with pre-defined ***Layouts*** that help position the widgets on screen and use CSS3 for flexibility and positioning to update UI quickly. This is in particularly useful on orientation change event. Coupled with ***Profiles*** that help with dynamic adaptation based on specific rules such as Tablet vs Phone, RWD is not a necessity with Sencha Touch.
- Backstage, Touch operates like a full-fledged philharmonic orchestra powered by probably the most advanced ***Class system*** of all JavaScript frameworks. Much of the functionality is based on Abstraction, allowing developers to create custom components, plugins or extended features using these powerful design patterns.
- That said, developing in Sencha Touch is sometimes more of ***configuring*** with a light touch of real JavaScript development. While that can help the learning curve, it makes their API documentation essential even to the seasoned touch programmers. Fortunately, its documentation is also amongst the best out there.
- Sencha Touch offers a unique take on HTML5 Mobile UI Frameworks because it requires that all UI code is written in JavaScript.
- That makes for a more precise experience, but it requires developers to have considerable JavaScript chops to get things done.
- It is a commercial venture, so it has some great documentation, tools and support.
- However, it is free as long as it is not part of a product that ships more than 5,000 units.
- Sencha Touch is able to create some great graphical charts, it supports the Yahoo Query Language and it has themes to support every popular mobile platform.

5.10.2 jQuery Mobile

jQuery Mobile is a touch-optimized HTML5 UI framework designed to make responsive web sites and apps that are accessible on all Smartphone, tablet and desktop devices.

It is a touch-friendly UI framework built on jQuery Core that works across all popular mobile, tablet and desktop platforms.

It is a user interface framework based on jQuery that works across all popular phones, tablet, e-reader and desktop platforms. Built with accessibility and universal access in mind, we follow progressive enhancement and Responsive Web Design (RWD) principles. HTML5 Markup-driven configuration makes it easy to learn, but a powerful API makes it easy to deeply customize the library.

Pages and Dialogs:

A page in jQuery Mobile consists of an element with a ***data-role="page"*** attribute. Within the "page" container, any valid HTML markup can be used, but for typical pages in jQuery Mobile, the immediate children of a "page" are divs with ***data-role="header", class="ui-content"*** **and** ***data-role="footer"***. The baseline requirement for a page is only the page wrapper to support the navigation system, the rest is optional. A page can be styled as a dialog that makes the page look like it's a modal style overlay. To give a standard page the appearance of a modal dialog, add the ***data-rel="dialog"*** attribute to the link. Transitions can also be set on dialog links.

Ajax Navigation and Transitions:

jQuery mobile includes an Ajax navigation system to support a rich set of animated page transitions by automatically 'hijacking' standard links and form submissions and turning them into an Ajax request. The back button is fully supported and there are features to prefetch and cache, dynamically inject and script pages for advanced use cases.

Whenever a link is clicked or a form is submitted, that event is automatically intercepted by the Ajax nav system and is used to issue an Ajax request based on the ***href*** or form action instead of reloading the page. While the framework waits for the Ajax response, a loader overlay is displayed.

When the requested page loads, jQuery Mobile parses the document for an element with the ***data-role="page"*** attributes and inserts that code into the DOM of the original page. Next, any widgets in the incoming page are enhanced to apply all the styles and behavior. The rest of the incoming page is discarded so any scripts, style sheets or other information will not be included. The framework will also note the title of the incoming page to update the title when the new page is transitioned into view.

Now that the requested page is in the DOM and enhanced, it is animated into view with a transition. By default, the framework applies a ***fade*** transition. To set a custom transition effect, add the ***data-transition*** attribute to the link.

Content and Widgets:

Inside your content container, you can add any standard HTML elements - headings, lists, paragraphs, etc. You can write your own custom styles to create custom layouts by adding an additional style sheet to the head after the jQuery mobile style sheet. jQuery mobile includes a wide range of touch-friendly UI widgets: **form elements, collapsibles, collapsible sets** (accordions), **popups, dialogs, responsive tables** and much more. For best performance, use the **download builder** to pick the components you need.

Listviews:

jQuery Mobile includes a diverse set of common listviews that are coded as lists with a ***data-role="listview"*** added. Here is a simple linked list that has a role of ***listview***. We're going to make this look like an inset module by adding a ***data-inset="true"*** attribute and we add a dynamic search filter with ***data-filter="true"*** and a text field.

Form Elements:

The framework contains a full set of form elements that are automatically enhanced into touch-friendly styled widgets. Here's a slider made with the new HTML5 input type of range, no ***data-role*** needed. Be sure to wrap these in a ***form*** element and always properly associate a ***label*** with every form element.

Responsive Design:

jQuery Mobile has always been designed to work within a Responsive Web Design (RWD) context and our docs and forms had a few responsive elements from the very start. All the widgets are built to be 100% flexible in width to fit easily inside any responsive layout system you choose to build. The library also includes a number of responsive widgets like responsive grids, reflow tables and column, and sliding panels.

Theming:

jQuery Mobile has a robust theme framework that supports up to 26 sets of toolbar, content and button colors, called a "swatch". Just add a ***data-theme="b"*** attribute to any of the widgets on this page to turn it black. Cool party trick: add the theme swatch to the page and see how all the widgets inside the content will automatically inherit the theme. When you're ready to build a custom theme, use Theme Roller to drag and drop, then download a custom theme.

5.10.3 Enyo

It is a mobile and desktop framework that uses JavaScript and HTML5. Developed by HP and the open source community, it's licensed under the Apache License. The Enyo style guide is suggesting double quotes instead of single quotes. Enyo also uses tabs for indentation.

Kinds

Enyo applications are built around object prototypes called kinds. These can be either components or controls. Kinds in Enyo are very modularized, reusable and encapsulated. Controls, on the other hand, are for controlling DOM nodes and manipulating them. Controls can nest other controls or components they're the "building blocks" for applications. A good example would be an app consuming an XML feed: a component would process the feed to JSON and rearrange the data. The views of that application representing the feed would be controls.

Libraries

Layout: Fittables, scrollers, lists, drawers, panels.

Onyx: Based on the original styled of webOS /Touchpad design but available for use on any platform.

Moonstone: Used by LG Smart TV apps but available for use on any platform.

Spotlight: To support key-based interactions and "point and click" events on remote controls and keyboards.

Mochi: Advanced user interface library. It has been maintained by the community since the team behind webOS released this abandoned interface from Palm/HP as open source. This library is not included on bootplate right now, but has very good design documents.

enyo-iLib: Internationalization and localization library, it wrap ilib's functionality on Enyo apps G11n was another library that has been deprecated on newer versions of enyo.

enyo-cordova: Enyo-compatible library to automatically include platform-specific Cordova library (WIP).

Use

The following projects are built with Enyo:

- LG Smart TV apps.
- Openbravo Mobile and Web POS.
- XTuple ERP Web and Mobile App.

Example

```
enyo.kind({
        name: "HelloWorld",
        kind: enyo.Control,
  content: 'Hello, World!',
});
new HelloWorld().write();
```

Supported Platforms

Enyo can run across all relatively modern, standards-based web environments, but because of the variety of them there are three priority tiers. At 2015 some platforms supported are:

Tier 1 Supported at High Priority:

Packaged Apps: iOS7, iOS6 (PhoneGap) Android 4+ (PhoneGap), Windows 8.1 Store App and Windows Phone 8 (PhoneGap), Blackberry 10 (PhoneGap), Chrome Web Store App, LG webOS.

Desktop Browsers: Chrome (latest), Safari (latest MAC), Firefox (latest), IE11, IE10, IE9, IE8 (Win).

Mobile Browsers: iOS7, iOS6 Android 4+ Chrome, Kindle Fire and HD, Blackberry 10, IE11 (Windows 8.1), IE10 (Windows Phone 8).

Tier 2 Supported

Packaged Apps: iOS5, iOS4 Android 2.3, Firefox OS (pre-release), Tizen OS (pre-release), Windows 8 Store App, Windows (Intel AppUp).

Desktop Browsers: Opera, Chrome >10, Firefox >4, Safari >5.

Mobile Browsers: iOS5, iOS4 Android 4+ Firefox, webOS 3.0.5, webOS 2.2, BlackBerry 6-7, BlackBerry Playbook and others.

Tier 3 Partial Support

Mobile Browsers: Windows Phone 7.5.

No support

Desktop Browsers: IE8

Mobile Browsers: Windows Phone 7, BlackBerry 6, Symbian, Opera Mini

Enyo Apps:

Here is a partial list of Enyo apps currently available on various platforms.

App Name	Developer Name	App Category	Available on
17 Day Diet Meal Plan	Realized Mobile	Health and Fitness	iOS
3D Tet	Bertram Stading	Games	Android, Other, webOS
Apollo (Pandora Radio Client)	JMTK	Music	BlackBerry, webOS
Healthy Habit Tracker	MachiApps	Health and Fitness	Android, iOS, Other, Web App, Windows
Photo Filters	Chris Van Hooser	Photography	Android
USA TODAY	USA TODAY	News	webOS

5.10.4 Montage

Montage is framework lets you develop rich HTML5 applications that use JavaScript both on the front-end via the browser and back-end via Node.js. Montage is designed to allow you to develop applications optimized for today and tomorrow's range of connected devices.

It is an open-source JavaScript framework for building scalable single-page applications. Its aim is to simplify the development and maintainability of expressive HTML5 applications by employing many of the foundations of proven native application frameworks. You can build rich UIs in the client and use a service-oriented back-end to handle data persistence and server-side logic.

Features

- Components and HTML templates.
- Bi-directional data binding.
- Data persistence.
- Serialization.
- Event Management.

Compatibility

Montage depends on standardized browser features and works best in modern browsers, including Google Chrome, Firefox, Safari 5+, Internet Explorer 10, Safari Mobile and Android browser.

5.10.5 iUI

User Interface Framework for Mobile Web Devices

iUI is a lightweight open source Web application framework consisting of a JavaScript library, Cascading Style Sheets (CSS) and images for developing advanced mobile web applications iUI is a framework consisting of a JavaScript library, CSS and images for developing advanced mobile webapps for iPhone and comparable/compatible devices.

iUI has the Following Features:

- Create Navigational Menus and iPhone-style interfaces from standard HTML.
- Use or knowledge of JavaScript is not required to create modern mobile web pages.
- Ability to handle phone orientation changes.
- Provide a more "iPhone-like" experience in your Web apps.

5.10.6 jQTouch

- jQT (formerly jQTouch) is an Open Source Zepto/ JQuery plugin with native animations, automatic navigation and themes for mobile WebKit browsers like iPhone, G1 (Android) and Palm Pre.
- It enables programmers to develop mobile applications with a native look and feel for the target device using HTML, CSS and JavaScript.
- jQT tries to emulate mobile platforms, like the iOS SDK, as much as possible even enabling the use of the WebKit application offline.
- jQTouch is currently the most used Mobile JavaScript library in the top million sites, shortly followed by JQuery Mobile, both of which are extensions of JQuery, the most popular JavaScript library used on the web.
- jQTouch applications are not developed like regular web applications, where in an index page will be loaded with links that lead to other pages and each page is loaded from the server every time a visitor clicks on a link.

- With jQTouch, all the pages are loaded once inside the **index.html** and each page is represented as a separate div element in the index page.
- jQTouch comes with javascript files and css files with themes. This defines the look and feel of the application.
- There are two themes that come with the plugin: **apple theme** and **jqt theme**.
- jQTouch applications are basically developed in a single file, usually *index.html.*

It contains the html code, javascript code and the styling.

Features of jQTouch

- Easy Setup.
- Native WebKit Animations.
- Image Preloading.
- Callback Events.
- Flexible Themes.
- MIT Licensed.
- Swipe Detection.
- Extensions.
- Improved File Size.

5.11 JAVASCRIPT MOBILE UI PATTERNS

In this section we take a quicker look at a few mobile-specific UI patterns.

1. **Clear Text Box Buttons**

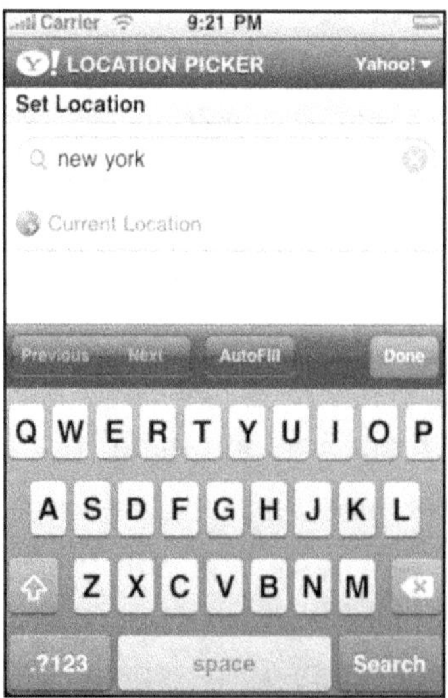

Fig. 5.5: Yahoo! website for touch devices

In their native UIs, touch devices have added a very nice feature to text boxes: the possibility of clearing all the text by touching a small X at the right-hand side of the box (as shown in Fig. 5.5). This is especially useful because of the lack of a keyboard on these devices. We can emulate this UI pattern easily by combining an image and a little JavaScript code.

2. Autogrowing Textareas

This UI pattern was created by the Google Mobile team and is currently used in Gmail. The problem is that if we have a large amount of text in a textarea, scrolling inside it is very painful in some browsers (Safari on iOS is one of them). The solution is to grow the textarea to fit the contents, so the user can use the normal page scrolling instead of the textarea's.

We can capture the onkeyup event and grow the textarea if necessary. We also need to capture onchange, because pasting in iOS does not generate an onkeyup event.

3. Floating Bars

A floating bar is just a full toolbar, a drop-down menu or a mixture of both that always remains at the top (or bottom) of the page when the user scrolls the content.

It is not suitable for focus-based browsers, because there will be usability issues when the user is tabbing between links.

For floating bars to work, the browser needs to support the scroll event. If the browser supports this event, the toolbar moving can be done automatically, using a smooth animation on some browsers. You can decide whether to have the floating bar appear at the beginning of the navigation or only after scrolling.

4. Cascading Menus

A cascading menu should be used for large toolbars, typically for touch devices. It can also be used in cursor-based browsers, but remember that in these browsers it may take the user a while to get to the desired zone of the screen using the navigation keys.

As these menus will typically be used on touch devices, we should not use mouseover events to open and close the menu bar and it is best to use onclick for both the opening and closing actions. We can also hide the menu when the user selects an option, scrolls the page or moves the focus to another object.

5. Autocompletion

An auto complete (or autosuggest) feature to reduce the user's typing, like the one in (Fig. 5.6), is a great feature, but it is not as simple to implement in a mobile site as it is in a desktop site. There are two kinds of auto completes: preloaded and Ajax-based. The preloaded ones involve downloading all the possible values to suggest (not recommended for more than 2,000 values) and storing them in JavaScript variables and then, if offline storage is available, storing them in the device for future usage.

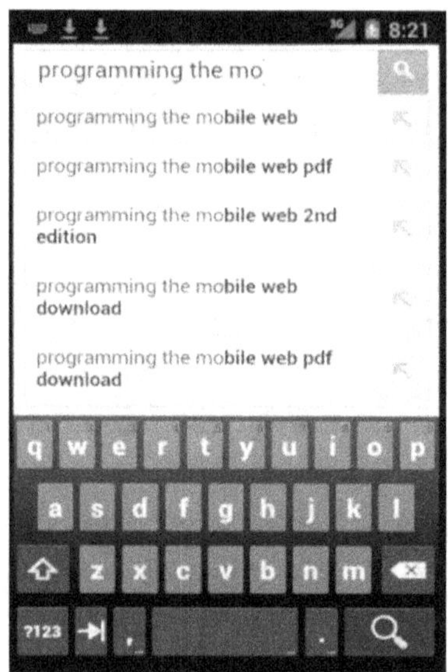

Fig. 5.6: Google.com auto completion on an android device

QUESTIONS

1. How J2ME is very much different from the computers?
2. What are the types of configurations in J2ME explain in detail?
3. What is profile in J2ME?
4. What are the features of HTML5?
5. List the standard attributes of HTML5 along with their function.
6. Write note on HTML5 document.
7. What are the different ways to execute javascript code?
8. What are the characteristics of cloud based browser explain with example?
9. Explain JS debugging and type of debugging.
10. What are the different types of background execution explain it?
11. Write note on JS supported technology.
12. What are the feature of standard JavaScript behavior?
13. Write note on Java Libraries.
14. List all Mobile Libraries and explain.
15. What are the different UI frameworks explain in detail?
16. Explain mobile-specific UI patterns.

✠ ✠ ✠

Unit VI

ADVANCED APPLICATIONS

6.1 GEOLOCATION AND MAP APPS

- "What is in your mind?" can be writen on Facebook and "what is happening ?" can be described on Twiter but future trend of social networking is "where are you?" and applications like Google Buzz, Brightkite, Gowalla, Foursquare individuals can use to answer it. To know where an individual is, or to find places recommended by other people, or to check in remotely at clubs, bars, and restaurants people can use their smartphone like Apple iPhone, Google Nexus One, or RIM BlackBerry with GPS facility.
- Location-based services (LBS) are major features of modern mobile web applications. From mobile websites, anybody can get the user's location using many methods. Mapping and LBS are very popular right now among smart phone users, so it is easy to find web services and APIs from different providers that we can integrate into anybody's mobile enabled websites.
- Typically, geolocation apps do two things first they report location of an individual to other users, and they associate real-world locations (such as shopping malls, Public Transport, Events, etc.) to anybody's location. These apps that run on smartphone devices provide a richer experience than those that run on desktop PCs because the relevant data you send and receive changes as your location changes.
- Smartphones today have a GPS chip inside, and the chip uses satellite data to calculate your exact position (usually when you're outside and the sky is clear), which services such as Google Maps can then map. When a GPS signal is unavailable, geolocation apps can use information from cell towers to triangulate your approximate position, a method that isn't as accurate as GPS but is has greatly improved in recent years.
- Some geolocation systems use GPS and cell site triangulation (and in some instances, local Wi-Fi networks) in combination to zero in on the location of a device; this arrangement is called assisted GPS (A-GPS).
- Use different techniques to determine the user's geographical location using his device, based on the platform, the browser, the operator etc. Most technologies involve server detection, but others depend on client detection, and even rely on the user's input.
- To consider, few aspects like accuracy and indoor location while detecting device location. First every location technology has some accuracy error and second it is difficult to locate user's indoor location inside building or office. Service providers can offer better services for the users inside the building if we can pinpoint what floor they are on or what department they are in.

6.1.1 Client Techniques

Different approaches from different device manufacturer are yield to provide exact location of device. These multiple approaches may predict different results about location of device.

The Global Positioning System (GPS)

- Is the first technique most people think of when location detection is mentioned. The United States government created GPS as a system for locating devices, using between 24 and 32 satellites orbiting the Earth.
- Many mobile devices come with a built-in GPS receiver that can read satellite data to determine location information (data must be received from a minimum of four satellites). In mobile devices, the accuracy error is between 2 m and 100 m. The user needs to have a sky view (outside), and it can take between 5 seconds and 5 minutes to calculate the location.

A-GPS

- Assisted GPS (A-GPS) is a software-based system available for mobile phones connected to carrier networks that can help the devices to determine their locations. The assistance can be in the form of helping the device to find a better satellite signal, or providing less-accurate information about the location of the user until the GPS has connected successfully.
- In 2006, started to use a Nokia N95 with GPS support. In city, it took 5 minutes to get location using GPS (with an accuracy error of 10 meters). A firmware update later added A-GPS support to the same hardware, allowing the same device in the same city to connect in 10 seconds, with an initial accuracy error of 100 meters. Cell information using the operator network's cellular towers, the carrier can triangulate the position of a mobile device.
- The accuracy will depend on how many cell towers are in range (the more densely populated location is, the more towers will be in range and the more accurate the reading will be). The carrier knows every cell tower's position, so it can make the required calculations to detect the device's location. Even knowing which cell tower a device is connected to can provide an idea of its location (near the location of the tower). This might be accurate to within a block, or up to some kilometers in rural areas.

WiFi Positioning System

- If a notebook with WiFi, go to Google Maps and click on the blue circle (the locate feature) then location identification is possible. If somebody is in a large city, he will probably be located very accurately.
- An individual just geolocated, and unless he have a 3G notebook, chances are that his notebook does not have GPS. This technique also works on a WiFi-connected iPod touch and on tablets. But how? The WiFi Positioning System (WPS) is a very clever technique that detects anybody's location using the list of wireless routers that are available in their area (even if you are not connected to them). This method relies on a pre-existing database of routers and their geographical locations.

- Skyhook Wireless is the leading provider, offering developer programs for most mobile and desktop platforms. Google has its own database and is also the provider used by Firefox. The main problem for us is that as yet there are no mobile browsers that give us the hotspot list.

6.1.2 Server Techniques

On the server, get the HTTP request headers. This is opportunity to locate the user without using any client technology, such as GPS, and in a way that works even for low-end devices.

Some techniques are describe below:

IP Address

- The main server technique for locating a user is reading the client's IP address. However, this is not as straightforward as it may sound. Depending on the users connection type (2G, 3G, WiFi), the IP address we receive may be the operator's WAP gateway address, a dynamic IP address in the operator's range, or the IP address of the WiFi connection. To further complicate our work, we need to bear in mind proxied browsers These browsers use a proxy server to connect to the Internet and to our servers.
- For example, if the user is browsing using Opera Mini, we will receive the requests from the Opera server instead of from the user's device. Likewise, if the user has a BlackBerry device and is using a corporate Internet connection, we will receive the requests from that connection, which could be based thousands of miles from the user's actual location.
- What should we do with the IP address? There are public lists of operators' IP addresses, and there are public and commercial solutions for determining the location of an IP address. The accuracy of this method can be country-level to city-level, although in some special situations, like when the user is using a public WiFi network, we can pin point the exact location.

Carrier Connection

- Some worldwide operators offer developer programs (both open and private) for web portals that allow any request made from a user to web server to carry additional headers containing information about the user (identity, location, and billing services).
- The GSM Association, which encompasses almost all the operators around the world, has launched an initiative called *OneAPI* that aims to provide web applications with access to all this carrier information through its APIs.

Indoor Location

- When users are connecting via WiFi hotspots in a single building, we can configure our routers to be queried about those users. Every WLAN user has a unique IP address in the network, so we can tell which hotspot a given user is connected to. With that information, we can identify the floor and zone where the user is located.

Language

- A less accurate mechanism is to use the accepted language of the browser. If the user has set up his device correctly, it should send a header indicating the preferred language, from which we can infer what country the user is in (for example, the browser may send us en-CA as the accepted language, meaning English from Canada). This results in at best country-level accuracy.

6.1.3 Detecting the Location

- There are two options for detecting the user's geographical location: using the W3C Geolocation API, available under the HTML5 APIs, or using third-party APIs, usually available directly from carriers. The W3C Geolocation API. The W3C standard way to query the user's position from JavaScript is called the Geolocation API. The Geolocation API does not rely on one location technology.
- Instead, it allows the browser to decide which method it will use. With this API implemented in a mobile browser, the navigator object in JavaScript will have a read-only property called geolocation that will allow us to interact with the API. Location querying is an asynchronous process. It can take some time to get the user's location (like with GPS); that's why the API relies on callback functions to give us the latitude and longitude. The user will need to give the site permission to obtain the geolocation data using the API.

Getting the Position

The first way to use the Geolocation API is to get the user's location using the getCurrentPosition() function of the geolocation object. It receives two callbacks: the function that will receive the position, and an error-handling function. The latter is optional. Optionally, it may also receive an object that configures some additional properties. The cords property has the following attributes, defined in the W3C standard:

- Latitude in decimal degrees
- Longitude in decimal degrees
- Altitude (optional) in meters above the ellipsoid
- Accuracy in meters
- Altitude accuracy (optional) in meters
- Heading (optional) in degrees clockwise related to true north
- Speed (optional) in meters per second

Handling Error Messages

The parameter received in the error handler is an object of class PositionError having a code and a message (useful for logging). The class also has some constant values to be compared with the code property. The constants are shown in Table 6.1.

Table 6.1: PositionError constants in the W3C Geolocation API

Error Constant	Error Constant Description
PERMISSION_DENIED	The user has denied permission to the API to get the position.
POSITION_UNAVAILABLE	The user's position could not be determined due to a failure in the location provider
TIMEOUT	The user's position could not be determined before the timeout defined in the options.

Tracking the Location

The second way to use the W3C Geolocation API is to track the user's location. With tracking support, we can receive notifications about location changes. For instance, we can make a sports website that tracks the user's steps, makes speed and distance calculations, and stores this information either locally or on our server using Ajax. The tracking process involves the watchPosition() method of the navigator. Geolocation object, which receives two handlers (for location detection and error management) and returns a watchId. The handler function will receive the same parameter as the getCurrentPosition() function that we saw earlier. To stop the location tracking we can call clearWatch() function.

Defining Optional Attributes

The third parameter of the getCurrentPosition() and watchPosition() functions can receive an object with the optional properties outlined in Table 6.2.

Table 6.2: Optional Properties for getCurrentPosition() and watchPosition()

Property	Type	Default Value
enableHighAccuracy	Boolean	False
timeout	Long (in milliseconds)	Infinity
maximumAge	Long (in milliseconds)	0

If the enableHighAccuracy property is defined as true, the provider should force the best accuracy in determining the user's location (such as GPS if available). The maximumAge property is useful when retrieving location data cached on the device. With this property, we can specify how recent we want the cached data to be if the data is older than the specified maximum age (in milliseconds), the device will have to get a new location.

Geolocation API 2.0

- The W3C is working on the next generation of the Geolocation API, including some additions to the current specification (mainly the ability to query about postal addresses). There are two optional Boolean attributes that we can use when we query about locations: requireCoords and requestAddress. The first forces the system to deliver co-ordinates, and the second defines whether or not we want to receive a civic address (street, number, city, country).
- When we get a location through getCurrentPosition() or watchPosition(), there is an optional address attribute in the argument (in the same place where coords exists). The address object may contain a set of properties including country, region, county, city, street, streetNumber, premises, and postalCode. Every property is optional, so how much information the browser will give us will depend on the current situation.
- Some carriers offer custom APIs that developers can use for free, for a monthly fee, or for a geolocation request fee.

GSMA OneAPI

OneAPI is a cross-operator API organized by the GSM Association. With this API we can access the user's location from our servers, using his phone number. Register as a developer and obtain a token to access the OpenAPI web services. The API supports SOAP Web Services and REST using HTTP.

Specific carrier's APIs

Table 6.3 shows other carrier geolocation APIs that we may use, using the network services after getting the user's permission.

Table 6.3: Carrier Geolocation API Availability

Platform	Carriers	URL
Verizon Network API	Verizon (US)	*developer.verizon.com*
BlueVia	Movistar (Latin America, Spain), O2 (UK, Germany), Telenor (Asia, Scandinavia, Eastern Europe)	*bluevia.com*
AT&T Location API	AT&T (US)	*developer.att.com/developer*
LBS	Sprint API Sprint (US)	*developer.sprint.com*
Orange Location API	Orange (France only at the time of this writing)	*api.orange.com*

6.1.4 IP Geolocation

There are a lot of free and commercial IP address geolocation services available for use on any servers. When using such a solution, we need to remember that a BlackBerry can browse through a corporate network, so the IP address will be the network IP address and not the user's. The same applies to proxied browsers like Opera Mini.

Reading the IP Address

We can read the IP address from the host using the appropriate mechanism for the server platform. For example, in PHP we read the address using:

```
$IP = $_SERVER['REMOTE_ADDR'];
```

Google's ClientLocation Object

Google provides a set of JavaScript APIs (Maps, Search) that can be used to create feature-rich dynamic websites. Whenever one of these APIs is loaded on a client, the Google Loader attempts to geolocate the user using the device's IP address. To add support for the APIs, we need to insert this script:

```
<script src="https://www.google.com/jsapi"></script>
```

To use the client location feature, we must then load an API. For example:

```
<script type="text/javascript">
```

```
google.load("search", "1");
</script>
```

6.1.5 Map Apps Integration

Some platforms, such as iOS, Windows Phone, and Android, include a native map application outside of the browser that we may want to open in some situations, such as to start a turn-by-turn navigation process.

Google Maps for Android

To invoke the Google Maps application on Android devices we can just point to *maps.google.com* and optionally send any parameters want to include, in the basic form *http://maps.google.com/?<attributes>*.

Attributes should be URL-formatted, as in *attribute1=value1&attribute2=value2*. Possible attributes include:

q: Query parameter; this can be a comma-separated coordinate preceded by a *loc:* prefix (*loc:lat,long*), or any search string, such as *starbucks*.

near: Applies a location definition for a query, as in *q=starbucks;near=san+mateo+ca*

ll: A comma-separated latitude and longitude for the map center

t: The type of map (*m*: map, *k*: satellite, *h*: hybrid, *p*: terrain)

z: The zoom level, from 1 (the whole world) to 23 (buildings, not available in all areas) On Android devices, the user will be able to decide if wants to execute URLs with the Google Maps native API or with the browser.

Directions and Navigation

To initiate a route algorithm and later a possible turn-by-turn navigation, use *http://maps.google.com* with the *saddr* (source address) and *daddr* (destination address) parameters, such as:

```
<a href="http://maps.google.com/?saddr=golden+gate&daddr=pier+39">
Directions
</a>
```

Street View

Android devices also offer the Street View service on Google Maps. To open a Street View panorama, we can use the nonstandard *google.streetview:* protocol. The parameters are:

cbll: The latitude and longitude, comma-separated (mandatory).

cbp: A series of optional parameters, such as yaw (center of panorama view in degrees clockwise from north), pitch (center of panorama view in degrees from −90 to 90), and the panorama zoom.

mz: The map zoom associated with this panorama if want to get these parameters, just browse to the street view want to link to and generate a link from desktop; see the parameters there.

iOS Maps

The Maps application on iOS has changed with time. From iOS 1 to iOS 5.1 the application is Google Maps, and from iOS 6 the application is Apple Maps. For the Google Maps application we can use the same *http:* protocol as in Android, so linking to *http://maps.google.com* will open the Maps application instead of the website until iOS 6. It accepts the same parameters as in Android. To initiate a route navigation, we can use the same syntax as in Google Maps from iOS 6.

Bing Maps

On Windows Phone, we can open the Bing Maps application using the *bingmaps:* protocol, which accepts the following parameters (a partial list):

cp: The center point a latitude and longitude, separated by a tilde ~ character.

lvl: The zoom level (1–20).

Where: A search query on places, locations, or landmarks.

q: A search query on a local business.

sty: The map style (*a*: aerial, *r*: roadmap).

trfc: Whether or not traffic information should be included (*0*: no, *1*: yes).

rtp: The route definition, with the source and destination addresses separated by a tilde ~ character; if either the source or the destination is undefined it will make a route from/to the current location.

Showing a Map

Once we have located the user (via a client or server solution), we may want to display a map showing the user's position, and/or a list of points of interest or other information superimposed on the map. To do this, we should use one of the available public maps APIs: Google Maps, Bing Maps from Microsoft, or Nokia. Use all these APIs for iOS and Android devices, as well as other HTML5 compatible devices; Nokia Maps does not just work on Nokia browsers.

6.2 OFFLINE WEB APPS

- HTML5 allows to create offline-capable web apps using a mechanism known as *application cache*. The concept is very simple. The user first opens the website in normal online mode, and it provides the browser with a package declaration text file called the manifest file, which lists all the resources like images, stylesheets, JavaScript, and so on. The next time the user visits the page, the HTML document is loaded from the cache, as well as all the resources in the manifest.
- First step is to define what we want? Do we want a full offline application? Do we want some pages or data to be updated from the server every time the application tries to access them? Do we want to have a local data cache and update it whenever online access is available?

- The second step is to define the manifest, or the list of files for the browser to download the first time the user accesses website. This list must include every JavaScript script, stylesheet, image, or other resource that want to access offline.
- Firefox is the only mobile browser that asks the user's permission before storing an application cache (AppCache) package in the local memory. For all the other browsers it's just a transparent action from a user's point of view.
- The architecture of website will be exactly the same as if all the resources had been downloaded from the server. Images, stylesheets, and JavaScript scripts will be loaded, but they will be sourced from the cache instead of the server.

We can use application cache for:

Performance Purposes

Cache from home page and all its resources, resulting in faster load times and reducing the number of requests to the server. Every time the user accesses URL it will load transparently from the local application cache and not from the network. The Google home page uses this technique on iOS and Android devices.

Installed Apps

Offer the user the option to install app and add an icon to the Home screen, so it can be launched from there. Installed apps do not require a web server to work. The Financial Times web app is a good example of this idea.

An Offline Web Experience

The website will be available even when the user does not have an Internet connection usually rely on other storage APIs for this. The Gmail web app for smartphones is a good example.

6.2.1 The Manifest File

The package list is delivered through a text file known as a *cache manifest*. This file must have as its first line the literal text CACHE MANIFEST. This line is followed by a list of all the URLs relative or absolute of the resources to download to the device. The manifest file must be served as text/cache-manifest and defined as the manifest attribute of the html element:

```
<html manifest="manifest.appcache">
```

The HTML file that is pointing to the manifest, as well as the manifest itself, will be stored locally in the application cache implicitly; do not need to declare them inside. If any file listed in the manifest fails to download while the package is being installed, the entire package is invalidated. That means that if we are defining resources on third-party servers, rely on these servers for apps to be installed.

The initial CACHE MANIFEST line can be followed by a series of relative or absolute URLs that to be cached for offline availability. We can comment lines by using a hash (#) at the beginning of the line:

```
CACHE MANIFEST
# This is a comment
ourscript.js
images/logo.gif
images/other_image.jpg
ourstyles.css
```

While there is no standard definition, the manifest is recommended to use the *.manifest* or *.appcache* extension and must be delivered with the right MIME type: text/cache-manifest.

Reusing the Manifest

If more than one HTML page that the user browses points to the same manifest URI, the manifest package will be reused and all the HTML files browsed will be added implicitly to the manifest as "master resources." That is, after a package has been installed, if the user browses to another page that points to the same manifest, all the resources will already be available offline.

6.2.2 Accessing Online Resources

If application attempts to access any resource that was not originally defined in the manifest file, the process will fail because the application is sandboxed offline. By default, all the resources are declared in an implicit CACHE: section. If know for sure that we are going to need some information from the Web, we can define it in the manifest file in a special section called NETWORK. To define a section, just end the line with a colon. So, if want a *countries.json* file to always be delivered from the server, we can change manifest to:

```
CACHE MANIFEST
# Resources that should be installed on the user's device
CACHE:
ourscript.js
images/logo.gif
images/other_image.jpg
ourstyles.css
```

Resources that should always be downloaded from the Web

NETWORK: countries.json

Then, *countries.json* will not be downloaded with the other resources and instead will be accessed online every time the application needs it. If there is no Internet connection, will not get this file, unless the browser has a cached version (using the typical web cache, not the application cache).

In the network section, can use wildcards, such as *, or folders; every resource in that folder will be accessible from the Web while in an offline operation mode. So, if want to have an offline application that can access the full Web if the user has a connection, can just use:

NETWORK: *

With this configuration only files listed before the NETWORK: section will be loaded from the offline package; every other resource will be loaded from the Web.

Fallbacks

Application cache has a mechanism to access external online resources but at the same time provide a fallback to avoid errors if the user is offline: the FALLBACK: group. In this section provide two URLs, space-separated; the first one can use wildcards while the second one should be a specific URL.

For example: FALLBACK:

images/profile.png noconnection.png

In this example, when the web app tries to get *images/profile.png*, it will bring it from the server if the user is online and will return *noconnection.png* as a fallback file if the user is offline. The fallback image is stored in the application cache package implicitly.

6.2.3 Updating the Package

- When the package is installed all the resources including the main HTML document will always be loaded from the local storage and not from the Web. Therefore, it's fair to ask: how can update a resource? What happens if want to update the theme CSS file, change an image, or add a new page link in the HTML document?
- Every time the user opens a cached web app, while the app is always loaded from the local storage, in the background the browser tries to get an updated manifest file from the server. If there is no Internet connection, nothing happens, and the local version is used.
- If there is a network connection available, the browser downloads the manifest file from the server and does a byte-by-byte comparison of the new version of the file with the local version from the original web app download. If even one byte has changed, the entire cached manifest is invalidated and every resource is downloaded again, using the new manifest file.
- We can force the browser to check for a new manifest file while the application is running, rather than waiting for the next time the app is launched, using applicationCache.update()
- If we change the contents of a CSS file but do not change the name of that file, the manifest will be the same, so the downloaded files will not be updated. This is an important point we need to change the manifest itself for the web app to receive the update.
- How should we change the manifest when we make an update to any of the listed resources? The change can involve something as simple as adding a space, changing the resource name or even including a comment line at the start of the manifest file containing a random value or the last-modified date, as in:

CACHE MANIFEST

webapp updated 2013-10-01

- If we make a single change for example, the date the whole manifest will be invalidated and the platform will download all the files again. Remember that the resources in the manifest will not be downloaded again until we update the manifest file or invalidate the AppCache.
- There is another problem that arises when dealing with manifest updates: if there is an update, the platform downloads all the resources in the manifest again, but this download process is done in the *background* while the previous files are on the screen. This means the user will not see the newly downloaded versions of the resources until reloads the application. In other words, if we change the manifest, the user must load the page twice to see the new version.

6.2.4 Deleting the Package

How do you remove a package from the application cache? The only way to do it is to deliver a 404 HTTP code when the browser is downloading the manifest while trying to check for an update. Therefore, if we want to delete a package we need to use Ajax or some other technique to communicate to the server that we want the package to be removed on the next reload. The server may physically delete the file, or just store a flag in some sort of server-side storage such as a session variable so that on the next manifest request for that user we force a 404 status. After that, we can reload the app or just force an update using applicationCache.update().

In some browsers, the user can delete the packages from an advanced configuration section, usually called "website data."

6.2.5 The JavaScript API

There is a global JavaScript object that helps us to know the status of the application cache. The object is applicationCache, and it has a status property that can have one of the values listed in Table 6.4.

Table 6.4: Status of the applicationCache Object

Value	Constant	Description
0	UNCACHED	This is the first load of the page, or no manifest file is available.
1	IDLE	The cache is idle.
2	CHECKING	The local manifest file is being checked against the server's manifest file.
3	DOWNLOADING	The resources are being downloaded.
4	UPDATEREADY	The cache is ready.

If the application cache status is 0, our document is loaded from the network; otherwise, it is loaded from the application cache.

We can use constants to ask about the current status. For example:

```
if (window.applicationCache!=undefined) {
// The API is available
if (applicationCache.status==applicationCache.UPDATEREADY) {
// There is an update waiting for reload
}
}
```

The applicationCache object has the methods update(), which will force an update check, and swapCache(), which will swap from the older cached versions of the resources to the newly downloaded versions (if the object is in the UPDATEREADY state).

However, the HTML document and all resources already in memory will not be updated until we do a full page reload (such as with location.reload())

If offline application needs to store custom images that are only for one user for example, pictures of the user's contacts, create a manifest file dynamically for each user or, even better, store the images in base64 in offline storage for usage as inline images later.

Cache Events

The applicationCache object has events that we can handle to manage every Situation. For example, if the user is accessing our website for the first time, we can show a "Downloading app" message while the resources are downloaded so the user will wait, increasing the probability of a complete download.

We can use the new events online and offline and the navigator.on Line property to detect whether the user has an Internet connection available or not.

The possible events that bind to listed in Table 6.5:

Table 6.5: Events Available for applicationCache

Event Property	Description
checking	The browser is checking the manifest.
downloading	The browser has started downloading the resources listed in the manifest
progress	A resource has been downloaded. The current HTML page and the manifest file count as resources, so this event will be fired n+2 times, with n being the number of files in the CACHE: and FALLBACK: sections.
cached	The first download process has finished properly
noupdate	The cached manifest has been compared with the version on the server, and no update is available.

Event Property	Description
updateready	There was an update, and the new resources have been downloaded properly and are waiting for a reload.
error	There was an error downloading a resource.
obsolete	When checking for an update it was determined that the manifest is no longer valid, so the web app has been deleted from the storage and will not be available offline the next time the user attempts to use it.

In a typical situation, we are going to:

- Capture downloading so we can show a message to the user and optionally an animated spinner.
- Capture progress to make a progress bar.
- Capture cached to hide the loading message and tell the user that the app was installed.
- Capture error to hide the loading message and tell the user about the situation.
- Capture updateready to inform the user that there is an update ready and ask the user if wants to reload now to access the updated app.

We can bind to these events using addEventListener. For example:

```
if (window.applicationCache!=undefined) {
// The API is available
applicationCache.addEventListener('updateready', function() {
// There is an update waiting for reload
if (confirm("There is an update ready. Do you want to load
it now?")) {
history.reload();
}
}, false);
}
```

6.2.6 Compatibility and Limits

Application cache compatibility is good in the mobile web, but on some platforms issues do arise that are difficult to debug.

Safari on iOS, the Android browser from 2.1, Google Chrome, Amazon Silk, the BlackBerry browser since 6.0, the Nokia Browser for MeeGo, Opera Mobile, Internet Explorer since 10, and Firefox support application cache. Cloud-based browsers do not support this ability, as they need an Internet connection to parse the website on the cloud.

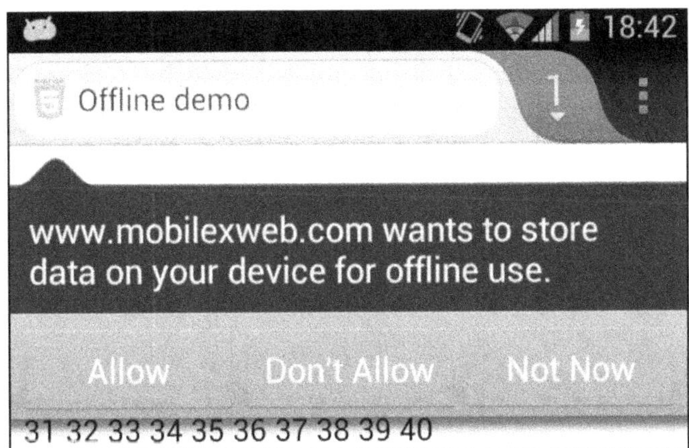

Fig. 6.1: storing an application cache package using Firefox

One of the biggest problems with the specification is the lack of a limit definition. How much space can we allocate for an offline web app? Is there any limit? If so, is it per URL or per domain? Usually, up to 5 MB there are no big issues on any platforms.

6.3 STORAGE

- The main problem in working offline is that where should a web application store vital statistics and other information when the device is not connected to the Internet? And if the device is not connected to the Internet, how can applications access helpful databases or information? Client storage solutions come to assistance, in two flavors: key/value storage and SQL databases, from JavaScript, without server interaction.
- Remember that client-side storage mechanisms should be used as temporary and volatile storages, as devices can be restored, lost, stolen, or upgraded. The data should also be stored somewhere else, usually on the cloud (a web server).
- Of course, we also have cookies, but they are simpler, only string storage and they are not guaranteed to survive in the browser. However, cookies are the only storage that is shared between the client and the server, through HTTP headers.

6.3.1 Web Storage

- The HTML5 Web Storage API defines two key/value stores through two objects: *localStorage* and *sessionStorage*. They are pretty much the same, but the scopes are different: while the local store is used for long-term storage, the session store does not persist after the user closes the tab or window.
- Both stores are used in the same way:

```
// Save an object or variable in the store
localStorage.setItem("name_in_the_storage", object_to_store);
// Read an object from the store
var object = localStorage.getItem("name_in_the_storage");
```

- We can also delete all the objects using *clear* or delete one key using removeItem. There is also a storage event that we can listen for with window.addEventListener that will be fired when the contents of the local or session stores have changed.
- Usually, on mobile devices *localStorage* is the preferred one as the browser session concept is more ambiguous than on desktops. Remember that from a user's perspective the browser may be opened and minimized, but in practice its session may be closed and out of memory. Therefore, *sessionStorage* is useful only for caching objects in memory that are volatile.
- If the user is browsing in private mode, *localStorage* will not persist values. The only exception is Google Chrome on iOS because of a UIWebView limitation.
- Storing information on the device is a synchronous file operation and it takes time, so it will harm performance if you store small items in a loop. Storing a big item once is preferred in terms of performance in some browsers. Just to give an example, it takes Google Chrome four times longer to store 100 elements of 10 kB each than 1 element of 1,000 kB. Version 2.x of the Android browser can take up to 4 seconds to store 1 MB in web storage.

We can only store string values in the local and session stores. We can convert all of the following to string form:

- Any basic JavaScript value, including numbers and Booleans
- Any noncyclic objects or arrays, converting them to JSON
- Images, converting them to data URI format
- JavaScript code to execute using eval()
- CSS styles to be applied in a style element
- HTML parsed code to be injected in the DOM

6.3.2 The Web SQL Database API

- The idea of having a relational database available in JavaScript sounds powerful. The WHATWG team has defined an SQL-based asynchronous API called Web SQL Database that is implemented using the open source SQLite engine. When this API came to the W3C discussion, it was neglected because it does not have any other implementation than SQLite, so it can not be a standard.
- Therefore, more W3C-friendly vendors, such as Mozilla and Microsoft, have decided to not implement this API and instead to go for the standard alternative, IndexedDB.
- While IndexedDB is getting more support as the database standard, there are still big opportunities for Web SQL Database in mobile environments, as Safari on iOS up to version 6.0 does not support IndexedDB. The Web SQL API is implemented in Safari, Chrome, the Android browser, the BlackBerry browser, and Opera Mobile; it's not available in Firefox or Internet Explorer.

- Even though IE does not support this API, Apache Cordova/PhoneGap supports it in Windows Phone native web app projects, emulating the feature using an SQL Server engine.
- The main method that defines the availability of the SQL database is the window.open Database() method, which creates a new database if the internalName does not exist, or opens it if it does. This method has the following signature:

```
var db = window.openDatabase(internalName, version, displayName,
sizeExpectable, [callback]);
```

- If we use a try/catch, we can capture errors during the operation. To execute nonrecordset sentences (CREATE TABLE, INSERT) we can use a transaction using the transact() method, which receives a function as a parameter. As a transaction, if one sentence fails, the others will not execute:

```
db.transact(function(t)) {
t.executeSql('CREATE TABLE countries (id INTEGER NOT NULL PRIMARY
KEY AUTOINCREMENT, name TEXT NOT NULL)', [], function() {},
errorHandler);
});
```

- The parameter after the query string is an array of parameters to be replaced in the query (using ? inside), the next parameter is the data handler function (not used in a nonrecordset query), and the last parameter is a function handler for errors in the query.
- To create a typical SELECT statement with recordset looping, we can use the following template:

```
db.transact(function(t)) {
t.executeSql('SELECT * FROM countries', [], countriesHandler,
errorHandler);
});
function countriesHandler(transaction, data) {
var record;
var id;
var name;
for (var i=0; i<data.rows.length; i++) {
// We get the current record
record = data.rows[i];
id = record['id'];
name = record['name'];
```

```
// Do something with record information
}
}
function errorHandler(transaction, error) {
alert('Error getting results');
}
```

- If you allow working offline you should implement a synchronization method, using Ajax to download changes from and upload them to the server.

6.3.3 The IndexedDB API

- The IndexedDB or IDB API is the W3C standard replacement for the Web SQL Database API. IDB is not yet available in Safari on iOS before version 6.0 or the Android browser prior to version 4.1, but it's implemented in Chrome, Firefox, and Internet Explorer (from version 10), and with time it will probably replace Web SQL on all platforms.
- The IDB API allows us to create and query databases, asynchronously or synchronously useful for web workers. Unfortunately, at first sight the API does not look so nice or easy to understand.
- The basic concepts include a *database repository* having multiple *object stores* (similar to tables) that contain objects (similar to records) indexed with a key (similar to a primary key). A database, or store, can only be accessed by a same-origin policy, as in the other storage APIs, meaning that we can not access databases cross-domain. IndexedDB provides support for objects to manage indexes, tables, and cursors in a particular transaction. The transaction is the only place where we can execute commands. With IDB there is no way to execute SQL commands.
- The example is given below which will show how to create a database, create an object store, and work with data.
- The main functionality happens in the global indexedDB object. Some versions of Firefox, the BlackBerry 10 browser, and Chrome up to version 18 use prefixed versions, so to be compatible with previous versions we should check for the prefix first or reassign the global object, as in:

```
window.indexedDB = window.indexedDB || window.webkitIndexedDB ||
window.mozIndexedDB;
```

- Opening a database is done using indexedDB.open() and we need to bind events using on<x> syntax or addEventListener, as in:

```
var dbRequest = indexedDB.open("myDatabase");
var database;
dbRequest.onsuccess = function(event) {
```

```
// The database object appears as event.result
database = event.result;
}
dbRequest.onerror = function(event) {
// Manage error
}
```

- A big difference between Web SQL and IDB is that when we call the open() method in IDB the database object is not returned. It is available as the result property of the success event parameter.
- To create the object stores and schemas we need to implement the upgradeneeded event, which will also be fired when upgrading database versions:

```
dbRequest.onupgradeneeded = function(event) {
var db = event.target.result;
// Let's create the object store for books
var objectStore = db.createObjectStore("books", { keyPath:
"isbn" });
}
```

- To execute commands on an object store we need to use transactions, which receive as parameters a single store name, an array of store names, or an empty array (for all stores) to query on, and the operation type (by default, read-only), as in:

```
var transaction = database.transaction("books", 'readwrite');
transaction.objectStore("books")
.add({ isbn: "1234567890", name: "Programming the Mobile
Web"})
```

- To get one element by key from the database, we can use a chained syntax, as in:

```
database.transaction("books")
.objectStore("books")
.get("1234567890")
.onsuccess = function(event) {
var object = event.target.result;
});
```

- To browse between all objects, we can use a cursor:

```
var allBooks = database.transaction("books").objectStore("books");
allBooks.openCursor().onsuccess = function(event) {
var cursor = event.target.results;
```

```
if (cursor) {
var key = cursor.key;
var currentBook = cursor.value;
cursor.continue(); // Move to next element and execute
// onsuccess again
} else {
// End of object store
}
};
```

6.3.4 The FileSystem API

The FileSystem API, also known as "File API: Directories and System," is a W3C draft specification more experimental in terms of storage compatibility that allows our domain to have its own full virtual *filesystem* in the device memory. Not confuse this API with the File API (useful to read files from the user's *filesystem*).

With this API we can create and manage folders and files in a virtual *filesystem* that may or may not have a corresponding private place in the real device *filesystem*. Some browsers may implement it using a database. The API does not allow us to work with the user's *filesystem* (private or public); we can only work with the files created by scripts in our domain.

We can request two kinds of *filesystem*, PERSISTENT or TEMPORARY, and create our own structure inside.

To retrieve a persistent *filesystem* of 4 MB, we can use the following code:

```
window.requestFileSystem(window.PERSISTENT, 4*1024*1024,
function(filesystem) {
// The filesystem was created/opened
}, function(event) {
// Handle error
});
```

With this API we can:

- Modify *filesystem* quotas
- Create and open files
- Append, replace, and delete files
- Create and delete directories
- Copy, rename, and move files and directories
- Read directories content
- Create *filesystem* URLs

With this API we also have a new URI, *filesystem*: that we can use to point from our web app to any file stored in our persistent or temporary storage.

6.4 NETWORK COMMUNICATION

Communication between mobile web apps and a server is usually a must-have feature. Modern mobile browsers have different APIs that will help us with this task, including the well known Ajax and HTML5 APIs

6.4.1 Ajax

- Ajax, originally an acronym of *Asynchronous JavaScript* and *XML*, is a technique that involves making asynchronous server requests without refreshing the page, interrupting the user's activity, changing the browser's history, or losing global state variables.
- The magic behind Ajax is called XMLHttpRequest; it is a native JavaScript object available in compatible devices that was based on an ActiveX object created by Microsoft in Internet Explorer 5.0. By basic support, means XMLHttpRequest 1.0 support with the ability to download text (sometimes treated as JSON) and XML.
- XMLHttpRequest Level 2 (XHR 2, sometimes called Ajax 2) is an extension to the original standard defined by the W3C. With this extension, we can manage a new load event instead of managing states in readystatechange; it also supports the progress event as well as the ability to upload and download binary information.
- Using XHR 2, a normal Ajax request looks like:

```
var xhr = new XMLHttpRequest();
xhr.open('GET', 'myurl', true);
xhr.onload = function(event) {
// xhr.responseText includes the server's response as Text
}
xhr.send();
```

- XHR 2 also added the responseType attribute, allowing us to read the result in different formats. We can set this to arraybuffer, blob, document, or json.

JSONP

- JSON with Padding (JSONP) is a hack for accessing a third-party domain's content without the cross-domain problems of Ajax requests to servers on which CORS is not enabled. Many public web services are offering this new way of communicating with third-party servers.
- JSONP uses a script tag generated by JavaScript pointing to a URL with a parameter we define, generally for a local callback function to be called when the script (and the data it fetches) is downloaded and executed.

- A very similar technique is used for scripting code: you download only a subset of the scripts in the initial download, and then you download the other scripts that you will need later.
- JSONP needs one feature to be working on the browser: the ability to insert a script dynamically from JavaScript. If this feature works, the browser should detect the new DOM script element and automatically download and execute this new resource. As this script will call your function with the data, you will be able to receive data from a third-party server.

Ajax with Offline Resources

Ajax can be used when we are in offline mode in two situations:

- When using web views, such as in Apache Cordova/PhoneGap apps. We can load resources from our application bundle (JSON, text, XML, or binary information) using Ajax, even if there is no web server running.
- When using application cache, if the URL we are trying to get is listed in the manifest file.

6.4.2 Server Sent Events

- Server Sent Events (SSE, also known as EventSource) is a network specification draft for enabling web apps to use HTTP for unidirectional real-time communication from the server to the browser. Basically, it's like an Ajax request that does not close the connection, so the server can send pieces of information to the client whenever it needs to.
- This API aims to replace the long-polling Ajax techniques, sometimes known as Comet techniques, which are not standard and may not work properly on mobile devices. If for some reason the client or the server closes the connection, the browser starts a polling mechanism, opening the connection again.
- SSE is compatible with Safari on iOS (since 4.1), Google Chrome, Amazon Silk 2.0, the BlackBerry browser for PlayBook 2.0 and BB10, Nokia Browser for MeeGo, Opera Mobile, and Firefox.
- To create an SSE request, we must instantiate an *EventSource* object with the script URL and using a messaging API event mechanism, as follows:

```
var request = new EventSource("/mySSEscript");
request.onopen = function() {
// An HTTP request has been opened. It can be called more than
// once if the connection drops
}
request.onerror = function() {
// Something went wrong or the connection has been dropped (and
// it will try to reconnect)
```

```
}
request.onmessage = function(event) {
// The server has just sent a message through the connection and
// it's available in the data property
var data = event.data;
}
// If we want to close the connection later, we call request.close()
```

- Every time the server sends a message, we will receive a message event handler call. The message data can only be a string.

The Server Component

- Usually this kind of real-time communication mechanism requires a server-side platform prepared for this kind of work (clients connected for long periods of time), so web servers like Apache or IIS may not be well suited to it. Solutions such as Node.js are much more optimized and prepared. However, SSE can be implemented with any server-side HTTP platform even PHP, as it's mounted over HTTP.
- To answer an SSE request, we must use the MIME type text/event-stream and follow the SSE protocol. The basic protocol involves answering with data: <data> and a line break. We replace <data> with the message we want to send to the client, which will be received in the message event.
- After sending a message, instead of closing the connection, the server should keep waiting in an event loop for new messages to send. Therefore, the server and the client are permanently connected, like a server that is taking a long time to respond and periodically flushing small pieces of information.

6.4.3 WebSockets

- While SSE is great for real-time apps, it has a big problem: the communication can not be done from the client to the server. WebSockets solve this problem, enabling bidirectional, full-duplex, real-time communication between the browser and a web server.
- WebSockets involve two specifications: the WebSocket API, which defines the JavaScript API, and the WebSocket network protocol. Because of their bidirectional nature, Web-Sockets do not use standard HTTP messages, and therefore a special server is required.
- There are some Apache-based projects to add WebSocket protocol supports, such as Apache WebSocket; on the Microsoft side, this protocol was added in Internet Information Server (IIS) version 8 in conjunction with ASP.NET 4.5.
- We can define WebSocket URLs using the ws:// protocol definition. From an API perspective, using WebSockets is easy: we just instantiate a WebSocket object and use the message event and the send() function to receive and send information from/to the

server. When we create a WebSocket connection we can optionally define the protocol name as the second argument:

```
var socket = new WebSocket("ws://myserver.com");
socket.onopen = function() {
// The connection was opened
}
socket.onclose = function() {
// The connection was closed
}
socket.onmessage = function(event) {
// We have just received a message from the server
var message = event.data;
}
// We may send messages
socket.send("Hello server!");
// We can close the connection from the client
socket.close();
```

- The WebSocket API is not like low-level socket implementations in other languages, such as C or Java. It supports only string messages, although there is a nonstandard extension supporting binary JavaScript data that works in some browsers.
- We need to provide a server solution for our WebSockets. There are frameworks available for almost any server-side language and platform, but remember that WebSockets are more suitable for event-driven platforms that can maintain several connections at the same time instead of closing the connection after the response.

6.5 DISTRIBUTION AND SOCIAL WEB 2.0

There is always lot of doubts regarding how to convert mobile websites using publicity and how to combine mobile applications with some social features. Some techniques regarding this are described here.

6.5.1 Mobile SEO

- It is Search Engine Optimization (SEO) refers to a set of best practices that you can follow to help your website be in the best possible place in a search engine results.
- In general, typical desktop SEO techniques apply to mobile websites, but some extra care must be taken.
- The 1st thing we need to know is that mobile search users are not the same as desktop search users.

- Mobile users are typically searching for something very specific, and we should do our best to make possible access to those resources.
- Mobile search engines (Google, Yahoo!, and Bing) localize the search results, so if your service is location-based, you should make sure that your location is properly defined in your text and code.
- In mobile search engines, the user only types a few characters and the engine tries to suggest the best possible results based on location and previous results, with mobile-specific content given priority.
- Search engines like Google will try to serve mobile-specific content first, but if someone is looking for the correct name of your application and Google does not know that you have a mobile website, the user will be redirected to your desktop site or to a go beyond mobile version of it produced by a Google server.
- If you appear in the search engine's databases, you will also be found using the native applications that many search engines are developing, including voice-powered search applications.

6.5.2 Spiders and Discoverability

The first problem is how to make mobile website known to the search engines. This can be different depending upon whether anybody already have a desktop website that has been crawled or not. If user already have a desktop website, he can give search engines the URL of your mobile site using the alternate link method:

```
<link rel="alternate" media="handheld" href="http://m.yoursite.com" />
```

User can also add his mobile site manually, using these links:

- Bing
- Google

6.5.3 Mobile Sitemaps

- Google has formed an extension to the Sitemap protocol for mobile web content discoverability, called Mobile Sitemaps.
- After creating an account in Google Webmaster Central, you can add your mobile site to Google database.
- You need to verify that you are the owner of the site, by inserting a temporal Meta tag or HTML file in your site. Once your site has been validated, you can submit a Sitemap for it.
- If you're mobile site is targeted to only one country using a non country top-level domain (like *.com* or *.mobi*), you can also define the geographic target for which your mobile site is prepared.

6.5.4 How Users Find You

Search engines are not the only way for users to discover your mobile website. Obviously, offline marketing is always welcome, but there are also other online features we should implement to facilitate discoverability. These include advertising the new mobile website to user's current desktop visitors and implementing newsletters and feed readers. The first problem to tackle is simplifying the user's first access to the mobile website. Many mobile users still do not know how to go to a URL if it is not on the carrier's home page, and many others will not want to type a long URL on a numeric keypad device.

SMS Invitation

A good solution is to include in your desktop website a form to collect the user's phone number and then send him a WAP Push or an SMS link. A WAP Push is a special message with a URL inside. This is generally a premium SMS and some carriers do not allow sending them from a website. An SMS link is just a normal SMS with a link inside. Almost every modern device with a browser will auto detect a URL inside a text message if it begins with *www* or *http://* and will convert the URL into a link that the user can click after receiving the SMS. The big question is how do we send an SMS from a website? The answer is not what you might expect there is not a simple or free way to do it. We have to use an SMS provider or gateway that, with a simple web service call, will send the message to users in one country or worldwide. We will have to pay for that SMS, but depending on the business, a new mobile web user will probably be worth the small expense.

Some SMS gateway providers include:

- Mogreet
- Lleida
- Clickatell SMS Gateway
- BulkSMS
- ClockWork

Email Invitation

If the user accesses his/her email mailbox from his/her mobile device, an alternative to SMS is to send the user a free email message containing the mobile URL.

Web Shortcuts

A web shortcut is a native application or web app that has an icon in the applications menu that launches the browser when it is activated. Adding a shortcut is better than adding a bookmark, because it will be installed just like any other application.

6.6 SOCIAL WEB 2.0

Mobile website will not be complete if user do not add some social features to it. In the current social networking era, social integration is a must-have feature to implement.

Authentication and Sharing APIs

Facebook, Twitter, and Google all offer APIs that can enhance the visibility of your mobile site thanks to the sharing features.

Facebook Connect

Facebook offers Facebook Connect for Mobile Web, an HTML5 library that lets our applications log users in using their Facebook accounts. With this API you can:

- Create a login mechanism easily.
- Get user session data.
- Call methods from the Graph API and prompt for extended permissions (access friends list, send private messages).
- Post on the Facebook timeline.

To use it, you will need to register an app on Facebook, implement the Facebook SDK, log the user in, and use the Graph API. To get detailed information and samples, visit Facebook developer site.

Twitter for Websites

Twitter for Websites allows us to integrate our mobile website with Twitter login. We can also access the user's account, such as for posting new messages or accessing the whole Twitter API.

Google APIs

Google offers different APIs that are useful for mobile websites, including Google Accounts Authentication and Authorization, useful to log in the user, and the Google+ API for sharing on that social network.

Sharing Content

For any content user can offer a *Share* service to publish the URL via Twitter, Facebook, and other social networks.

For most social networks, you should use the same URL you would use for the desktop website. On the server, the social network scripts will redirect mobile users to the mobile website.

For Twitter, you can Use a Link Like this:

```
http://twitter.com/home?status=<your message here>
```

Twitter has a limit of 140 characters, including an optional URL using *http://*, which should be URL-encoded in the status variable. For long URLs, you should use a shorter service API.

For Facebook, you can share a link using:

```
http://m.facebook.com/sharer.php?u=<url to share>&t=<title of content>
```

QUESTIONS

1. What are the different location techniques which are use determine the geographical location of a device?
2. Write a note on server technique and client techniques.
3. Explain W3C Geolocation API.
4. Explain IP Geolocation and their mechanism.
5. What is MAPS? Explain maps application.
6. Write note on Bing Maps.
7. What are different steps of Offline Web Apps? Explain in detail.
8. What is mean by updating package and deleting package?
9. Explain how Client-Side Storage work.
10. Explain Communication between our mobile web apps and a server.
11. Explain Mobile SEO.
12. Write an note on How Users Find You.
13. Enlist different Mobile Web Social Features.

Sample Question Paper For In-Semester Examination (30 Marks)

Time : 1 Hour **Total Marks : 30**

1. (a) Give the importance of Mobile Development. How it is useful for the business world. **[5]**

(b) Differentiate Mobile Web and Mobile Application. Give advantages and disadvantages of both. **[5]**

OR

2. (a) Explain Java Script Object Notation (JSON) with an example. Compare JSON with XML. **[4]**

(b) Explain following with advantages and disadvantages: **[6]**

(i) Adaptive mobile website

(ii) Dedicated mobile website

(iii) Mobile web application

3. (a) Explain following terms associated with mobile device display: **[4]**

(i) Resolution

(ii) Pixel density ratio

(b) Which tools are available for the mobile testing? Give the steps to use android emulator. **[6]**

OR

4. (a) Explain preinstalled and user installable mobile browsers in detail. **[6]**

(b) What is WAP? Explain WAP1 and WAP2.0 standards. **[4]**

5. (a) Explain XHTML MP (XHTML Mobile Profile) document structure with example. What are the advantages of XHTML MP? **[5]**

(b) Which are the different mobile strategies to provide the best possible experience to every mobile device? Explain any one in detail. **[5]**

OR

6. (a) What is WML? Explain with example. Give advantages and limitations of WML. **[5]**

(b) Explain different tests to check HTML5 compatibility levels. **[5]**

✠ ✠ ✠

Sample Question Paper For End-Semester Examination (70 Marks)

Time : 2.30 Hours **Total Marks : 70**

1. (a) Explain Titanium and jQuery frameworks. **[4]**

(b) Explain Java Script Object Notation (JSON) with an example. **[3]**

(c) Describe Physical dimensions associated with mobile device display. **[3] OR**

2. (a) Explain following with advantages and disadvantages: **[4]**

(i) Adaptive mobile website (ii) Dedicated mobile website

(b) Write similarities and differences between JSON and XML. **[3]**

(c) Describe various input Methods for mobile device. **[3]**

3. (a) What is WAP? Explain WAP1 and WAP2.0 standards. **[4]**

(b) Explain following WCSS extensions: **[6]**

(i) WCSS access key extension (ii) WCSS input extension

(iii) WCSS marquee extension **OR**

4. (a) Explain different user installable browsers. **[4]**

(b) Explain following form attributes of HTML5: **[6]**

(i) Placeholder (ii) Autofocus

(iii) Autocomplete (iv) Required

(v) Form (vi) Formaction

5. (a) What is device detection? Explain possible problems and solution. **[6]**

(b) What is device Interaction? Explain specific platforms support both an API and a URI scheme. **[6]**

(c) Describe Standard Vector Graphics. **[6] OR**

6. (a) What is mean by Client-Side Debugging? Explain all debugging tool. **[6]**

(b) Describe on image formats in detail. **[6]**

(c) Explain in detail Video player API and HTTP Live Streaming. **[6]**

7. (a) Explain with example standard attributes of HTML5 along with their function. **[8]**

(b) Explain **[8]**

(i) JS debugging and type of debugging (ii) Cloud based browser **OR**

8. (a) List all Mobile Libraries and explain in detail. **[8]**

(b) What are the different UI Frameworks? Explain in detail. **[8]**

9. (a) What are the different location techniques? Which are use determine the geographical location of a device? **[8]**

(b) Explain : (i) W3C Geolocation API (ii) IP Geolocation **[8] OR**

10. (a) Enlist different Mobile Web Social Features. Describe all in detail **[8]**

(b) What are different steps of Offline Web Apps? Explain in detail with example. **[8]**

✠ ✠ ✠

www.ingramcontent.com/pod-product-compliance
Lightning Source LLC
Chambersburg PA
CBHW080905020726
47502CB00008B/2351

* 9 7 8 9 3 5 1 6 4 9 1 7 5 *